It Started with a Kiss

ALSO BY MARINA ADAIR

The Eastons

Chasing I Do
Promise You Me
Crazy in Love

Heroes of St. Helena series

Need You for Keeps
Need You for Always
Need You for Mine

St. Helena Vineyard series

Kissing Under the Mistletoe
Summer in Napa
Autumn in the Vineyard
Be Mine Forever
From the Moment We Met

Sugar, Georgia series

Sugar's Twice as Sweet
Sugar on Top
A Taste of Sugar

Sweet Plains series

Tucker's Crossing

It Started with a Kiss

A SEQUOIA LAKE NOVEL

MARINA ADAIR

Montlake
Romance

Published by Montlake Romance, Seattle

www.apub.com

Amazon, the Amazon logo, and Montlake Romance are trademarks of Amazon.com, Inc., or its affiliates.

ISBN-13: 9781503939684
ISBN-10: 1503939685

Cover design by Damonza

Cover photography by Regina Wamba of MaeIDesign.com

Printed in the United States of America

To my husband, Rocco,
and the rest of the Santa Cruz Search and Rescue Team,
who put their own lives on the line to reunite families
and keep them safe.

CHAPTER 1

If life was an adventure, then Avery Adams needed to fire her travel agent and demand a refund. She wasn't a demanding person by nature, but that's what happened when the universe issued an early expiration date on living—it gave you cojones. So Avery issued herself a new passport on life and was ready to put some stamps in each and every column.

Her first destination required crisp mountain air, fireside s'moretinis, and a real get-back-to-nature kind of adventure—one that would hopefully give her the skills needed to live out loud.

Avery looked through the windows of the local Moose Lodge at the imposing Sierras, a rugged mountain range that cut through Northern California and towered over her quaint hometown of Sequoia Lake.

"Before you begin your climb, you want to make sure you give the chest harness a final tug to ensure it's secure," she said as if she were the foremost expert on extreme adventures. As if her entire world—up until a year ago—hadn't consisted of managing retirement portfolios at the local bank and listening to couples talk about their senior cruise to Alaska.

She bent over slightly to click the last carabiner into place, securing the leg straps to the chest harness.

There was something so poignant about that sound, about how with one click the device restricted her freedom and pressed down on her scar, a reminder that she was strapped in and fully committed to the climb.

"I'll tug it," Mr. Fitz offered, his bony fingers already reaching out to help. Or grope. Avery couldn't be sure, so she stepped back out of range.

Mr. Fitz was three thousand years old, with teeth too white to be real, and, even though he looked like a harmless old-timer in his Too Big to Throw Back fishing hat, his eyes were laser pointed at Avery's chest—which was prominently on display because of how the harness fit her body.

"I'm fine." Avery swatted his hands away right before they made contact. "But thank you for the offer."

Mr. Fitz backed off, taking his seat, but he looked awfully disappointed.

Senior X-Treme Team, the town's invitation-only fly fishermen's club, had asked Sequoia Lake Lodge to their monthly meeting, since the first topic on their agenda was to finalize their big summer excursion. And since Avery was Sequoia Lake Lodge's adventure coordinator, it was her job to go out into the community and solicit new customers. If she secured all twelve members for this excursion, then she'd meet her entire quota for the month in one fell swoop.

She straightened her shoulders—an impossible task due to the climbing harness—and held out a clipboard to the crowd. "Now, if that answers all the questions, let me tell you about the amazing views from—"

Mr. Fitz's hand went up.

"Mr. Fitz?" she said thinly since this was his fifth question.

"If I fall on this climb, will you be there to catch me?" he asked, and a dozen gray heads bobbed in support.

"Your harness is secured to a safety line and a main line," Avery said, reiterating verbatim the lodge's safety manual, which outlined the precautions taken in any excursion that included chest harnesses. But to ease the concerned looks, she added, "Plus your adventure guide is with you every step of the way to make sure your trip is exciting and safe."

Another hand flew up. The Captain, as he preferred to be called, was the president of Senior X-Treme and seemed to be the ladies' man of the group. With his silver-streaked hair, captain's hat, and deck shoes, the man looked as though he'd just stepped off his boat and was ready to impress. He was also trying his hardest not to look at Avery's chest. "If you fall, can I catch you?"

"I don't go on excursions. I coordinate them," she said, leaving out the part that with every party confirmed, she got a bonus adventure for herself.

A series of disappointed mumbles filled the room, and she dropped the clipboard to the table, silencing the room with a bang. "Now, will all of those in favor of Senior X-Treme starting off the season with the Sierra Point climb please raise their hands?" she asked in a tone that usually had her customers signing on the dotted line.

Not a single hand went up. Which was odd since she'd come here to pitch the Emerald Bay fly-fishing day trip, and the group had specifically asked her to explain the Sierra Point climb, even going as far as having her demonstrate how the harness worked. And since that trek had a special place in her LIVING FOR LOVE passport, she'd suited up.

Only now, she was afraid she'd secured the carabiner incorrectly. Even though she'd followed the directions exactly, she couldn't seem to loosen the harness or get the carabiner to open. Not that she'd let them know that.

"Mr. Fitz, how about you?"

Mr. Fitz shook his head. "My wife would have my head if she knew I was even thinking about climbing Sierra Point. That's a young man's trail, and I had a new hip put in last year—no way could I take the pressure of that harness."

Avery had made it through a surgery of her own last year, and she could tell him, without a doubt, that healing bodies and harnesses were a tricky combination. But that the pressure would be worth the thrill he'd feel when he got to the top and looked out over the Sierra Nevadas.

"Then why did you ask about the trip in the first place?"

Mr. Fitz looked at the floor, his ears going pink. In fact, most of the men were avoiding eye contact. A clear sign that Avery had been played. "You weren't planning on booking any trips today, were you?"

"We've been doing the fly-fishing excursion on the north side of the lake for nearly twenty years," Prudence Tuttman said from the back row, not sounding all that excited about going for number twenty-one. She was the only female in the group, outweighed the heaviest member by twenty pounds, and held the county record for gutting the most fish in under a minute. "Dale has taken us out on every one of those trips."

"Dale couldn't make it today," Avery said. "So he sent me here to finalize things."

Dale Donovan used to be the top-rated adventure guide at Sequoia Lake Lodge, fitting since he'd owned the lodge for more than forty years. He'd survived a helicopter crash, three avalanches, and the loss of his youngest son. Dale was the kind of man stories were made of. Only lately, his memory had been slipping, and on bad days he struggled to remember his own story—which was why his wife had hired Avery.

When she wasn't booking trips, she was managing the schedule and rechecking any and all safety equipment he touched—stealthily.

Pride was a tricky thing, she knew, and she was careful not to take that from him too.

"Really, because Brody said he was going to take us this year and he was sending you down to handle all of the paperwork. Said he had some big trek today so he didn't have time for paperwork," the Captain said, and Avery snorted.

No one had time for paperwork. It was the nature of paperwork!

"So Brody sent me here to finalize *his* excursion?" Avery tried to hide her disappointment that she wouldn't get the credit—or the bonus—for booking her first group-sponsored trip, even though she'd wind up doing all the legwork.

"Yup. And he said to ask about Sierra Point." Mr. Fitz paused, his eyes going right back to Avery's chest harness. "Said if we asked about harness safety, you'd probably put it on. We weren't sure it'd work, said you would see right through it, but he was confident that you'd put it on, even said he'd buy the first round if he was wrong."

Of course he had. Brody was tall, built, good looking, and the most requested guide at Sequoia Lake Lodge. And he knew it. He was also four hundred kinds of asshole and considered himself above menial tasks, such as putting his equipment away when he was done with an excursion.

When he wasn't busy hitting on mountain bunnies and charming hotel guests, he amused himself by making Avery's job difficult. This stunt was one in a long line of many already that week. Thank God it was Friday.

Avery worked hard to school her features, careful not to let them see her sweat—because once again her fatal flaw of predictability was being used against her.

Being nice doesn't mean being someone's doormat, she told herself. It was not her job to makes Brody's life easier.

"What if I were to tell you that as Sequoia Lake Lodge's official adventure coordinator, I have the ability to customize your trip," Avery said. "Give you exactly what you're looking for."

"We've been pitched custom excursions before, but our group isn't large enough to absorb the cost," Prudence explained. "We asked Dale, but he couldn't seem to come up with one that would fit within our budget."

It was true that customized trips were always on the higher end in pricing and usually reserved for corporate retreats and large group events, but with all of the seasonal specials and their senior discount, finding something new and exciting within their means shouldn't be too difficult.

"No sense in signing up for a journey that you've already taken." Avery pulled her calculator and the excursion price guide out of her travel pack, setting them on the poker table that the Moose Lodge provided as workspace. "If you guys are bold enough to chase a new view, I know I can craft the perfect customized trip for your group *and* come in close to budget."

Well, if that didn't get their attention. The excitement in the room rose until it crackled, but it was Mr. Fitz who spoke up. "I guess the Emerald Bay fly-fishing trip has become old hat for us."

A few amens sounded from the group. The Captain even took off his hat and leaned in closer as Avery started scribbling down some rough numbers.

"At least with Emerald Bay we know what we're getting into," Prudence cautioned the group. "This bean counter doesn't even know how to unlock that carabiner. How is she going to come up with a trip we'll like?"

The "bean counter" held up the Sequoia Lake Lodge handbook. "Because I am a master planner and know this book inside and out." When they didn't look convinced, she added, "What's the fun in knowing exactly what you're going to get?"

"Knowing it won't suck," Prudence said.

"Adventure is about trying new things, straying off the known path." No one spoke. "And if you book today, I'll take ten percent off the total."

She wouldn't get her bonus trip, but she'd get the credit for bringing in her first custom trek, which would go far with her boss. If there was one thing that Dale admired, it was assertiveness.

And if there was one thing seniors loved, it was a deal.

CHAPTER 2

Twenty minutes later, Avery walked down the front steps of the local Moose Lodge and onto Lake Street, painfully aware that the safety harness was jammed and not coming off anytime soon. The sun was setting behind the lush peaks of the Sierra Nevadas, streaking the sky a brilliant orange. A cold evening breeze blew through the thick canopy of ponderosas and crape myrtle trees that lined the main drag of town.

Avery shifted her bag, which housed the signed, customized excursion contract for the Senior X-Treme Team, farther up on her shoulder and waited for the thrill of landing her first big client to come.

It didn't. Odd, since once upon a time, say just a few months ago, coming out on top would have had her flushed with excitement, and okay, for a small moment in there, when all twelve sets of eyes had been riveted on her, the adrenaline of a job well done had made a brief appearance. Fooling her into actually believing she was one step closer to reaching the top of Sierra Point—and putting a special stamp in her book.

But that was just it. Avery had been Sequoia Lake Lodge's acting senior adventure coordinator for most of the season, yet the closest she'd come to a real adventure was waking up to a band of raccoons partying in her cabin. They'd torn through the screen door and made off with a box of Oreos, peanut butter, and two pairs of her favorite underwear—which told her they were male raccoons.

Avery had hoped her job would entail more than senior center visits, working the farmers' market booth, and helping lost guests at the lodge find the restroom. So far, she had spent more time talking about all the different trails the Sequoia National Park offered than actually taking one. Turned out, adventure coordinating wasn't all that different from managing retirement funds, except her desk was outside and travel insurance covered more than lost suitcases.

Even the pine trees glistening with frost couldn't distract from the feeling that she was once again sitting idle, waiting for life to find her. Instead of waiting for the net to appear, she needed to leap.

Determined to get out of the harness so she could talk to Irene and Dale about running this trek on her own, she headed toward the purple Victorian with light yellow trim at the end of the street that had Sips and Splatters and a paintbrush in a martini glass painted on its leaded windows. It wasn't a hardware store, but she'd seen enough framing tools to know the owner possessed a screwdriver and a set of hands strong enough to pry open the carabiner. Convincing Dale she was ready to take clients into the great outdoors while stuck in basic climbing gear wouldn't make the kind of impression she was going for.

Only, before she reached the shop, she noticed the Closed sign hanging in the window. She also noticed a big, shiny, black ego-trip of a truck with mud tires, a lift kit, and a mountain bike secured to its top.

The truck was parked directly under the town's flapping banner—which read Come for the Adventure, Stay for the People—and practically on top of her Mazda's bumper. Not only did it have a toolbox in its bed, the box appeared to be unlocked—and its owner nowhere in sight.

Avery found herself laughing at the situation, but a good part of her wanted to cry. Like her Mazda, Avery had spent the majority of her life boxed in. First by her mother's illness, then by her own, which had led to doctors and medical regimens, and finally Carson. And she'd taken it all with a smile, doing her best to make herself as little of a nuisance as possible.

The idea of approaching life carrying a big stick didn't appeal to her; she'd always preferred to walk softly through life, to ask permission before rifling through someone's personal effects. But look where that had gotten her. Booking a private trek that someone else would get to lead.

Ready to make a few waves of her own, and since no one was around to grant or deny her access, Avery reminded herself that living loud required no permission. And to further cement that idea, she pulled out a journal from her purse. It was made of a buttery leather, had a vintage map of the world burned into the cover, and the page corners were softened from time and love.

Avery lightly traced a finger over the branded message on the bottom.

"Don't go where life leads—lead your life in the direction you want to go," she whispered, her voice thickening with emotion.

Her mother had given it to her the day Avery started dialysis, right on the heels of discovering that Avery had not only inherited her mother's petite stature and blue eyes, but also her kidney disease. She'd seen her mother struggle with kidney disease, so when at fourteen Avery learned she too would one day need a new kidney, it was as if her entire world ended. It was her mom, a two-time transplant survivor, who had given Avery the courage to hope and the strength to fight, even when Avery felt as if she was losing every battle. More importantly, her mom had given her something to fight for and someone to fight with.

When times got rough and treatments got longer, they scoured travel magazines at the hospital together, clipping out pictures of all of the places they'd go and the things they'd do when Avery's name made it to the top of the transplant list. It had all started with an article on an amazing island in the Pacific that had endless beaches, exotic animals, and a surplus of suntanned surfers.

As time went on the clippings grew, and little mottos for life and affirmations about enjoying the journey were added to the pile. Until her mom's body rejected her kidney and Avery had lost her biggest ally and her closest friend.

She also lost the will to keep clipping, keep dreaming. Some days it was even hard to keep fighting. That's when Avery met her mom's friends from Living for Love, a local bereavement group that helped people reclaim their life after loss. They stepped in and held her when it was rough, cried with her when it was agony, and eventually gave her a goodbye note from her mom when things became unbearable. Even in death, her mom was there for her, encouraging and challenging her, and in that moment Avery made a promise to stop waiting to get her life back and start living.

She'd started with pasting their favorite clippings, along with photos and funny memories, into the journal to create a living memory book inspired by the strongest, most vibrant person she knew. And what started out as a way to remember her mother's courage had turned into something bigger. A way to honor all the women she'd met through the hospital or at Living for Love.

Women who would never get the chance to leap.

Wiping a tear from her lash, Avery carefully thumbed through the pages that detailed and highlighted the hopes and dreams of those women. A small smile teased her lips as she flipped past the map of Disneyland showing all of the hidden Mickey ears in the park, the article about the jellybean factory in California that gave out free samples, and stopped when she found what she was looking for.

An unopened letter from her mother. Beautifully patinaed with age, the corners worried from years of love. Avery carefully pulled it from its sleeve and turned it over, her heart catching at the faded, familiar scrawl on the back flap of the envelope:

Life is meant to be lived loud, Avery. In the moment and without fear or apology. Don't wait for the net to appear. Jump and let the wind rush beneath you.

Yet there Avery was, about to crest the one-year mark with her new kidney, and she was still waiting for the net. Still waiting until she was ready to really absorb her mother's final words. Waiting for someone to give her permission to fly, when so many couldn't even breathe.

Avery scanned the street again for passersby, then suppressed the urge to jump up and down to test out what the rush of wind felt like because that kind of motion in the harness would end badly, and instead she reached over the side of the truck to play with the latch on the toolbox and—

"Look at that," she said to herself.

With one toggle the latch came undone, two and Avery had the lid propped open and was staring at a handy-dandy screwdriver sitting on the top, as if waiting for a stranger in need to happen by.

She was a stranger, and she was in need, and when she happened by no one was there. So in theory, no one would know she'd borrowed the tool for a second or two.

Palms sweating and heart racing, Avery did one last quick scan of the area, then snatched the screwdriver and quickly stuck the flat edge inside the opening of the carabiner. With a calculated twist she wedged open the two metal clasps and—

"Shit. Shitshitshit!"

The screwdriver launched itself up into the air only to come down and land near the storm drain. Avery scrambled to catch it before it rolled out of sight, but her short legs combined with the restrictive harness made retrieval without face-planting into the Greater Sierra sewage system impossible, leaving her standing in a harness and watching the stolen tool roll into the drain.

She couldn't leave without coming clean and promising to at least replace the screwdriver, but she couldn't stay too long either because Dale headed for home around sunset. And if she didn't catch him tonight, her adventure would have to wait until Monday.

And Avery was tired of waiting, so with the first hints of orange peeking over the mountains, she pulled out her brightest lipstick—Fearless Red with a gloss luminous enough to flag down passing planes—which she'd bought when she'd decided to start living loud. Propping her knee on the hood of the truck, she gripped the back lip of the hood for leverage and pulled herself up.

She perched on top of the hood on all fours, took a bold breath, and ever so carefully scrawled across the front windshield: I OWE YOU A SCREW—

Damn it! Her lipstick, warm from the day's heat, broke and rolled down below the wipers and out of sight. She leaned forward and slipped her fingers inside the crevice to get it, thunking her forehead against the windshield when she realized it was right out of reach.

"Either you were going to write in your ex's phone number or this is my lucky day."

Avery slowly turned her head, and what she saw sent her heart to her toes. Leaning against a lamppost, looking relaxed and incredibly dangerous in a pair of battered hiking boots, stood a mountain of hard muscles and pure testosterone. He wore low-slung cargo pants with a million and one pockets holding a million and one surprises, enough stubble to tell her it was five o'clock, and a Sequoia Lake Lodge cap.

She reread what she'd written and felt her face flush.

"This isn't what it looks like," she said, because it was so much worse. Two seconds into living loud and she was caught defacing the truck of a man she had never seen before, but she could tell by the well-worn but well-kept Gore-Tex mountaineering boots that he wasn't a weekend warrior.

He was apparently a Sequoia Lake Lodge member—and a serious climber. That she was stuck on the hood of his truck in a climbing harness told him that she wasn't.

"I figure you're either testing out a new lip color or making a declaration, in which case you might as well save us both some time and give me your number."

"My dad warned me about giving my number to handsome strangers. He said they either call or they don't, but either way you're in for a world of hurt."

"Handsome stranger, huh?" He pushed off the lamppost and approached the truck, his hand extended. She ignored it under the pretense of looking for her lipstick. "Easy fix. Name's Ty."

Just that. Ty. With a shrug. As though Mountain Man was too badass for anything more than a couple letters thrown together—and big enough to get away with it.

In her experience, big, badass men who pretended to be bulletproof were the first to take cover the second that whole "through sickness and in health part" came into play. Unfortunately, big, badass men who dropped five hundred bucks on a pair of hiking boots also tended to drop serious cash on adrenaline-pumping excursions—most likely at Sequoia Lake Lodge. Which meant she needed to appear somewhat neighborly.

And normal.

Eyes making direct and unwavering contact, she said, "I'm Avery. Avery Adams."

"Well, Avery Adams, if you aren't making an offer, then my guess is you mistook the hood of my truck for a mountain." He chuckled, and she found herself smiling back.

He had a great chuckle—warm, deep, and a little tired. While living loud might not require permission, she decided that in this case it did require an apology.

"It's not an offer, just my way of saying sorry," she clarified, giving her most apologetic look, which was completely wasted on him since he was too busy staring at her ass to notice.

"And just what does one need to do to receive that kind of apology?" When she went back to looking for the lipstick, he added, "You know, so I can be prepared."

"Underestimate me," she said, then smiled over her shoulder. "Or keep staring at my ass."

Mountain Man grinned. Slow and sexy and completely annoying. "I was staring at your harness. It's really wedged up there. Looks painful."

Avery was well aware that she was sporting the biggest wedgie known to man, and yes it was not a comfortable experience, but she'd rather die than admit that to him. The man looked competent, capable, and like the kind of guy who could spot weakness a mountain away. And this wasn't her finest moment. "I'm fine."

"You sure?" He stepped even closer, turning his ball cap around to get a closer look and—*holy cannoli*—Mountain Man was seriously sexy. Rugged sexy with a strong jaw, soft whisky eyes, which were currently sparking in her direction, and a confidence that said he was prepared and ready.

For anything.

And why that made her stomach flutter she had no idea. Avery was on a self-imposed, flutter-free solo adventure at the moment. No fluttering allowed, sexy stranger or not.

"Yes, just part of my job."

"As what?" His eyes were back on her harness. "A window washer?"

Shrugging off the little voice reminding her she was on the hood of a truck in a pair of strappy sandals, pressed capris, and a safety harness, she said, "As an adventure coordinator."

She had to give him credit—he didn't laugh. But he wanted to, she could tell. Why was it so hard for people to understand that she was perfect for this job?

Sure, she might have been hesitant at first too, but after settling in she realized that she had all of the skills required to be awesome at her job. She just needed time to gain her bearings, and then she would be proficient. And as Avery had learned over the years, with proficiency came respect. And confidence.

Something she needed a shot of right then. Fully embracing her new mantra, *Leap like you aren't afraid*, she said, "So as you can imagine, this is nothing I can't handle."

Flat on her belly, she held on to the lip once again, annoyed that she was going to have to scoot to the end since her legs were too short to reach the ground. Something he seemed to notice because before she'd even reached the grille, one big hand closed around her waist, the other on the back of the harness, and suddenly she was airborne.

"Put me down," she ordered, her legs flailing as she tried to twist herself to face him. It didn't work. "What part of 'I got this' did you not understand?"

"The part where you got it." He placed her on the ground, and she spun to look at him and felt her heart stutter. The man was bigger than she'd originally thought, so tall in fact that she had to take a step back just to glare up at him. He was grinning, the big jerk.

"Yes, well, I would have had it." At least she hoped that she would have, but she wasn't entirely sure. That little flight had her a bit off-kilter.

That he was staring at her made it even worse, so she channeled her inner awesomeness, the same way Lilian had taught her to do when facing down unexpected outcomes, and stared back, not noticing how well he filled out his fitted tee or how her belly quivered when he smiled. Hard to do when her body revved every time he so much as breathed.

"Interesting," he finally said. "Your eyes are dilated and you're breathing hard. Admit it, you like me."

"Not possible." Only it was. Go figure, the first time she had a reaction to a man in three years, and it had to be a lodge guest. Which meant that it was time for her to leave. "Just thinking about your tool."

He grinned even bigger at her statement, his eyes twinkling with humor. Avery felt her cheeks heat. "Ah, then you're thinking about how to apologize again. Even better. Does this mean I'm on your IOU list?"

She rolled her eyes, not amused.

"No?" He studied her for a long minute, then leaned in and whispered, "How about now?"

Both of those big hands, strong enough to break granite, wrapped around the front of her safety harness—bringing his fingers right within grazing range of her nipples, and they noticed—then tugged her close. So close she could feel the afternoon heat roll off his skin. He smelled like fresh mountain air, pine trees, and sex—not the kind of sex that could be penciled in between meetings, but the kind that lasted for days on end with only body heat for sustenance.

And if that thought wasn't enough to get her moving, then the reminder that she'd lost her best shot at happily ever after when Carson decided his love only covered the "in health" part of the deal did.

He'd not only hesitated when she'd explained her kidney was slowly killing her, but he'd walked out when she'd needed him most.

Turned out the only dead weight Avery lost in the surgery was Carson, and even though it had been a rough time in her life, she was a stronger person for it. Now she was pain-free, Carson-free, and ready to move forward.

In theory, she was making progress. Her feet were moving in the forward direction. Only Ty's hands were still on her harness and—*oh my God*—he was staring at her lips. Like a wild bear settling on his prey, and she was pretty sure he was either going to throw her over his shoulder and take her back to his cave or kiss her. Either way she couldn't seem to get traction. Unless she counted shuffling closer.

Page six in the living memory journal she'd been assembling flashed in her head, reminding her of her late friend Bella's wish to kiss a stranger on a rain-slickened street, and her belly heated. Avery hadn't kissed anyone since Carson, let alone a stranger, but Lake Street was slick with an early-spring frost, and this stranger looked as if he was about to kiss her.

His grin went full watt, and her breath caught as he closed the last shred of distance and whispered, "You're welcome, Avery Adams."

Avery felt the pressure in her chest release on one big whoosh as the harness slid down her legs, the straps clanking against the concrete. She was free. "How did you do that?"

"Extremely talented fingers," was all he said, but her body tingled all the same. "Now, how about we celebrate your newfound freedom with a drink?"

"I'd really like that, but tonight I have to live loud."

"This is your lucky night then, because it doesn't get any louder than a Flaming Pig's Ass, the house specialty." He gestured with his head to the building behind him. With walls made of logs, copper-rimmed windows, and a massive door with antlers, it looked like a giant hunting lodge. A hand-carved sign declared that you were entering BACKWOODS BREWHOUSE territory. "Closest to death you can come and not wind up in the ER." His voice lowered to a soft gravel. "And if that isn't enough for you, Widow Maker's always looking for a new victim."

The historic brewery, once the local watering hole for miners during the gold rush, was as famous for its extensive beer selection as it was for its mascot. Weighing in at more than a half ton of steel and mechanical hide, Widow Maker was the toughest ride this side of the Rockies. In fact, making it a mere eight seconds was so rare that anyone who rode him past the buzzer was crowned a backwoods king.

"Does the title come with an actual crown?" she asked.

"You make it eight seconds and I will make you a crown." He looked her up and down—so slowly that her toes curled into her barely-broken-in hiking boots—then smiled. "Although I didn't take you for the princess type."

She smiled back. "I'm not."

But Caroline Peters was.

Being a princess for a day was at the top of that little girl's wish list—right under beating leukemia and going to Disneyland. Avery had met Caroline at a hospital in Reno, when Avery was undergoing final treatments in preparation for her transplant. Caroline was sweet, determined, and desperately wanted to have a Cinderella moment— something Avery could relate to.

Gaining that title by riding a mechanical bull would only make Caroline smile bigger. And anything that made that little girl smile was worth potential bruises and humiliation.

"But who knows, maybe after a stiff drink and watching you craft a crown out of paper napkins and beer coasters I might change my mind," she said, her heart racing at the idea of doing something spontaneous and social. Not to mention paying it forward for a five-year-old leukemia patient whose friends had stopped visiting when her beautiful red curls went away.

"Great. You can treat me to the first round since I saved your—" His eyes dropped to her backside, and he smiled. Before he could finish, she threw the harness over her shoulder and took her first real step into living loud.

CHAPTER 3

Tyson Donovan had come into town looking for something to distract him from the fact that instead of being twelve thousand feet up the side of the Andes in Peru and a safe five thousand miles from his past, he was back in Sequoia Lake for the unforeseeable future.

He'd found his distraction all right. She was sexy, a bit sassy, and surprisingly unpredictable for a woman who looked like a kindergarten teacher. A combination that usually spelled trouble. And trouble was something Ty had spent his youth perfecting and the last fifteen years trying to prevent.

Yet, instead of heading for home, he found himself following her into the bar.

It was the curls, he decided. They were blonde, wild, and pulled into a sexy little ponytail that his fingers itched to unravel. And damn, she smelled good. So damn good he wanted to lean in and take another sniff. He also wanted to know what it would take to get her to come through on that promise she'd scribbled on his truck.

She studied the menu like it was a matter of national security, then wrinkled her nose at him as if he'd stepped in dog shit and trailed it in behind her. Obviously not a beer drinker.

"The wine list is on the back," he said, leaning past her to flip the menu over, his chest pressing into her back.

Avery Adams, adventure coordinator, looked up at him through those blue eyes of hers as though she'd forgotten he was there. Then she frowned, obviously irritated by his presence. Not the normal reaction he elicited from women.

"Never trust a menu that offers two wines, red and white," she said, closing the menu.

"Smart woman. Personal recommendations are a much safer bet." He leaned in even closer, making sure to invade her space even more. "The Flaming Pig's Ass Porter is the house special. Confidence in a glass."

"So the warning above the bar claims."

"Not into beer?"

"Not all that big of a drinker," she clarified, then without further explanation she flagged down the bartender. "Excuse me."

And wouldn't you know it, she snagged the attention of Harris Donovan, part-time brew-master and full-time chopper pilot for Sequoia Elite Mountain Rescue. He was also Ty's cousin.

Even though Ty worked out of Monterey County as the head of the swift water rescue team and Harris was stationed out of Sequoia Lake, they'd worked more than a few missions together. With Harris running rescues from the air and Ty rappelling into some of the most dangerous waters in the Pacific, the two of them had gotten into—and out of—some pretty squirrelly situations. Both on and off duty.

Only now, Harris was smiling at Avery as if she was his next mission, and Ty suddenly regretted coming inside. Partly because he wanted to keep the news of his homecoming quiet until he saw his parents, and Harris, who up until two seconds ago had been his favorite cousin, was headed his way—and he tended to gossip like a schoolgirl.

But mainly because Harris was flashing that charming grin he used when looking to get laid. Ty knew the grin well, had taught the prick its power back in high school when he'd had doggie eyes for Shelby Steel, the first girl to upgrade from a training bra. Those double-barreled Donovan dimples had gotten him up close and personal with Shelby's silk and all of her secrets. That he was flashing them at Avery had Ty firmly planting his ass on the barstool next to her.

Which was ridiculous. Avery might be sexy in a hot-librarian kind of way, but she was not his type.

She was also off-limits. His trip home was packed, and unfortunately there was no room in his schedule for a fling with a crazy cutie.

"Well, hey there, tiny," Harris said, leaning in close, charm dialed to "let's get naked." "Haven't seen you around in a while."

Avery self-consciously fiddled with her hair. That she'd done it while gifting a shy smile Harris's way told Ty the two had a history. One that went beyond bartender and patron. That she'd avoided Ty's gaze, as if uncomfortable with his presence, told him that they also shared a secret. One he wasn't privy to.

"Life's kept me busy lately," she said, and Harris's expression changed. Not enough that anyone else would notice—his smile was still there, as was the lethal dimple he was working—but his eyes softened.

What that meant Ty didn't know, but he didn't like it.

"Kicking ass and taking names as I hear it," he said, and Avery blushed as if the prick had dropped to a knee and promised her the world. "So, what can I get you?"

Some fucking privacy? "How about decent service?" Ty said, resting a palm on the bar top.

Harris's gaze settled on Ty and went wide with surprise. "Jesus, man, when the hell did you get back into town? Shouldn't you be lying on a beach somewhere, working on your tan?"

Harris reached across the bar and gave him a side hug, and even though Ty wasn't big on hugging, it felt damn good. He'd spent a decent portion of the past few years conquering one deadly terrain after another, sometimes searching for lost swimmers, sometimes searching for forgiveness. But no matter where he was he always managed to keep himself pretty isolated, except in Sequoia Lake. One of the reasons he avoided coming back.

"I pulled in about an hour ago," he said, aware that Avery was dividing her focus between the two of them. Funny how he'd been trying to get her attention for the past ten minutes and she chose now to acknowledge him, when all he wanted to do was disappear.

"Does your dad know you're back?" Harris asked cautiously.

Ah, yes, the other reason.

Dale Donovan: husband, father, respected adventurer, and town hero. Also the man whom Ty had spent a lifetime trying to impress and never failed to disappoint.

"Not yet." He'd considered going straight to his parents', but he needed a little time to decompress from the trip and prepare himself. Telling the one person in town who didn't want him back that he was settling in for the near future took some working up to. "And I'd like to keep it that way."

Being home was hard enough. Being home around this time of year was a painful reminder of everything he'd lost. Something his cousin understood firsthand.

"Well, happy to have you back." Harris looked from Ty to Avery, and his smile said he understood *that* too. Not that there was anything to understand—Ty had just been too long without sex. That was all. "Now what can I get you? On the house."

"On the house? Thanks, Harris." Avery tapped her chin with her finger, and after a drawn-out moment of dramatic contemplation—in which she wasn't looking at the menu—she said, "A Shirley Temple, please."

"That's a pretty prissy drink for someone who just scrawled 'I owe you a screw' on the front of a stranger's truck," Ty pointed out.

"And a Flaming Pig's Ass," she added with a smile that had him nervous.

"You do know that it's a pint of porter with a lit shot of wild turkey and 151 dropped in?"

She slid Ty a glance. "So I've been told."

"You can't leave your seat until you finish it, and if you don't finish, then you have to buy a round for the entire bar," Harris said.

Her eyes lit with excitement, which made no sense. He'd sweet-talked her into a corner, she knew it, and all that was left was for him to sit back and see if she was as stubborn as she seemed. Only she was grinning as if she'd planned this all along.

"I know the rules," she said, smiling, and damn if Harris didn't smile back. "I guess the glass better wind up empty then."

"I don't like it, but I'll make it." Harris walked off to prepare their drinks.

When it was only the two of them, Ty said, "Big words for someone who was stuck in a safety harness for most of the day."

"Less than an hour, and it was a single clasp."

"Tell that to my screwdriver," he said, leaning in and tucking an escaped curl behind her ear. "One chance encounter and it will never be the same."

"*The same* is overrated," she said on a breath, her cheeks turning an adorable shade of pink. *And look at that.* Something flickered between them. It was raw and hot and something he hadn't felt in a long time.

Chemistry. The kind that wouldn't disappear until he did something about it.

She knew it too, because she was zeroed in on his mouth, which worked for him since he'd been thinking about that mouth of hers pretty much nonstop since he saw her. When he wasn't fixated on her mouth, he was trying to get a better glimpse of her heart-shaped ass, which the safety harness had highlighted to perfection.

Helping her out of it had been a damn shame, since it would have been so much more fun to watch her parade around with the harness shrink-wrapping her clothes around every one of her delicious curves.

She might be petite and a little slender for his taste, but the woman was a bombshell.

She was also breathing heavy. He could see the pulse beat at the base of her neck as clearly as the hesitation in her eyes. Oh yeah, Little Miss Live Loud might pretend to be all fearless and devil-may-care, but being impulsive wasn't her normal MO.

Ty was a ninja at making rapid assessments of subjects. A skill that had saved his ass too many times to count. Being able to size up a person's nature and accurately predict their next reaction in a matter of seconds was crucial when hanging from a chopper and looking down at the rough waters of the Pacific with a terrified and often irrational subject in tandem. And Avery was about as close to being a balls-out kind of person as she was to being a princess.

The way she nervously licked her lips told him that the most spontaneous thing she'd ever done was borrow his screwdriver. So he decided to call her bluff. "So this living loud thing—I don't buy it."

She didn't back down and didn't lean away; instead, she zeroed in on his mouth and said, "I'd like to prove you wrong."

Being wrong went against Ty's nature. Always right and never in doubt had saved hundreds of lives. But if the determined heat in her pretty blue pools were anything to go on, Ty would be willing to man up and admit defeat this one time. Because he'd bet that being on the losing side of this discussion would taste like heaven.

Only Harris, the slowest bartender in town, chose that moment to tap into his super speed and reappeared with their drinks in record time.

He cleared his throat, and when Ty made eye contact, his good old cuz was looking back with a grin that made Ty want to punch him in the throat. "Here're your drinks."

"Thank you." Unabashed, Avery beamed up at Harris and then pointed to her Shirley Temple. "That's not for me, it's for him," she said, turning those pearly whites Ty's way. "For him to drink while he's making me my crown. So can you put an extra cherry in it and an umbrella? A pink one?"

Harris choked on a laugh. Not that it stopped him from reaching under the bar and placing a prissy pink umbrella right in the center of Ty's drink. "He offered to make you a crown?"

"Yes, he did, for after I ride Widow Maker and am crowned princess for the day."

"Although I'd pay good money to see ham-hands there craft you a crown, Widow Maker's incapacitated at the moment."

Avery looked toward the big pen in the corner, covered with red mats and a giant yellow Out of Service sign, and her smile dulled.

"What happened?" Ty asked, willing to call in a favor to get Widow Maker back in the ring if it meant he could watch Avery give him hell.

"Ladies' night and seniors' Shot4Shot landed on the same Wednesday. Had to call in the sheriff." Harris shivered. "Got a cleaning crew coming in later this week, so he'll be back to business as usual by the weekend."

"Bummer." She sounded genuinely disappointed. "I guess my coronation will have to wait."

"The night is just getting started," Ty said. "Tons of time to live loud."

Avery turned around and met Ty's gaze, and *hot damn*, he didn't know what was on her mind, didn't care.

She gave one tug at his shirt collar, and their lips collided, hard and with heat, and he was game for whatever she had planned. Because if this was what living loud tasted like, then he wanted a second helping. Not only did Avery pull him close enough to smell the evening chill on her skin, she pressed her mouth to his in a kiss that was so unexpected it had every part of him begging to take the leap.

Because right there, beneath the flashing neon Buzz Saw Brown Ale sign and in front of Harris and half the town, Avery Adams, adventure coordinator, kissed him. And *holy hell*, the woman could kiss.

It started out slow, and a brush of air escaped her mouth, as if she'd surprised herself. There was a warmth, then a heat, and finally those lips of hers parted, ever so briefly, in a move that was as seductive as it was addictive. And just when Ty was about to go in for a second taste, she lifted her head and smiled.

It wasn't smug or wicked, like he'd expect, but sunny and a bit giddy. As if she was delighted with herself. He wanted to keep the get-to-know-you party going, but then Harris laughed, and he realized that a public venue wasn't the place.

Her bedroom, perhaps?

"What was that for?" he asked, his voice raspy.

"Bella."

Ty knew how to kiss. Period. In fact, his kisses had garnished a lot of praise from the ladies: *luscious, mind-blowing, addicting, clothed foreplay,* and his favorite, *panty-melting.* But they'd never been coined beautiful. A little flowery for his taste, but he'd take it because "bella" had Avery's face flushing, her eyes gleaming, and her lips curling into a shy little smile. So he agreed. "Definitely bella."

"A reminder to live loud and in the moment." A hint of romance tinged her voice. "Trying that something new we talked about."

"Damn shame the moment's over."

"Ah, hell," Harris mumbled as he approached and saw the just-been-kissed expression on Avery's face, and he rolled his eyes.

She looked at her shot and grinned up at his cousin. "You got a light?"

"I'm going to regret this, aren't I?" But Harris pulled out his lighter all the same.

"Not if you let me light it," she said.

Harris held up his hand in mock surrender. "Have at it, girl."

She took a lighter and carefully lit the floater of 151. Her eyes sparkled with excitement when it caught, and then she scooted the glass full of porter beer, and herself, a little closer to Ty. Her hair brushed his cheek as she dropped in the shot and whispered to him, "Remember, if you don't finish it you have to buy the bar a round."

Before Ty knew what was happening, she had the safety harness in hand and was swishing that fine ass of hers toward the door. Ty went to hop down and follow, but Harris grabbed his arm and looked at his Flaming Pig's Ass and then burst out laughing. "House rules, cuz."

Right. Couldn't leave until the drink was gone.

"Where are you going?" Ty called out to Avery—from his freaking barstool.

She stopped at the doorway. "I said I'd buy you a drink, not have one with you. Like I said, not a big drinker. But it looks like tonight *you* will be. Enjoy, and sorry about the screwdriver!"

A little finger wiggle and she was gone. Just like that. Leaving him with a hangover in a glass and a hard-on in his pants.

CHAPTER 4

"What's the deal with Avery?" Ty asked Harris, his intentions strictly professional, of course.

"She's local. Not a regular of the bar, but local," Harris said, still laughing even as the door swung shut. "Keeps to herself, on the shy side, but seems to be a sweetheart. Too nice for a guy like you."

Ty almost laughed. Hard to picture the woman who'd offered him a screw and a kiss in under thirty minutes as shy. But beneath the excitement and boldness of the moment, he could sense a quiet gentleness as well as an adorable naïveté that was shockingly refreshing.

So where had she been hiding? Sure, Ty had chosen a career that kept him busy enough to spend the majority of his time everywhere but here, but he came home on rotating birthdays and all of the expected holidays. Yet he'd never come across Avery.

Odd since Sequoia Lake was, like most of the tourist towns in the Sierras, a destination for many, home to few. When the bass weren't biting and the powder wasn't falling, the town would shrink to less than six thousand. So hiding a face like hers in a place that small would be damn near impossible.

Good thing Ty loved tackling the impossible—almost as much as he liked being right.

"Everyone around here likes her, including me, so watch yourself," Harris warned.

"Hey man, she kissed me."

"Right, and the Flaming Pig's Ass was what? You being neighborly?"

"We were just having fun," Ty said.

Harris flipped his ball cap around and leaned in so that Ty could see the whites of his eyes. "It's always fun until someone gets hurt."

He palmed his cousin's face and shoved. The asshat didn't move. "It was a little meaningless flirting with a girl who lives here and knows I don't. Plus, she's not my type. Too sweet, too young." And way too vulnerable for a guy like Ty.

She might have been all rainbows and happy-go-lucky, but he could see the shadows beneath her eyes. Noticed how hard she worked to appear sunny, when it was clear that she was exhausted. The kind of exhaustion that came from challenging the universe.

"I think she was a few years behind you and Garrett in school," Harris chimed in.

Ty placed a hand on his chest to slow the familiar shot of pain before it took him down. It had been fifteen years since his brother passed, but the sound of his name still brought back all of the sorrow and regret. Not to mention guilt. A giant rucksack full of guilt that pressed down so hard that sometimes it was impossible to breathe.

Only eleven months apart, Ty and Garrett had been more like twins growing up. Best friends. And when Garrett died it felt as if a part of Ty died with him.

"Thanks for taking Dad up the mountain last week," Ty said. "I should have guessed he'd be determined to make the trek, even though he's about a decade too old to make that climb."

It was a hike every Donovan man made with his pops on his eighteenth. It was the same hike Harris had made on his eighteenth—and the same hike Ty attempted when he'd been a cocky seventeen-year-old, desperate to prove he was ready for bigger and better. Ty had made it to the top of River Rock—in record time. Came home with a touch of frostbite, a fractured wrist, and what should have been bragging rights for a lifetime.

Only Garrett's competitive nature had kicked in, and refusing to be out climbed by Ty, he had come along for the climb. They'd made it back to the bluff, but then Garrett slipped on some loose rocks and slid down the mountainside and into the river. Garrett was an expert swimmer, but with the snowcaps melting and the rivers rushing, the current was too difficult to navigate in the dark.

And for the first time in his life, Ty wasn't fast enough to make a difference.

"Your dad called and told me he was going to River Rock. Said I could tag along or get out of his way. I offered up the chopper." Harris shrugged as if it were no big deal. But it was. It was a huge fucking deal in every way that mattered.

"I saw the pictures on Facebook. He looked happy, so thanks," Ty said, hoping the genuine appreciation in his voice wasn't smothered out by the disappointment.

Not that *that* was a new emotion when it came to his dad. Since the funeral, Dale hadn't bothered to invite Ty to a single anniversary climb. Not one. Whether it was simple oversight or something much more difficult to acknowledge, the rejection burned long and hot.

Why he expected Garrett's fifteenth anniversary to be any different, he couldn't say. But for some stupid reason, Ty had hoped he'd get a call. An email. Something. But when communication had been nonexistent, he got the message.

It seemed Dale had skipped the invite, choosing to honor his son's life with Harris and some of his buddies instead. Didn't stop to think that making the trip with Ty might lead to some kind of understanding. Then again, understanding required an honest conversation, something

Ty and his dad had never seemed to reach. For as long as Ty could remember, his dad was more interested in talking about who he wanted Ty to be instead of who Ty really was.

The difference now was Ty had found some kind of peace with who he was, and now he wanted to find the same acceptance with who he'd been.

"He said you were working that mudslide in Santa Barbara—didn't want to bother you."

"I would have come," Ty pointed out.

"I know you would have. But I also knew that they needed every hand they could get for that rescue. They were even pulling guys in from Reno and Portland."

Ty let out a deep breath. "Yeah, this time of year I can barely get a weekend off."

"Yet you're here."

He was there all right, and not for a vacation. "Lance Meyers was the representative sent on behalf of Cal-SAR to oversee SAREX. My dad didn't have a thing ready for the meeting."

Harris stilled, his eyes going into *Oh shit* circles. Fitting since this was an *Oh shit* moment of epic proportions. "Isn't SAREX in two months?"

"Yup." SAREX, the annual Northern California Search and Rescue intensive training, was a huge moneymaker for the lodge, bringing in specialized teams from all over the state. Hundreds of extreme first responders came to train, learn new skills, and enjoy the mountains. Sequoia Lake Lodge had been the host for the past fifty years, and it had gained them a lot of recognition in the S&R community. That combined with the local Type 1 terrain attracted adrenaline junkies from around the world and made Sequoia Lake Lodge the premier destination in extreme adventures.

"By the time Lance called to let me know about the botched meeting," Ty continued, thankful that Lance, a friend from the academy, had thought to call him, "his boss, needing to know if they should move the training to a new location, had already sent an inspector out to see if the lodge was up to code." Ty blew out a breath. "We failed the inspection, by the way. But based on the history with the lodge—and me—Lance said he'd give us some time to make the upgrades and he'd send an inspector back out. I figured if Lance was calling me, it must be bad, so I took a personal leave."

If they lost SAREX and word got around that they'd failed a safety inspection, it could be a huge hit to the lodge—and the community who relied on the tourists for their economy. He owed Lance big-time.

And Ty hated owing anyone anything.

"How long did they give you?" Harris asked.

"Three weeks."

"Three weeks?" Harris laughed as if Ty were delusional. "I take it your mom didn't fill you in much on what's going on."

A knot formed somewhere between his ribcage and his stomach, and then it started twisting. "Just that ski season had been rough and they'd hired some extra help to get the lodge back in order for SAREX."

Harris gave a low whistle. "Man, you must be slipping with the ladies."

"Why do you say that?"

"First your mom gave some BS story about hiring new help, and you believed her, even though you know Dale is a tight-ass when it comes to outsiders working in his lodge. And second, the girl next door, who has no game, zero"—his hands made a zero—"just played you."

"She wasn't playing me." Ty picked up the Flaming Pig's Ass and took a hearty swallow, grinning like an idiot even as the liquid burned him inside out. "That's what flirting looks like, in case you forgot in your old age."

"You're two years my senior," Harris said, picking up an empty mug and pouring himself a beer, sans the shot from hell.

"You haven't seen the flip side of nine o'clock in over a year."

The ass just grinned, so genuine and content a part of Ty prickled with jealousy. "When you share breakfast every morning at five with the prettiest girl in the world, giving up beers with the guys isn't all that much of a sacrifice."

"No arguments from me." Ty lifted his glass, because if he had a pint-sized pixie like his goddaughter, Emma, looking at him like he hung the moon, he would probably trade in late nights with the guys too.

Harris clinked rims. "Good, I'll let Emma know you'll be over bright and early for pancakes tomorrow. She keeps asking when Uncle TyTy will be back so you can watch that *Frozen* DVD you bought her for Christmas."

Ty groaned at the thought of hearing that soundtrack one more time, but he couldn't keep the smile from creeping in. Emma was damn cute. He'd missed the little tyke. And with her mom out of the picture, Ty didn't mind watching her princess movies with her.

Not that he wanted a family of his own—more people to be responsible for. But he understood why other people needed that. The love, the connection, the belonging. That kind of vulnerability wasn't someplace Ty was interested in visiting again.

Ever.

"Oh, and in case those beach babes and eternal spring-break hookups are clouding your judgment," Harris said, "what happened a second ago wasn't flirting. That was kissing a stranger or some kind of girls' night out BS small-town ladies do for entertainment."

Ty opened his mouth to argue but then realized Harris was right. The lipstick innuendo on his window, the bull, and that kiss . . .

"Well, shit."

He'd been played. He was probably some kind of scavenger hunt item to be checked off and giggled about by a bunch of hot ladies during their next wine tasting.

"I'll give her the weekend to gloat." Ty sat back, knowing by the Sequoia Lake Lodge employee logo on her shirt that he'd see her Monday.

"You sure about that?" Harris asked. "This is Sequoia Lake—by tomorrow it will be all over town, and come Monday your mom will be inviting her to dinner."

"I don't think I have to worry about that," Ty said with confidence. Avery didn't seem the type to gossip lightly. Plus, once she learned who Ty's mom was, he doubted she'd want to tangle with that. "Monday is soon enough. I know where she works."

Harris looked over the rim of his beer. "She know where you work?"

"Exactly my point." Because come Monday when he called a staff meeting at the lodge and started cleaning up the mess his father had created, she'd figure it out.

Too bad fooling around with his employees was not how he operated. Because he might have found the one thing that could have made his stay a little more enjoyable.

"To you coming home." Harris held up his beer.

"To Garrett."

◆　◆　◆

"I can't believe he did that. In front of everyone," Grace Mills, the town's self-appointed hall monitor and one of Avery's best friends at Living for Love, gasped, brushing a bold red streak down the middle of her flowerpot, making it look artsy.

"It wasn't in front of everyone," Avery explained, making the exact same stroke on the exact same spot on her flowerpot. Only instead of a statement, it looked like she'd cut her finger and bled all over her project.

It was the last Sunday of the month, which meant the ladies of Living for Love had gathered to work on their community projects.

This year the group was making Love Blooms, hand-painted terracotta flowerpots filled with blooming bulbs to be delivered to long-term hospitals in the area. The idea was to bring a little sunshine to an otherwise sterile existence.

Avery had once been the recipient of a Love Bloom, and she was beyond honored to pay it forward and brighten someone else's day.

Sips and Splatters, the local art school and wine bar that Grace managed, had agreed to help with the project, and she invited them to their famous Monet and Martinis class. While a few of the ladies were there for the art lessons, the majority showed up for the free martinis and bottomless gossip. Because when the ladies of Living for Love had an "outing," everyone's prattle was fair play.

And Avery had done her share of playing this weekend—with the hot stranger she'd met on the ice-slickened street. But since that wasn't the "he" her friend was referring to, she ignored her tingling lips and said, "It was just the gift shop girl, and Dale only expressed his concern that me taking out such a large group for my first solo trek might be too risky."

"Too risky?" Grace plopped her brush in the jar of water. "The only thing you're in risk of with that group is Mr. Fitz wanting you to hold his pole."

"Dale is cautious," Avery said with a smile as if the act alone would diminish her disappointment that the experience she needed to hike Sierra Point was that much farther out of reach.

Dale was known as having the toughest guidelines of any lodge in the Sierras. He knew better than anyone how deadly those mountains could be. And Avery wasn't asking him to make an exception to the rule—she just wanted the same rules to apply to everyone.

Since being hired on, two other coordinators had been tapped, trained, and promoted to guides. Sure, they both had prior climbing and survival experience, but Avery was a fast learner, yet she couldn't even get Dale to agree to a start date for her training. "I lack the skills and experience."

"Skills?" Grace snorted. "What kind of skills does one need to babysit a bunch of old retired men while they compare fish stories?"

"Dale just wants to make sure I'm ready before I take on my first solo trek."

"Do you feel ready?" Olivia Preston asked as she walked up behind them, drops of evening mist still clinging to her coat from the outside. Olivia was the newest member of Living for Love and the third bestie in their trio.

Avery considered this, thought through every skill she'd need to possess to handle a simple fishing hike with a group of seniors. "I think so."

"Then get yourself to a place that you know so and tell him you're ready."

"And if he disagrees?"

"Then agree to disagree, because unless you want to go back to living in a bubble, you've got to fight," Liv said, shrugging out of her coat. "And if he's still being stubborn and can't see past the sick woman you once were, well, then send him my way."

Liv was one of the top nurses at Mercy General. Known for her nurturing bedside manner, her attention to detail, and most importantly, her ability to cut to the heart of the problem, she would convince Dale to listen to reason.

"And if that doesn't work," Grace said as she took Avery's brush and extended the lines of the red blob, making it into a beautiful redbird, "get creative."

Right, that whole *don't wait for permission* mantra she'd adopted. Easy in theory, but hard in application for a woman who'd spent her entire life waiting. On tests, on doctors, on her name to rise to the top of the list.

After the transplant had taken, Avery had to wait in that recovery room for three months until a panel of experts told her she could finally go home. Even then, she'd been given a list of approved food and drink and activities.

Now she could finally plan a life past her lab results. She just needed to remind people of that.

"Be assertive. Fight. Get creative. Got it," she said.

She might not have convinced Dale to let her take out Senior X-Treme or earned that princess crown for Caroline, but she was making steady progress. Her energy was slow coming and she still bruised easily, but she'd gained back a few pounds and her skin was looking less pasty, plus she'd spent most of yesterday filling out page six in her memory journal—making one more person's final wish a reality.

Avery's wish had been that her dear friend Bella was with her so she could tell her that kissing a stranger in the heat of the moment led to the exact kind of heart-fluttering and soul-melting magic Bella had dreamed of. That two days had passed and Avery's heart was still feeling the aftershocks.

Or maybe it was her blood pressure still stabilizing. Either way, she placed a hand over her heart to keep it steady, then set the brush in the water jar and grabbed a martini. Even with her kidney 2.0 she couldn't drink the whole thing, but a sip wouldn't kill her. "Who knew living loud could be so"—*exciting, thrilling, mind-blowing*—"overwhelming."

"It's the pushover part that gets me," Grace said, taking a martini of her own.

"Tell me about it." Liv slid into her seat, and bypassing the art project altogether, she went straight for a martini—fisting two. "I spent that past hour negotiating with a five-year-old over the importance of eating your broccoli."

Grace and Avery exchanged looks.

"Don't judge," Liv said. "It's the rules of Mom's night out."

"Funny, I thought we were here for our monthly Living for Love craft night." Grace waved her paintbrush in the air as proof.

"I believe the invitation said 'Monet and Martinis.'" Liv held up her glass. "Plus, I ate all of my broccoli. Now tell me why he said no so we can figure out how to get him to say yes."

"He didn't technically say no," she said, and Grace coughed something that sounded a lot like *bullshit*. "Okay, he also didn't say yes. He said when I've had the proper training we can talk."

"Oh, he's good." Liv leaned back in her chair, her lips twitching with irritation—and admiration. "That is some serious parenting skills right there. I tried that with Paxton tonight. 'You can have dessert after you finish your greens.' It still took a few gags, a convincing argument about green foods equating to green poop, and a story about some boy who grew hair on his chest from eating green things, but he finished every last speck."

Huh, Avery might need to take a lesson from little mister Paxton. A whole hour? She had caved in two seconds flat.

"Then he said instead of dessert, he wanted a hamster."

"I thought he wanted a dog," Avery said.

"Until I told him a dog was a lot of responsibility, and maybe when he's bigger."

"Saying no without saying no," Grace said. "Smart."

"That kid's smarter. We tracked his height for over a week, and when he realized that the line hadn't moved, he pointed out that a hamster is smaller than him, and he's even big enough to carry the cage."

"How did that go?" Avery asked, her cheeks a little hot at the realization that Dale had used the same trick and—unlike Paxton—she'd fallen for it.

"I told him he made a valid point and I'd look into it, and then I gave him a second helping of dessert." Liv shrugged. "Mommy misdirection at its finest. Making a promise with no expiration and distracting him with a treat."

"But that's what this new year is all about, remember?" Grace said, pointing her brush at Liv. "Eight months ago we sat in that awful hospital room, waiting on Avery's doctor to read the verdict, and we made a pact. We said no matter the results we weren't going to let fear and heartache hold us back from living."

"I know, and a hamster sounds like an easy first step, right?" Liv let out a long, tired sigh. The kind of sigh that went soul deep and ached to release. "Did you know they only live a few years? Opening my heart up to a cute little critter that has the life expectancy of snow tires isn't something either one of us is ready for."

Last year, after Liv's husband was killed in a snowstorm, she'd relocated with her five-year-old son to Sequoia Lake and took a nursing job at Mercy General, where she and Avery met. Without family of her own nearby, Liv hoped being near her in-laws would help with the healing. But when his parents, unable to live among the memories, decided to relocate to Palm Beach, Liv bought their house—and Avery brought her to Living for Love.

Since then the three had been inseparable.

"How do you know you're not ready if you don't try?" Grace said.

"And what if I get the hamster, he dies, Paxton goes back into that silent place where I can't even reach him, and I realize, whoops, we weren't ready? What then?"

"You try again," Grace said, her voice thick with compassion and understanding. "Every loss ached until I thought I would pass out from the pain, but I never regretted opening my heart up to the possibility of love."

Powerful words coming from a woman who had lost more than any one person should be able to lose and still smile. But Grace always smiled, even when her body rejected every attempt at expanding her family—which ultimately cost Grace her marriage. "Maybe this is Paxton's way of telling you he's ready to try love again."

"Maybe," Liv said quietly, but Avery didn't think her friend would be opening up her heart anytime soon.

Avery had taken a step, a huge one, and her head was still swimming at the memory. "I fulfilled one of the wishes in my living memory journal this weekend."

Liv's eyes went round. "You lived out someone's wish?"

"And you waited this long to tell me?" Grace sounded about as upset as a kid at Disneyland.

"I wanted to wait until you were both here." Avery looked around to make sure all of the busybodies were busy painting, then lowered her voice. "Also, because I didn't want to broadcast it."

"Oh my God," Grace said. "You're blushing, which means it was a juicy one. Was it birthday-suit BASE jumping?"

"No," Liv said. "Her doctor hasn't cleared her to do physical activity that could bruise the kidney."

Plus, BASE jumping was Avery's dream, and the purpose of her journal was to live out other people's wishes for them when they were no longer able to.

"Wait." Liv snapped her fingers. "She streaked naked through town with Hugh Jackman."

"Nope." Avery still wasn't sure how she was going to pull that off, but she would figure something out to make that wish happen. "And what's up with people wanting to be naked all the time?"

"It's called foreplay, which leads to sex," Liv said as if she were getting some regularly.

"We should all try it again sometime," Grace said, and they all laughed.

It felt good to laugh, and it felt even better to say, "It wasn't sex, but it did include a hot stranger."

Grace's hands flew to her mouth. "You did Bella's wish."

Avery nodded.

"You kissed Bella Reed's infamous Parisian suitor?" Liv asked in case there was another Bella in Avery's journal.

"He wasn't a Parisian, or even European, but yes."

Liv's eyes went misty, as did Avery's. Bella wasn't just another Living for Love sister. She had been one of their closest friends, the fourth member of their posse, and a woman whose life had barely begun when loss struck in the form of cancer. It took her breasts, then her freedom, and eventually her life—but it never touched her sense of romance.

"Oh my God." Grace grabbed her hands, bouncing up and down in her chair. "You kissed someone. You. Avery Adams, the girl who ran to the bathroom crying when Billy Long kissed her under the monkey bars at recess, kissed someone? Wait." Her smile faded. "Was it Carson? Please tell me it wasn't Carson."

Avery snorted. Last year the idea would have thrilled her. Not anymore. Avery didn't want to live her life as if there were a clock ticking.

"It wasn't Carson." Carson had never shaken her foundation like Ty had. "It was a stranger I met on Lake Street. I bought him a drink, and then I kissed him. That was it."

"If that was it, then why are you smiling like that?"

"Like what?"

"Like you're floating."

"I'm not floating." Avery looked at the ground and, yup, her feet were firmly planted on the floor. Didn't mean she was on solid ground, though. At first, she'd convinced herself that the weightlessness was an overload of adrenaline and testosterone—two chemicals she hadn't had a lot of recent experience with.

But as the strange lightness grew, she began to wonder if it was the kiss itself—or what the kiss represented. Either way she felt different. Invincible.

Ready to finally climb Sierra Point.

She pulled her phone out of her pocket and dialed.

"What are you doing?" Liv asked.

"She's calling the hottie." Grace scooted closer, so close she was practically pressing her ear to the phone.

"I'm calling Dale. Telling him I'm ready to lead a trek."

Grace gave a fist pump in the air. "You tell him."

"And if he needs to train me, then he needs to set a concrete time."

Grace slowly lowered her hand to a *go get 'em, kid.* "Okay, not as balls-out as I thought, but it's a step in the right direction."

"Be strong," Liv coached. "Tell him who you are, why you're calling, and don't show fear. Then word it in a way that he can't say no." She turned to Grace. "The first time Paxton did that I was so thrown I let him have an ice cream sundae for dinner. In his Batman underwear."

"A way he can't say no. Right."

"And don't let him distract you," Grace said over the ringing. Then to Liv, "What did you call it?"

"Mommy misdirection."

"No mommy misdirection." Avery squared her shoulders and made a conscious decision not to get distracted right as the phone was picked up.

"Hello?" A sweet-as-pie voice came through the cell.

"Hey, Irene, this is Avery. I'm calling for Dale."

Clear, to the point, no backing down. She was halfway there. Wow, that was easier than she thought. She gave a thumbs-up to the girls.

"Oh, hey, sweetie, how's the art class going? I'm so sorry I couldn't make it. Rough night here."

Avery looked around and realized that Irene wasn't there. Which explained why she was answering her home line. "Rough night? Are you sick?"

Irene was the founder of Living for Love. She was the heart and soul behind the group, and the one who had kept it running all of these years. After the sudden death of her youngest son, the community rallied, showering her family with love and constant support to help them get through that trying time. So when Irene got to a place where she could breathe again, she started Living for Love as a way to pay back the kindness she'd received and to offer other women in the community a place to come when they needed support.

Avery's was the first family she'd helped.

In thirteen years, Irene had only missed two events. That she wasn't there tonight meant she was either sick, stuck in bad weather, or zombies had attacked.

"Dale took a nap and woke up a little confused, so I figured it was best to stay put."

Or that.

With a deep breath, Avery sat back down. "I'm so sorry. Is he okay?"

"Just one of his spells," Irene said, but her tone told Avery she was beginning to believe that it was more than a few spells. The in-patient care center Avery had frequented in her teens when she'd undergone experimental treatment also housed dementia and Alzheimer's patients. She wasn't a doctor, but she was pretty sure Dale was in the early stages of one or the other. And Irene wasn't ready to admit it yet. "Are you returning his call?"

Avery looked at her phone. No missed called. "He called?"

Irene sighed and so did Avery. "He said he did, but who knows. He was supposed to get a hold of you and let you know that Brody took a fall today. Thank goodness he was out with a group of nursing students from Reno State."

"Lucky him," Avery said through clenched teeth.

Brody was a former X Games athlete who had a thing for co-eds, nature bunnies, and level one trails. When he combined the two, trouble usually ensued, but he'd most likely taken a fall right into a nurse's bed and wouldn't come up for air until ski week ended and classes were back in session.

"Did you see a doctor's note?"

"Not yet, but he did call me from the ER," Irene said, releasing a deep breath. "We had to cancel his last trek of the day and need to cancel his schedule for the next two days, which Dale said he'd have you do."

Knowing that faking ER sounds would be a staple in a guy like Brody's playbook, she closed her eyes and took a second to calm her irritation before saying, "Okay, I'll call the clients as soon as I hang up."

"This couldn't have come at a worse time. With Dale not feeling his best, canceling on clients will look so unprofessional, especially after that failed safety inspection, not to mention—"

"A failed safety inspection?" Avery cut in, wondering why, as the coordinator and office manager, she hadn't even known there was an inspection to fail. "Why didn't you tell me? I would have put it on the calendar and made sure we were ready and in inspection shape."

"Dale said he had it handled and, well . . . If we can't get it together by the next inspection, we will have to order all new ropes and safety harnesses if we still want to host SAREX."

Still want to host? Avery had booked the entire lodge for SAREX. If Sequoia Elite Mountain Rescue backed out, the lodge would lose a ton of money. Not to mention the repeat business they counted on. "We'll get it handled."

"I hope so." Irene sounded on the verge of tears, which in itself was not all that uncommon. The woman cried at greeting cards and YouTube cat videos, but this sounded different. Heavy.

And Irene was the sunniest person Avery knew.

But she understood the older woman's worry. SAREX was a huge moneymaker for the lodge and community. It was also a huge point of pride for Dale. He had pictures of his staff with every year's team posted around the lodge, dating all the way back to the sixties. A hit like this could explain his level of agitation the past few days. It could also explain why he'd been so curt with her about training.

"We will, I promise. And I promise to take care of the schedule." Avery swiped the calendar on her cell that connected to the one at work. "You don't worry about a thing. Marshall has been asking for more hours, so I can give him Brody's group treks, and I can pass his beginner climbing class to Clay." The adventure coordinator who had been hired after Avery, yet promoted within weeks. "That leaves a beginner solo hike and a fishing excursion."

"I knew I could count on you." Irene released a telltale sniffle that indicated the crying was back to business as usual.

Grace was shooting her a *Don't get distracted* look, and Liv was mouthing, *I have got those hikes handled, as in I will do those hikes.* Avery waved them both off. She was beyond distracted, and she needed to handle this mess so that Irene could be there for her husband.

"You and Dale can always count on me."

In unison, her friends let out an exasperated sigh and slumped back in their chairs. Avery sent Dale well wishes, and after a few more instructions about office matters, she ended the call. But when she turned, her friends were staring at her with big, troubling grins.

"What? Brody is *injured*." She threw up air quotes around the word. "I need to call him and see how long he plans on faking an injury."

Last time Brody had gone hiking with a lady in the medical profession it ended in a six-day medical leave. The pediatrician had been single, stacked, and interested. Brody had handed over a note, written on official doctor's stationery, diagnosing him with bronchitis. Coincidently, it was the same week Dr. McBenefits requested for her vacation from the hospital.

Brody had come back with a tan and a just-been-laid look, while everyone else needed a vacation from juggling schedules to fit in all of the clients.

"Note or not, it's my job to fill the schedule or cancel on the customer."

"Or you fill the schedule and put yourself in for the hike," Liv suggested.

The idea alone had Avery's stomach fluttering with excitement. But as soon as the first flicker happened, it died. "Dale said no to me going at it solo until he trains me more. I don't want to cause him any more stress, and I doubt he will be in any condition to train me before six o'clock in the morning."

Grace's smile became a full-out grin, and Avery had known her long enough to understand that meant trouble. For Avery. "Dale said no to you taking on a group trek by yourself, not you doing a solo trek."

Avery considered herself an honest person. She'd never cheated on a test in her life, fallen through on a promise, and never, ever led someone she respected astray. She'd learned life was too precious to behave otherwise.

But facts were facts. Dale hadn't said no to taking a single client out alone, he'd said no to her taking out a group of clients at the same time. The only people who booked solo beginner walks with a guy like Brody were senior ladies who wanted an afternoon being charmed by a playboy.

"I did promise Irene I would handle it." And breaking a promise was as bad as a lie as far as Avery was concerned. "How hard can a beginner hike be anyway?"

CHAPTER 5

The sun was barely peeking through the pines as Avery set her pack on the ground. It landed with a solid thud and sank slightly into the damp soil. Not a good sign since she'd have to carry it for the entirety of the five-mile hike around Cedar Rim.

Five miles wasn't all that bad, and the trail was rated beginner, meaning her grandma could cover it in less than three hours. But her grandma hadn't gone through major surgery eleven months ago—and wouldn't be expected to carry a thirty-pound pack.

Kneeling down, Avery ignored the cold as dew seeped through her jeans and opened her bag to see if there was anything she could leave behind. Unfortunately, every item was listed as a necessity in the official adventure guide's handbook she'd studied late into the night. Water, first aid kit, compass, map, high-protein meal, two ways to make fire, and emergency shelter and bedding.

In her boots, flannel top, orange puffer vest, and knit cap, she looked like a legit adventure guide. She even had the boots and equipment of an adventure guide. Problem was, she didn't have the body of an adventure guide.

Maybe she could lose the sleeping bag and kindling. Who needed *two* different ways to make fire? Or maybe she needed to call the client and cancel.

It was late March, but the ground was still frozen over, and the air was so cold she could see her breath. Even with her layers and the puffed vest she'd borrowed from Liv, she was shivering. Her hands were cold enough to freeze-dry ice cream.

She was in over her head. A position Avery had spent most of her life familiarizing herself with and had yet to master.

With numb hands, she pulled her cell out of her pocket to find the number of the client, only instead the phone lit and her favorite picture filled the screen. Her parents sitting atop Sierra Point on their honeymoon. Her mom looked like a real-life Daniel Boone, with her fur-lined hat and boots—only she was sporting two red braids and a grin big enough to change the world.

And her dad was happy, so genuinely happy and in love Avery reached out to touch the image as if the act alone could bring that side of him back. Avery hadn't seen him smile like that since she was diagnosed. Then when her mom died it was as if all of her dad's happiness died with her.

Blinking back tears and the hope that things could be different, Avery put her phone away and squared her shoulders. Sierra Point was a million times harder than the Cedar Rim trail, and Lilian had conquered that climb eleven months after her first transplant. If her mom could face down that behemoth of a mountain, Avery could surely handle a little hike in the cold.

So what if her pack was bulky and the client had specifically requested a trail she'd never hiked. She was well read in the world of wilderness, knew every plant in the area, and had two ways to make fire. She'd never actually made fire on demand, but how difficult could a skill that required four steps be?

Not to mention, Avery had one of the best assets a survivalist could possess. Something more important than gadgets and brute strength.

A positive attitude. And not just any positive attitude. One strong enough to see her through death and back—twice.

Avery had come here today to find an adventure, and that's what she was about to get. And the best part? She was going to help someone else find theirs.

Adjusting her shoulders—and her attitude—she breathed in deep. The scent of pine needles and distant snow burned her nose in a way that reminded her how good it was to be alive. Two things that were a miracle in their own right.

Grabbing her pack, she slung it up and over her shoulder, swaying a bit from the momentum—and the weight. She slipped her arms through the straps and waited for the bag to settle—which it did, far enough back to send her wobbling to the side and—*oh God*—into the trunk of a giant sequoia. The force of the impact jarred her heart and sent a fall of pine needles and morning dew raining down.

The needles landed in her hair, poking her scalp, and the dew— don't even get her started on the dew—felt more like ice drops. Then, to her horror, she felt something slip beneath her collar and roll slowly down her neck.

Her eyes slammed shut as she chanted, "It's just water, it's just water." But it wasn't water. Water didn't have prickly little legs and—*shit shit shit*, were those fangs?

Avery never considered herself squeamish by any means, but this didn't feel like the average run-of-the-mill house pest. This felt a like something Godzilla would attack over the skyline of Tokyo.

So when she released a noise that sounded like a mountain goat bleating for help, she told herself it was justified. Then she told herself to kill it before it killed her.

Lunging forward, she spun around, swatting her hands, hoping to either confuse what she was sure was a big, hairy spider, or make him fly off—and spun herself headfirst into a wall.

A rock-hard wall. With ripples and dips that smelled like heated dreams and the morning sun.

"I got you," the wall said with some serious morning gravel to its voice.

Avery lifted her gaze to meet a pair of deep brown simmering pools, and she felt her body hum with a surge of adrenaline.

"You," she breathed, taking in the familiar grin and stubble that had haunted her dreams. It was the stranger from the bar. *Her* stranger from the bar. "Ty."

He wore dark gray craghoppers with one of those fitted black body armor shirts that only looked good on guys with big biceps. His black beanie was pulled low, highlighting his scruff. He looked rugged, ready, and so damn good—too good for six in the morning.

"Morning, angel," Ty said, his eyes lit with humor. "The brochure boasted about its superiority in customer experience, but this is impressive." He looked at her hands—which were cupping his pecs. "Nice, but unexpected."

She snatched her hands back and smoothed them over her braids. A few needles scattered to the ground—and onto his boots. His expensive, well-loved but well-worn boots. Boots a hard-core climber would wear.

"You're my client?" she asked, her fingers coming to rest on her lips, which were already tingling. His gaze tracked the movement, then trailed down her body, taking in every inch of her, and his grin went dangerous.

Her body was suddenly warm and toasty, and the morning was looking up. A hike in the woods with her own personal mountain man? Avery wanted to kiss the universe in thanks.

"I booked it under a friend's name." He looked her up and down. "And you don't look like Brody."

"Right." She straightened and tugged the bottom of her vest. "Brody's nursing an injured ankle, so I'm stepping in to handle his clients for the day."

"Huh," was all he said, but his gaze slipped to her mouth, her neck, and lower until he reached her pack and stopped. He took a few seconds to size up her preparedness, then cocked a single brow in question. "Where are we going? Girl Scout camp?"

She straightened. "I had us taking the Cedar Rim trail, which goes around the back side of Sequoia Lake. But this is your adventure, so if you'd rather spend the afternoon with Girl Scouts, I can call up the local troop. I'll warn you, though, last month they roasted marshmallows and told campfire stories." She leaned in to whisper, "Some were not for the faint of heart. But I hear the troop moms make a mean campfire s'more-tini."

"Not sure I'm a s'more-tini guy."

If one guy could make sipping a s'more-tini masculine, it was no doubt Ty. The man oozed enough alpha vibes to have a grizzly scurrying for cover.

"Me either, but they're supposed to be like dessert with a kick." And she'd been waiting for the all clear from her doctor to try one.

"As tempting as troop moms and s'more-tinis sound, I'll have to pass." He looked at her pack again. "You got any climbing gear in that gypsy camp strapped to your back?"

Even though she waved a nonchalant hand and gave an impressive unfazed snort, her stomach knotted with unease. Not only was climbing equipment the one thing she hadn't packed, but rock climbing sounded a bit extreme for a beginner. "The trail we're taking doesn't have any extreme inclines, so climbing gear isn't necessary."

"Really, I thought Canyon Ridge required it."

He was calling her out. It was clear.

This was the point in the conversation where Avery should have conceded, admitted she was barely qualified for their scheduled hike. But he stood there looking so capable and smug, like an Olympic athlete and Thor all wrapped up in one delicious package, and she didn't want the moment to stop.

"Canyon Ridge is one of our most difficult treks. Not for the faint of heart." Or someone who'd had a semi-recent transplant. "It's a class four with several near-vertical rocks. A strict skilled-climbers-only trail."

His posture was relaxed and confident—so confident that she could scarcely breathe.

"Good thing I have a strong heart. And my skills? Well, let's just say there isn't anything I can't handle," he said and dropped his pack.

Avery knew he had some serious skills, skills she wouldn't mind exploring more. As for being handled, she imagined his hands were more than capable. But since her heart was lodged securely in her throat—and swelling—she had a hard time getting excited. Because there, on the back of his pack, was a simple white-and-blue nylon patch that read SARTEC I. The Roman numeral one meant that when nature fought back and the end of the world was closing in on humanity, *he* was the one person she'd want on her side.

The SARTEC? Well, that meant she was screwed.

Not only had she kissed her first—and possibly now her last—client, she'd kissed a type-one search-and-rescue badass who was as elite as they came—and undoubtedly there for a surprise inspection. An inspection that if Avery screwed up could lead to single-handedly losing Sequoia Lake Lodge's biggest account.

He pulled two harnesses out of his pack. "You ready to get vertical, angel?"

Normally, Ty would take one look at those panicked baby blues and go into rescue mode, assessing what needed to happen to pull her through this situation happy and unscathed. But he wasn't here to rescue a wannabe wilderness hottie, no matter how adorable her pigtails were. Sadly, he wasn't here to get laid either.

No, Ty had walked away from his team at the height of flood season to rescue his family's lodge. To figure out what was really going on and see how bad things had become. He needed to see firsthand how dire the situation was, so he could determine the best course of action. There was no room for distractions.

Ty took in her jeans that were more fashion than function, her ridiculously bulky vest that only served to hide all of those sweet curves, and her just-out-of-the-box boots. "Unless, of course, I need to reschedule for when Brody gets back."

Panic flashed in her pretty eyes, and for a moment he thought she was going to back out. Only her stubborn side seemed to outweigh the smart one at that moment.

"What? No, of course not. Here at Sequoia Lake Lodge we pride ourselves on providing extreme adventures while adhering to the strictest safety guidelines."

He looked at her pack again and almost laughed. "Prepared for anything, I take it?"

"A good adventure guide always is." He wanted to argue that she wouldn't know the first thing about being a guide, but then she smiled, sweet and determined, and he decided to let her hang herself. "Give me a second to run and grab some supplies more suited to your adventure."

"You might want to swap out your boots too."

She looked down, her face a sign that she didn't see anything wrong with her boots. But to her credit she said, "Right," then started to turn around. "And, uh, would it be unprofessional if I asked you to look down my shirt?"

Ty let out a startled laugh. Avery Adams might be the worst adventure guide in the area, but she was damn refreshing. "Is that a part of the experience?"

Her face flushed. "Not normally, but I think I have a stowaway, and he's sinking his little fangs into my neck."

"Normally I'd make you buy me dinner first, but since this is a special situation, I'll make an exception." He gave a quick twirl of the finger. "Turn around and drop the pack." She did and it landed with a thump.

What did she have in there? Bricks?

Tackling the most immediate problem first, he pushed her braids to the side, exposing the creamy length of her neck. His chilled fingers slid down her skin and she gave a little shiver, from the contact or the spider he couldn't tell, but her breath hitched.

He spotted the pokey hitchhiker. "Found him. Hope you aren't afraid of spiders."

"Nope." She slammed her eyes shut. "Nothing much scares me. I just don't think it's fair he should get to tag along for free when you've paid for the trip."

"Uh-huh," he mused. "Then you'll be happy to know it wasn't Mr. Fangs."

She whipped her head around, and *bam*, he felt a jolt of awareness. "It wasn't Mr. Fangs?"

"Nope." He detached it from her bra strap—her black lacy bra strap—and held it up for her to see. "A blood-sucking pine needle."

The look of relief on her face was almost as amusing as watching her try to haul her pack back down the trail toward the lodge. To her credit, she made it back in record time, same boots with a little mud smeared on them for effect, and a few more things added to her pack.

Not less as he'd hoped. But that didn't stop her momentum—or determination. Nope, Dora the Explorer set off up that steep mountainside as if she were a woman on a mission. It was as impressive as it was frustrating.

Twice she slipped, and twice he was convinced she was finally going to admit she wasn't skilled enough to lead this trek. Both times she caught herself, until they were staring down Canyon Ridge, a hundred feet of near-vertical granite face that was jagged, unforgiving, and damn scary for someone who had lost a fight with a carabiner a few short days ago.

"Need help?" Ty asked as Avery stared over the cliff to the basin below.

He was geared up, clipped in, with his pack attached to the end of the rope, ready to be lowered to the platform below.

"Nope, I'm good," Avery said, and even though her harness was on and she'd clipped in, her rope wasn't routed properly.

"Either you're so good that rappelling down in a near free fall is your style, or you might want to check your ATC."

At least she looked at the rappelling device, proving she knew what it was. Then she blew her lead by looking back at him as though she hadn't a clue as to what was wrong. He offered her another out. "Or we can pass, hike a little east of here, and take Poppy Alley back to the lodge."

The safety-conscious part of Ty that made him the best at what he did prayed that she'd take it. But the risk taker who had a thing for pushing the limits—and apparently determined women—hoped that she'd plunge ahead.

To his surprise and horror, she actually smiled. It was equal parts nerves and excitement—and man was it a turn-on. "And miss the wind rushing beneath my wings? Or uh, my body. No way."

She undid her rope, then rethreaded it the exact same wrong way. "How long have you been in search and rescue?"

"What gave me away?" he asked as he reached for her ATC.

"I knew when I met you the other night that you were a serious wilderness guy, but the badge on your pack clued me in." She looked down as he began to pull out her rope. "What are you doing?"

"Teaching you a new way to tie off," he said, ignoring her hands trying to bat his away.

"My way works fine," she announced. "In fact, it's the preferred method according the lodge's safety handbook."

"What, from 1976?" He snorted. "Think of it this way—it will give you a new-and-improved method to impress your next client with."

Smart girl, she gave in. "I do love learning new skills."

He tugged her harness to get a closer hold on her rope, only he tugged a little hard. She stumbled forward and right into his arms, giving him a glorious view of those lips, which just a few nights ago had given him quite the ride.

He heard her breath catch, and he looked up higher—into those piercing lake-blue eyes—and realized he wasn't the only one remembering that kiss. He also wasn't alone in wanting to revisit that night.

She swayed closer, and he got a good whiff of her perfume, which was fresh and airy. Sexy without trying—just like her.

Jesus. He focused on her harness and away from those lush lips. What the hell had gotten into him? It was a kiss. A single, mind-blowing kiss. But nothing to wax poetic over. And so what if she was sexy? There were lots of sexy women.

Sexy women who weren't trying to kill him by tackling a cliff.

"The key to wilderness safety is continuous education and always refining your skills," Avery said.

"Where did you read that? In some kind of self-help book?" he asked while refeeding the rope through the ATC correctly. Because the first rule to wilderness safety was always be prepared, and the only thing this woman was prepared for was a picnic by the lake.

"No."

"Well, you sure as hell didn't read it in that book that told you how to feed your ATC," he said, securing her rope with a prusik, and then, in case she was so stubborn she wanted to go through with the descent, he clipped his safety rope to her harness.

He was willing to see how far she'd go to hang herself, but he wouldn't let her get hurt.

"Education comes in many forms," she said primly.

He looked her in the eye. "And do you have any practical form of education?"

Well shit, she hesitated. Long enough to have Ty wondering if she'd ever even been on a hike. There was no way Dale, with all of his strict rules and iron-fist views, would have hired a guide like Avery. Not unless things were worse than Ty realized.

Yup, this was the moment he needed to call bullshit on her little charade. Except they weren't rappelling quite yet, and there was something about the way she wholeheartedly threw herself into this role, determined to see it through, that intrigued him. Just like there was something about the way her eyes sparkled with life, even though he could see the faint smudges of exhaustion beneath that had him wanting to protect her.

"Have you ever rappelled down a hundred-foot wall?" When she opened her mouth, he clarified, "In real life?"

She shut it, then shook her head.

"At least tell me you aren't afraid of heights?"

She clasped her hands in front of her as if she were sitting in church talking to Pastor Ryan. "Why would I bring us all the way up here if I were afraid of heights?"

"Good question." One he noticed she didn't answer. "Look down."

"What?"

He crossed his arms. "Look down without cringing. If heights aren't an issue, it shouldn't be a problem."

"And miss that view?" She waved her hand to encompass the miles of snowcapped mountains blanketed with evergreen pines that circled Sequoia Lake. "Nah. A good adventure guide always focuses on the climb ahead"—this time she pointed to the crystal-blue waters of Sequoia Lake—"assessing and picturing his or her next move."

"You sound like the old handbook they keep in the lodge office."

When she smiled coyly, Ty dropped his hands and looked up at the sky for divine intervention. Because if this was a sign of how lax management had become, that was the only way he could possibly get the lodge ready to pass an inspection in a few weeks.

"You're afraid of heights yet were planning to take a client over Canyon Ridge. What were you thinking?"

She took a big breath and slowly let it out. "That I was taking a client out on a beginner hike."

She had him there. Ty knew at first glance Avery wasn't qualified for this trek. He could have ended it at any moment. But he'd wanted to see how far she'd take it. And—this was where he started questioning his judgment—he wanted to spend some more time with the woman who'd made regular appearances in his fantasies as of late.

Even worse, he'd wanted to impress her. Now here they were about to go over the edge of a gnarly cliff with a rope tied like she was going out for her slipknot badge.

"I know I misled you," she went on. "But I didn't want the lodge to lose the booking, and I had no idea I'd get a secret shopper."

"Secret shopper?" Cute and crazy—tempting combo.

"Yes, and my boss has been so busy getting ready for your inspection that when Brody got hurt, I told him I'd handle it. And he trusted me to handle it, which is normally a completely reasonable thing to do, but I wanted to prove to him that I could handle being a guide, so I took the booking. Myself. Without his knowledge."

"Not knowing who's on the mountain and what's happening with employees is a huge liability." How ironic that he was repeating what his dad had told him years ago. "Not knowing you're taking out clients is almost worse than him hiring an unqualified guide."

He watched her throat work, could see the genuine apology—and concern—in her expression. "Dale didn't hire me, his wife did," she admitted. "And I'm not a guide, I'm a coordinator. A fancy office manager, really. Dale was clear that I would not be allowed to take out clients until I was trained."

"Yet here we are," he said.

"I know, I went against his wishes, and he'll probably fire me, but he wasn't a part of this. But it was a beginner hike. I thought a little old lady wanted to see the new blooms, and I figured how hard can it be. Then you showed up all handsome and rugged, flashing those type-one biceps and changing the route, and, well, I didn't want to mess this up." She let out a wistful sigh that did something strange to Ty's chest. "As you can see, I am fully responsible for my actions, so please don't fail Dale on another inspection."

Pretty and loyal. An interesting combination. Almost as interesting as her thinking he was there in an official capacity, which meant she had no clue that he was Dale's son. She'd kissed him without knowing he was the sole heir to the crumbling empire. Oh, the irony kept growing.

Avery swayed back and forth, her hand visibly shaking. She was ready for the worst, ready for him to throw down the ruling that would ruin the lodge.

"Why didn't you just tell me that when I asked for the Canyon Ridge package?" Maybe she wanted to impress him, or spend more time with him, or go in for a second kiss.

"The client is always right."

Or that.

"Seriously? That's your answer? The client is always right? Well, they're not right if they get you killed. And believe me, I have seen the results of weekend warriors who think they're invincible. It's not pretty."

"You're too capable to get me killed," she said with a smile.

"Even pros can get people killed." Something he knew firsthand.

"I know," she said gently. "So what are you going to do?"

Ty had not a clue. He wanted to wring her neck, and then he wanted to wring his dad's. What he didn't want to do was think about how this could have turned out. About what could have happened to Avery if he hadn't been the one to pull this trek.

Some other guy would have taken one look at that sweet body and even sweeter smile and said, "Let's jump." And she would have jumped and—

Shit. Ty let out a breath, trying to quell the giant knot making a pretzel in his stomach. When that didn't work, he leveled her with a glare to let her know how serious he was—how serious the situation was. And how seriously pissed he was that she'd complicated an already complicated matter.

Avery was not qualified to work in the field, a fact his father would agree with—had they not had it out over the condition of the lodge. Ty had been blunt, Dale had been defensive, and both were chased out of the kitchen without dessert. No, Ty was going to have to handle Dora the Explorer all on his own. Which created problems of its own.

First, he could see how things had snowballed out of control and that she'd only wanted to make the lodge look good. Second, it was clear how much she wanted to be an adventure guide. Third, and most importantly, he knew that she tasted like spring water and salvation.

Jesus, his guys would give him so much shit if they heard that Kingfisher, a title he'd earned for his ability to calm the wind and the waves at will, was going menstrual over some chick he'd just met. Yes, he admired her zest for life, and her fascination for pushing the limits was a total turn-on. But he knew all too well what could happen when one pushed too far.

"Ty, I know you're really mad. And I know that you want me to know how mad you are." She scooted closer, and had it not been for all of the layers of sweaters and vests, they would have been touching. "But if intimidation is your goal, you might want to stop that." She waved a hand at his face.

"Stop what?"

"Looking at me like that. It's really misleading."

"I'm the one who's being misleading?"

"Well, you sound all angry bear, like you're contemplating tearing my head off, but then you're looking at me all . . ." There went her hand again.

"All what?" To be sure he got his point across he furrowed his brow.

"All warm and gooey, like you want me to kiss you again, but you're not happy about it."

He wasn't happy about any of this—the way his heart was racing, how one smile lit him up, and he especially wasn't happy that she was right. Something that must have shown on his face because the corner of her lips tilted into a smile that was all sunshine and forgiveness, and damn, Ty wanted to take a taste.

"You offering, angel?"

"No," she said with genuine distress. "I know I messed up, and my kissing you again would only make things worse. Kissing you now that I know you're the inspector? That would be beyond unprofessional."

"Let me get this straight," he said, trying not to smile. Letting her know she was amusing him would only ruin the scowl he'd conjured up. "Lying to the inspector isn't unprofessional, but kissing him is?"

She swayed back and forth as she considered this. When she finally spoke, her eyes locked on his—never wavering. "I'd like to say I didn't lie, but I did because holding back information is just as bad. I didn't want to let my boss down. I made a promise I shouldn't have, then got caught up in the excitement of proving I was ready—"

"Even though you weren't—"

"And I really thought I was doing the right thing for the lodge—and my boss. But"—she lifted one delicate shoulder—"if I kissed you? That would be selfishly for me without regard to how it would affect others, and that would be wrong."

He laughed at her logic. "So your lie was for the greater good, but the kiss would be for selfish desires?" She nodded. "Well, thank God I'm not the inspector."

She started to smile, then that tilt of hers went full watt, so bright he felt it hit him right in the chest. "You're not?"

"Nope."

If he was smart he'd turn around and head back down the mountain. Being close to Avery when he was this amped was like diving headfirst into trouble. Something he'd known the second he caught her on the hood of his truck. And kissing her again, inspector or not, would only further complicate things. But there was something about a woman like Avery and her never-back-down attitude that was impossible to resist.

"Then this shouldn't be a problem."

He didn't give her time to reply, just lowered his head and sank into those lush, full lips that had been keeping up him up at night and driving him crazy all morning.

Avery Adams might not be skilled at the art of rappelling, but the second her arms circled his neck and that soft body of hers pressed into his, Ty found himself in one hell of a free fall.

Silly challenge or not, there was enough chemistry between them to spark a forest fire. In fact, Ty couldn't remember the last time a kiss lit him up so fast and hot. She didn't miss a beat, taking it from a truth-or-dare brush of the lips to a hands-gripping-his-shirt, have-to-have-you kind of display. And for one insane moment, their worlds aligned and their bodies melded together like magnets and they rode the fall together, giving in to the gentle sweep of sensation.

"Wow," she whispered, her breath skating across his lips. "You kissed me."

"I did." And if she wasn't an employee he'd kiss her again.

"Oh my God!" Both hands flew to her mouth to cover the perfect circle of joy. "If you're not the inspector, then we didn't fail the inspection."

"No, we didn't," he said, hating the way her eyes lit with relief. Because the worst kind of blow was the one that you never saw coming. And Ty hadn't played this round fair. "And since I don't plan on failing it, I'm sorry, angel, but you're fired."

CHAPTER 6

Ty sat at the dining room table, surrounded by pictures and family heirlooms, all passed down through the generations, and he found it hard to breathe.

He could trace his Donovan roots back to Sequoia Lake since the eighteen hundreds. His great-grandfather operated a twelve-horse team over the pass, bringing in much-needed supplies to the area and wagon trains of people to settle the land. His grandfather opened the first hotel as a way to attract summer tourists from San Francisco. And Dale, the most successful of the Donovans, had turned that nine-room inn into one of the largest year-round adventure lodges in the Sierras.

Sequoia Lake Lodge had hosted Olympic teams, X Games athletes, and even a few politicians over the years. Through hard work and laser focus, Dale had made it the brightest spot in gold country and the Donovan family the golden family.

Ty had the same Donovan fever for adventure, only his tastes tended to fall into the extreme even for his family. Garrett's dream had been to follow in Dale's footsteps, make a life on the mountain and one day take over the lodge, but Ty had wanted more. He'd memorized every trail by sixteen and knew there were other things he wanted to see, bigger mountains he wanted to climb. He had an urge to explore where others had yet to venture, to expand the company to include other areas—a vision his father hadn't shared.

A difference in opinion that made their father-son relationship a difficult one. What Dale saw as his son's legacy, Ty always viewed as a jumping-off point. It wasn't that he didn't admire what his dad had created or appreciate everything Dale had taught him—he just knew there was more he wanted to do. But running a lodge was a family business, and it was expected that the Donovan boys would stick around to do their part. Something Ty tried to embrace, but when Garrett died he knew any chance he had of sticking around was gone.

So he'd left. And now he was back, and it was as if no time had passed.

"You had no right to fire her," Dale said, his voice that of a drill sergeant, even though his frame wasn't as imposing as it had once been.

"She was a problem waiting to happen," Ty pointed out, wondering if they could skip dinner and go right to the good night parting. His mom, sensing his need to run, passed him the potatoes.

"Well, she was my problem to deal with," Dale said. He'd passed the meatloaf, sweet rolls, and salad, yet he hadn't put a speck of food on his plate.

"Yet there we were, staring down Canyon Ridge with a Duraflame log and a slipknot. Had I not stepped in, there might not have been anything to handle." Ty pushed the bowl his dad's way and smiled. "Potatoes."

Dale ignored this. "If you hadn't shown up like you did, I might not have been too distracted to notice."

And here they went. No matter what transpired it always boiled down to one thing: Ty was in the wrong. And maybe he was at times, but in this particular situation he'd made the right call and they both knew it.

"What happened to calling ahead?" Dale added. "Guests do it all the time. The lodge might have been filled and—"

"You don't need to call ahead. Your room is always waiting for you. Isn't it, Dale?" Irene said, placing a roll on Dale's plate. When he didn't answer, she held a heaping spoonful of brussels sprouts over his plate. "Isn't it, dear?"

Dale eyed the offending sprouts and then reached for another roll. "No one wants that small room anyhow, with all your stuff clogging up the closets."

"And no one wants to hear you grumble. Confrontation is bad for digestion," she said. "Now, please pass the potatoes."

Dale did as told, then, as if he couldn't hold it in, mumbled, "Letting go of staff in the middle of a trek is bad for business—makes it look like we hire incompetent guides. Was that your goal? Come here and make me look bad?"

"Dale," Irene scolded.

But Dale wasn't done. He set the plate down and leaned in, flashing that look of frustration Ty had come to associate with his visits. "What else am I to think? The boy shows up here, sand still in his hair, spouting about how bad everything's gotten while he's been relaxing in the surf."

First, Ty had worked his ass off to become the top in his field. And second, he hadn't even gotten started on how bad things were. Not only had he heard rumors that some of the male guides were exploring a lot more than just the rugged peaks with the female lodgers—the whole reason behind his scheduled hike with Brody—but he'd spent several hours after his morning with Avery combing through the lodge's equipment.

He'd need to do a deeper inspection, but what he found made him nervous. He hadn't told his dad he knew about the failed inspection, didn't see a need to. Dale would have taken that news like an attack on the Donovan name. Having his son call him out on it would only hurt his pride, and that wasn't why Ty had come.

He swallowed back a bitter taste of frustration and tempered his words. "I didn't come here to step on your toes or upset you, Dad. I happened to be there when a problem arose, and I tried to handle it how I thought you would."

Dale blinked, as if in all of the bluster he hadn't even considered what he would have done. "Well, you're not me, and you haven't been around long enough to know what decision I'd make."

"Fair enough," Ty said, even though he knew Dale would have fired Avery on the spot. "Next time, I'll let you handle the situation."

"There you go thinking that there will be a next time," Dale said. "Like I can't handle my business."

Ty put up his palms in surrender. "Look, there's a lot to be handled between now and SAREX, and you're short-staffed. I figured you could use some help, so I took some vacation time and came up to offer my help where it's needed."

"Who says I'm shorthanded?" Dale asked, sounding so confident that he had everything handled. A ridiculous stance, since they were down two senior members.

Then he remembered Avery with her knitted cap and determined eyes and shook his head. "I thought Mark took a job in Donner and Brody was injured."

When Dale looked at him as if he were the ridiculous one, Ty looked at his mom to make sure he hadn't misunderstood the situation.

"That's right." Irene patted Dale's hand and lowered her voice to the same soothing level she used when one of her boys skinned a shin or scraped an arm. "Remember Brody turned his ankle Sunday, then the doctor told him to take it easy for the next few weeks?"

Dale looked at Ty, and for a moment his dad looked tired and confused. Almost lost. Then in the blink of an eye, he gave that same dismissive shrug that used to shatter Ty's world. Now it just pissed him off.

"Since this is your vacation, don't feel you have to waste it on heavy lifting," Dale said and dug into his dinner, grumbling something about the time for being needed had long passed.

"Well, I'm here now," Ty said.

Dale let that sink in. "And you're going to stay until it's done, or until you're bored with mountain life? Because if so I need to schedule that in."

Jesus, there was no pleasing his dad.

"I could leave now if that's what you want." Dale remained silent, stoic and stubborn. And Ty had his answer. He stood and tossed his napkin on the table. "Thanks for dinner, Mom."

Ty had barely made it to the coat rack when he heard the door to Dale's home office slam shut. Ty rested his forehead against the window and took a breath. When had things between him and his dad become so bad? Growing up, seeing the other's point of view had never been easy—it was what happened when two people were so much alike.

But after Garrett died things went from hard to impossible, and Ty knew that there was nothing he could do to make it better, short of trading places with his brother. A swap he'd do in a heartbeat if possible.

Ty looked out the window, staring out at the twinkling lights that ran the length of the mountain until they looked like stars lighting the inky night sky and reflecting off the glass lake below. Sequoia Lake Lodge sat in the middle of fifty acres of family-owned pines and trails, and it was surrounded by another two hundred acres of the most incredible national forest in the Sierra Nevada.

Ty had been a lot of places, seen a lot of things over the past decade. But no matter how breathtaking or challenging, no place got to him like Sequoia Lake. There was something so humbling about how small the moon looked above the steep mountains and unforgiving peaks. Maybe that was the draw, that he had conquered—and still could—something so unforgiving.

Only what was the point? He'd never found any form of forgiveness here.

A comforting hand settled on his back. "He just misses you."

"Yeah, I got that when he asked what day I was leaving so he could start the countdown."

"He doesn't handle loss well," his mom said with quiet apology. "Like most Donovan men, he'd rather be the one pushing than risk having something he cares for pulled away."

"Well, he doesn't have to push—I got the point."

"You're both so convinced of the other, neither of you are really taking the time to see what's happened. I've tried to bring you two together so you can see what I see in each of you," she said, her voice heartbreakingly sad. "But you Donovan men are too stubborn for your own good."

Ty gave the lake one last look, then faced his mom. "I'll try talking to him."

Irene touched his cheek. "When you do, be sure you're ready to listen."

Ty wanted to say he was an expert listener, that it was just when it came to being told what a failure he was that he tuned out. But seeing his mom so upset made his gut ache, so he covered her hands with his. "Sorry about dinner."

"It will make wonderful sandwiches for the weekend."

Ty grabbed his coat off the rack, ready to tell her that he wasn't going to be here come the weekend, but the sad look in his mom's eyes had him taking a deep breath and placing it back. For every time his father had made him feel misunderstood and like a disappointment, his mom had taken him into her arms and hugged away the hurt.

Irene Donovan was all heart and gentle compassion, and Ty had promised himself years ago he'd never be the cause of her tears again. "You got any coffee in the pot?"

She gave him a watery smile, then wrapped her arms around his waist and leaned in. She smelled like sugar cookies, lavender soap, and coming home. Even though Ty knew home wasn't a reality for him anymore, he allowed himself to pretend—for a moment—and did some leaning of his own. Into the past, and into his mother's gentle strength, resting his cheek on her head and breathing in until his heart slowed and his soul was at rest.

"I've got a pie cooling in the kitchen," Irene said.

Ty lifted his head and looked down into his mom's face. "Pie?"

"Well," she said, patting his cheek. "With a smile like that, I should have started the dinner with pie—it might have ended better."

It might have ended with world peace. His mom's pies were that good.

Not good, legendary. They were the only thing Ty had dreamed of more than a hot shower when he and his team had been tracking a lost family for six days down the Colorado River—in November.

When Ty had been twelve he'd ripped his knee open racing Garrett down a ski slope on bikes in the summer. He'd hobbled home knowing he'd need stitches, only his mom had just taken one of her olallieberry pies out of the oven, so he'd covered his gash with Garrett's hoodie and sat at the table.

When his mom discovered the cut, he'd received sixteen stitches, three weeks' grounding, and a pretty severe tongue lashing. All easier to take with a bellyful of pie.

"I think there's even ice cream in the freezer," she added, heading toward the kitchen. "And even though firing that sweet girl wasn't your finest moment, I don't see why you can't have two scoops."

Ty followed her, grabbing a stack of dishes and bowls from the table. "She was about to take me over Canyon Ridge. Firing her was me going easy."

"She had you there with her, so all would have been well," Irene said with so much confidence and affection in her eyes it made Ty squirm a little as he crossed to the sink. "It would have been a perfect first descent for her. Poor girl, she's been waiting for her shot."

Poor girl his ass. Although he had felt like a jerk when after they'd made the hike back, she'd apologized again, then thanked him for the hike as if he hadn't just kissed her and then fired her. "*She* wasn't qualified, and *I* was the client."

Irene took the bowls out of his hands. "No, honey, you're one of the best climbers on this mountain, and you didn't pay, so that makes you a plus one."

Ty snorted, because that was exactly how he imagined Avery justifying the morning to herself. "She didn't know that."

He opened the dishwasher and stacked the dishes, grabbing a couple of clean bowls from the cabinet when he was done.

"She probably took one look at those strong, capable arms and decided there was no one else she'd want to fall with." Irene set the pie on the counter. "And she is such a sweet girl. I hope you put your best foot forward."

"It wasn't a date, Mom."

"No, of course it wasn't." She grinned up at him, the gleam in her eyes one of mischief. "Funny that your mind went there, though."

So funny it gave him heartburn. "What's going on with the lodge?"

"You know?" Irene's easy smile faded, and she pulled out a stool, resting against it as if she needed the added support. "Of course you know, and your work friends told you more than they told us, otherwise you wouldn't be here."

"You make it sound like I don't visit," he teased, but a small knot of guilt lit his stomach. "I was up here for your birthday." Which was what?

Eight months ago. Man, how did a good son go eight months without seeing his mom when he was a half-day's drive away?

A good son didn't. Period.

"I know you visit, honey. Just like I know coming home is hard for you." She took his hands in hers, and Ty wondered when her hands had become so frail.

"It's not hard," he said, and she clucked. "Okay, it isn't Hawaii, but if you and Dad need me for anything, all you have to do is ask and I'll be here."

"And if you were the one needing help, would you come here?" Ty's face must have projected the wrong answer, because Irene's voice turned sad. "I didn't think so. Which tells me that if you're here, then it must be bad."

At this point sugarcoating it wasn't going to do anyone any good. His mom needed to know what they were facing. And Ty needed one of his parents thinking straight when it came to updating the equipment—and the direction of the lodge.

And maybe it would give him a chance to make amends for breaking his mom's heart.

"It's bad. In fact, we need to hire some help if we want to make the next inspection."

"I knew there were problems," she said, her voice so strained Ty's rescue instinct went into hyper mode. "I've been so focused on your dad—driving him to all his appointments, making sure he was okay—that I haven't been keeping as close an eye on things."

"Why are you driving Dad around?" Dale didn't ride shotgun; he steered the vehicle. Always.

Irene's shoulders caved. "He ran to the grocery store a few months ago, and when he wasn't home by dinner I got worried. Sheriff Watson showed up around nine and said he found Dale on the side of the road looking at a map." She let out a small sniff. "I guess they were doing some kind of construction on the highway, and he'd taken the detour and got turned around and couldn't find his way back."

"The grocery store is less than a mile from here. How did he get lost?"

"I don't know," she said, sounding exhausted. "Sheriff Watson said Dale seemed agitated and confused when he pulled up, so even when your dad *insisted* it was just his night vision, Watson *insisted* on following him home."

"I bet that went over well," Ty deadpanned.

"Oh, your dad was so embarrassed," Irene said, full of concern. "Blamed it on the public works department, said they needed to post more helpful signage and increase street lamps on that road."

"What did the sheriff say?"

"That he didn't want to see Dale driving at night until we saw a doctor." Irene shrugged. "We saw the eye doctor that next week, and his vision is fine. I tried to have him get a second opinion, but you know your dad."

Stubborn as the day is long.

Ty leaned back and let out a long breath, hoping to relieve some of the building pressure. It didn't help. In fact, he wasn't sure at this point how he could be of help. Getting the lodge back in order sounded like it was just the start of the problem.

"Why didn't you call me?"

Irene's face softened, to the point where Ty felt a familiar ache deep in his chest.

"Would it have made a difference? Would you have come any earlier?"

"If I'd known that there was a problem," he said, then wondered if that was the truth.

Outside of a death in the family or natural disaster, there wasn't much that would get him home around the holidays. Coming home was painful enough. Around the holidays the guilt was suffocating, tightening around his throat as a reminder that his family would never be complete. No matter how hard he wished it different.

"I could have reasoned with him," Ty said. "Made him go to the doctor again."

"Which is why I didn't bother you. You two don't need another reason to argue. Plus, I think it's stress. Your dad is under a lot of pressure right now, and the stress is really getting to him," Irene said, looking down at her folded hands. "He hasn't been sleeping much and has a hard time staying alert during the day, and sometimes his mind goes a little fuzzy."

"Mom," he said quietly. "This lodge is too big for the two of you to handle. You need to hire someone to help manage it." A suggestion he'd brought up before but was always met with hostility.

Ty knew firsthand how debilitating prolonged stress and sleep deprivation could be on a person. It affected a person's mood, energy levels, and cognitive abilities. Add fear over the lodge's well-being and it was no wonder his dad was acting so strange.

Bottom line—Dale was getting older. It was natural that he'd need some help with the heavy lifting that came with running a lodge this size.

"I think it's time to look into that," she said, sounding overwhelmed at the idea. "But you know how your dad can get about new people. I'm trying to respect Dale's wishes and do what's right for the lodge, and all I seem to be doing is letting everyone down."

Ty softened his voice. "You didn't let anyone down."

In fact, he had a sinking suspicion she was the only one holding things together. Irene had been the glue struggling to hold the family together after Garrett, and she was still struggling to please them all. Sadly, all of the love in the world couldn't heal this family, but Irene was nothing if not persistent.

A few broken skis and snowmobiles would be one thing, but whatever was happening went much further than losing Mark and Brody. And Ty was going to get to the bottom of it.

He couldn't bring back Garrett, but he could save the lodge and lighten his dad's load in the process. All he needed was to get the most stubborn, independent man in the world to agree to accept the help.

"I'll fix this, Mom. I promise."

And Ty had vowed to never again make a promise he couldn't keep.

◆ ◆ ◆

By Wednesday, Ty had a good grasp on the logistics of hosting SAREX, and he had covered three group hikes and a solo climb. With the morning clear, he went down to the boathouse early to meet Harris, hoping to get a jump on cataloguing the water equipment. Knowing what he was facing would be important in making a plan of action. Feeling suffocated by the enormity of it all, he watched the sun peek over the red tin-roofed structure that hung over the end of the dock, and he tried to focus on the way the water rhythmically lapped at the pylons.

It didn't help.

Ty and Harris were only an hour into checking out the boats, and Ty was ready to call it. Between the lodge's skiffs, Zodiacs, and hoppers, there were thirty-three poweredboats to check. Ty had checked twenty so far. Seven were dented, five needed new batteries, and two were begging to be scrapped. All problems that could have been avoided if the equipment manager had done his job and stowed the gear right.

And don't even get him started on the schedule. His dad was still using his trusty Post-it system, meaning one had to trust that Dale remembered to post everyone's schedule. It was a miracle more bookings didn't get lost.

"How does it sound?" Ty asked as Harris pulled their Coast Guard Delta—a forty-foot sportsman fishing cruiser—into the boathouse, the boat letting loose an audible sputter as it got closer. The cold bite of the morning air frosted his breath and sent small clouds billowing into the sky.

Harris cut the engine. "Like it sat idle all winter. I'll have to check the fluids and lines to see what the problem is, but it doesn't look good."

Not a good diagnosis coming from the gearhead of the family. There wasn't an engine Harris couldn't fix, period. The guy had rebuilt his first helicopter by the age of fifteen.

"Who lets a sixty-thousand-dollar boat sit all winter?"

"You know who, man. The only reason I got this close to it is because your dad is still sleeping. If he caught me on his boat he'd rip me a new one," Harris said. "After Mark quit, I set Dale up with a few local guys who do good work. He took one interview and then said he didn't need some millennial telling him how to run his fleet."

"Him and his vast knowledge of all things Sequoia Lake aren't doing much better," Ty said. "Isn't there anyone he likes in the area?"

"The only qualified mechanic in town who your dad hasn't pissed off is Nelson."

Ty grimaced. Nelson had a habit of turning a simple oil change into a complete engine rebuild. He was cranky, slow as slush, and predated the glaciers.

"I'll call around to see if any mechanics from Reno or Truckee are looking to relocate." Ty took a small notebook from his back pocket and scribbled FIND MECHANIC at the bottom of his ever-growing list. "Can you see if you can isolate the problem so we know what we're looking at parts wise?"

Harris let out a low whistle. "I'll see what I can do, but parts for this bad boy are special order."

"We can rush them if needed. That's our biggest cruiser," Ty pointed out. "Sequoia Elite specifically requested to use it for the water operations training."

It was the main reason the lodge had invested in the boat to begin with. Having the largest rental boat on Sequoia Lake brought in groups of fishermen in the spring, large families in the summer, and all kinds of first responders during training season.

"What about one of the C27 Zodiacs?" Harris asked, pointing a thumb over his shoulder to the civilian version of the boat that the Navy SEALs were famous for using.

Ty shook his head. "They hold half the bodies. There's no way the water recovery team could all fit in there. They'd have to divide their class down the middle and hold two courses."

Harris stepped off the boat and onto the dock, wiping his hands on one of the garage rags. "It's an option."

It was an option, just not an ideal one. A huge part of training was working hands-on with your team. Tackling new scenarios and pushing past one's limits was only part of it. The time spent together built a cadence that was essential for creating trust. In the field, Ty didn't have time to second-guess. He needed to make a call and know, without hesitation, that his team could execute. And when shit got real, there wasn't the time to make a call. Every member had to go off instinct—instinct that was built during these kinds of intense trainings.

"I'll help as much as I can, but I'm pulling a sixty next week." Harris tossed his life vest on the hook. "So you might want to consider having a backup plan."

Like packing up his bag and heading back to Monterey? Rescuing a terrified sumo wrestler during riptide sounded easier than passing inspection. "I am the backup plan."

Harris picked up his tools and fell in beside Ty as they headed up the stone pathway toward the back of the lodge. Neither of them said a word, Ty deep in thought, desperately searching for a plan B. Harris knew his cousin enough to give him the silence he needed to think. By the time they reached the office, Ty had worked through every possible solution.

"We just need to get through this inspection" was as far as he got.

"And after the inspection?" Harris asked, opening the back door.

"We get through SAREX." A solid plan.

"Then what?" Harris asked as they made their way past the kitchen and into the corridor of offices that housed the people who kept the lodge running. "You leave, go back to paradise and your life far, far away, and next year you'll have the same problems."

"I know." Ty ran a hand over his face, his eyes as scratchy as his chin. It was the problem that had kept him up all night. And okay, thinking about firing Avery hadn't helped.

Ty was a fixer by nature, and his first instinct was to charge into trouble and rescue those in need. Yet he'd been back home for less than a week and already he was back to ruining lives. And he'd just started cleaning house.

"We need more manpower," he said, looking at the wall of employee photos lining the hallway. Dale had a way of getting some of the country's best to pass up offers to work at Aspen or Breckenridge and instead come to a tiny western town in the middle of the mountains. It was people like that who made Sequoia Lake Lodge so successful over the years. It was a level of expertise Ty needed to find if his dad's business stood a chance.

"At the rate you and Dale are going, you'll fire or scare off everyone but Leslie in billing, and only because she came with the lodge." Harris stopped. "Did you really fire Avery after that kiss?"

"She told you I kissed her?"

"I was talking about the kiss at the bar. I guess you're talking about something else."

"Yeah." It was something else all right.

Harris shook his head. "What did you do for fun after, kick a puppy?"

Ty ignored this and thought back to his dad the other night. How upset his mom had been when she'd confided in Ty about the effect the stress was having on Dale. "This place needs qualified manpower. A team that will keep things going after I'm gone. Maybe even a general manager to oversee things, make sure nothing falls through the cracks. The lodge is understaffed, and my dad isn't running as tight of a ship it seems."

"How are you going to do that?"

"Start making some calls," Ty said, opening the office door and stopping short.

There were files strewn all over his dad's desk, a week's worth of mail stacked up, and the phone was going ballistic. In fact, the only calm place in the middle of that storm was the receptionist's desk.

Which was occupied by Avery—and meticulously organized.

She was in control of her surroundings—her fingers clicking the keyboard, the phone to her ear, and she was entering something on a fancy spreadsheet as if she hadn't been fired. She even wore a pair of khakis, a company blue tee that matched her eyes and hugged her to perfection, and a black ball cap that said No Fear.

She looked up and smiled. "You might want to answer the calls coming in first. I'd help, but I'm on hold." She pointed to the phone next to her ear, and Harris laughed.

Ty jabbed him in the gut and said, "Get the phone." Harris crossed his arms. "Please?"

"Fine, but you have to play Ice Princess with Emma on game night."

He had no idea what Ice Princess was, but it couldn't be so involved that he couldn't watch the game, so he said, "Fine."

With a shit-eating grin, Harris picked up the phone. "Sequoia Lake Lodge, this is Ty Donovan, town's biggest ice princess, how can I assist you?"

Ty rolled his eyes, then approached the reception desk. "I thought I fired you."

"You did, but that was when I was acting as an adventure guide," Avery said, flipping through a file on her desk. "A position which, I agree, I need more training for. Which is why I am back to being Sequoia Lake Lodge's adventure coordinator and customer service representative."

He wanted to smile, so much his cheeks hurt, but it would have ruined his bad mood. "My mistake, I must have been unclear. But when an employee poses as a guide, putting a guest in danger, they lose all of their jobs. The fake ones and the real one."

Locating whatever she was searching for, she made some swirly notes on a Post-it. "You weren't all that honest either. Or professional," she whispered, and Ty felt his neck heat. "But I'm willing to overlook it and start over. Good morning. I'm Avery Adams. Nice to meet you."

Standing, she smacked his chest, sticking the Post-it note to his shirt.

He shot her a look, which made her smile bigger, then glanced at the note. "Is this you slipping me your number?"

"No, that's Brian's number. And although I think you two would have a lot in common—dominating mountains and building fire from toothpicks and Saran wrap—he's married. He's also a mechanic from Incline who's looking to move his family here to Sequoia Lake so he can afford a house. He booked your dad for a snowshoeing trip around the holidays and made Dale laugh. I'd say he's your best bet." She lowered her voice. "And I wouldn't give my number to a coworker."

"Good thing I fired you," he said just as quietly, then peeled the note off. "How did you know I need a mechanic?"

"Because I'm good at my job."

He laughed. "A fact that I could easily argue."

"Ah, but we're starting over, remember?" He didn't remember anything, but the sweet scent of vanilla and crazy cutie was messing with his ability to think. "And while, admittedly, there is room to grow as a guide, I rock at coordinating and managing. You can ask my old bosses—they'll say I'm organized, efficient, motivated, and a fast learner. All I need is someone to see that I have—"

"No," he said, backing away from the desk because he had a sick feeling that her smile could charm him into just about anything. And he couldn't hire her back, no matter how good a kisser she was. Not when he knew the first chance she got to spread her wings, she'd go BASE jumping off Sierra Point.

"But you need a beginners guide, and what I lack in experience I make up for in—"

"No," he repeated, then said it softer, because he could already see her heart swimming in her eyes. "I'm sorry, angel, but rules are rules."

With a giddy clap, as if she'd just been promoted to zip-line instructor, she bent down and rifled through her bottom drawer. When she came up, she was holding a leather-bound book that was the size of a phone book and had a picture of Sequoia Lake Lodge on the cover. "Show me."

"What?"

She pushed the book—the same book his dad had used to keep Ty in order—his way, then clasped her hands. "Show me where that rule is. Because I've been working for Dale for a few months now, and he says everything I need to know is in this book. Which is why I've read it forward and backward, and I don't remember that rule. Anywhere." She smiled up at him. "So show me. Please."

He pushed the book back. "Being educated and being experienced are two different skills, and I don't think that this—"

She held up a finger, silencing him. "No."

"I'm sorry?"

"No problem at all, Mr. Lismore."

It took him a moment to realize she was talking to whoever was on the other end of the phone.

"Like I was saying, I can fit you in tomorrow at three . . . Oh, a picnic, how romantic . . . Let me see if we have anything closer to lunch."

She pushed hold, swiped the mouse, and up popped a beautifully coded spreadsheet, complete with client names, contact info, and trail preferences, each one assigned to a guide.

"Art Lismore is staying in the Alpine suite and wants to change his morning fishing trip tomorrow to Sunday, then book a nature hike around the lake at eleven so he can surprise his lady friend with a champagne picnic. Can you take him?" She blinked up at him. "Ty?"

"Oh, are you talking to me again?"

She nodded. "Yes, can you take him? Brody is still out, Marshall is taking the Rotary Club on a daylong fishing trip, and everyone else is booked." Her eyes went all dreamy. "I think Art is going to ask Helga from 305 out on a date. They met last week in the lobby when he was checking out. Then he heard she and her sisters were staying through the week and"—she wiggled her fingers, like little celebratory sparklers—"here he is. Looking to impress."

Ty didn't have time to ask how Avery knew all of that information—it was probably in one of her spreadsheets. He barely had time to cover Brody's schedule. Taking on another booking would be crazy. Especially one involving a couple of seniors who wanted to get frisky on the shoreline. But he couldn't disappoint a lodge guest. Part of the draw of staying at the lodge was guaranteed preference on booking adventures.

"How long we talking? Because I have at least five hours left in the equipment room." That didn't even touch how long it would take to finish up at the boathouse and find a new mechanic. "I need to get an accurate count of the climbing equipment, make sure we have everything we need for SAREX, and if we come in short, I need time to order extra supplies and equipment."

"Between the picnic basket, Helga's walking cane, and a little romantic time"—she waggled a brow—"it might take a little longer, but it should be a beautiful walk."

"Give it to my dad. This kind of hike is right up his alley." It was an easy hike, and it would get Dale out of the office and into nature, where he could decompress by impressing the clients with his vast knowledge of the local vegetation and history.

It was a perfect solution.

"Dale isn't doing hikes much anymore, and I have to make sure it's okay with your mom first."

"Good luck with that." Ty laughed. Dale never asked permission from anyone—not even Mother Nature. Hell freezing over wouldn't stop his dad once he had his mind set to a task. "Getting him out in the fresh air might loosen him up a little."

Avery didn't seem to agree. "I'll still check with your mom." There was a beat of silence that grew and expanded until Ty felt that knot in his gut tighten. Her gaze was unwavering, so intense it could penetrate a Kevlar vest. "But if he can't, I can take it," she said, as an afterthought, and he got her little plan.

"And have them end up rappelling down River Rock? No." She hadn't even been hired back officially and already she was pushing for more responsibility. Responsibility that would free up time he desperately needed. Until someone got hurt.

God, this was a mess.

"I've got you down, Mr. Lismore," he heard her say, and he reached out for her to hand him the phone.

"No, you don't have him down."

She put one of those elegant pink-tipped fingers to her delicious lips—then shushed him. Harris chuckled, fully amused, so Ty shared his own special finger with his cousin.

Avery ignored all of this. "I'll make sure that the kitchen prepares you the perfect romantic picnic, and I booked you on Poppy Alley. It's half the distance, but the view is incredible." She paused, listened intently, then gave an understanding tut. "I hear ya, but a lady likes to look good when being romanced, and walking around the lake requires hiking boots, and no one wants to be romanced in hiking boots when they can wear some pretty flats." Her eyes sparkled first, bright and alive, and then her warm laugh filled the air. Genuine and real and sexy as hell. "Yes, Helga does love her designer shoes . . . plenty of aphrodisiacs, got it."

She hung up. "It *is* Helga, the widow from Reno who comes here every March with her sisters. He came back for her. Isn't that sweet? I had to say yes."

"You *had* to say yes?"

"When Destiny works her magic, you always say yes," she said, not a note of apology in her voice.

"Great, and will Destiny be sending some of that magic my way when I run out of time before the next inspection?"

She looked unconcerned. "You don't need magic, you have me."

"Sweet Jesus." The woman was more than driven, she was a bully. A cute, adorable bully who was so enthusiastic it made saying no to her difficult.

No wonder Dale had hired her. She probably cornered him with one of those smiles of hers, then flashed that dimple at the right moment. Good thing he wasn't into crazy cuties with dimples.

Or he hadn't been up until that kiss.

Ty pulled out the chair and sat, resting his head in his hands. No matter how many different ways he looked at it, this was too big for any one person to fix. Even a master fixer. Being down two key people meant equipment wasn't being properly cared for, the guides were double-booked, the schedule was shit, and he had an entire event to plan. "Avery, look—"

"Before you tell me to cancel on Mr. Lismore, let me remind you that Poppy Alley is a twenty-minute one-way hike. You can probably make it back to the lodge in half that time. You only lose thirty minutes out of your schedule, and a VIP customer gets a day to play hero to a pretty lady."

Which meant he'd likely come back year after year.

Smart woman had taken an impossible situation and turned it into a winning solution. What surprised him more was that her solution wasn't her looking out for her job, like he'd originally thought. She was looking out for the customer. He wasn't about to tell her she was fired—that would be silly since she'd never been rehired. He was going to say that she was inspired.

But that might lead to what other talents he thought were inspired. And that would lead to the main reason why this could never work.

"And that's it?" he asked to be sure. "You aren't going to use it to get me to hire you back?"

"I really want this job, Ty. I love the clients and working outdoors, and I love learning about the mountains I've lived on my entire life but never had the opportunity to explore." She lifted a delicate shoulder.

"Right now, though, I truly just want to make sure Mr. Lismore gets *his* chance to explore them with his lady friend."

Ty wasn't sure if he should believe her, but he couldn't detect an ounce in insincerity. She really wanted this old man to have his day in the sun. "If I take the booking, will you promise not to dispute my decision?"

"I promise not to dispute it . . . today. But tomorrow—"

"Avery," he moaned.

"You need me and you know it. I might not be what you picture when you think *adventurer*." She stood and spread her arms to encompass her tiny frame. "But I have spent the past five years managing people's retirement accounts and expectations. I can balance what people want with what they need and give them options within their limitations that still excite them. Combine that with my knowledge of spreadsheets, event coordinating, and people skills, and I am uniquely perfect for this job."

Ty took in her khakis, which had pleats, he noticed, and the efficient way she pulled her blonde curls through the back hole of the ball cap, as if she took a great deal of time to look like she'd just thrown on the hat. Then he looked at her soft expression, the confident way she approached her insecurities, and those big hope-filled eyes, and he agreed.

She was uniquely perfect. For him.

Which made hiring her a bad idea. Ty took off his beanie and ran a hand through his hair.

"I've got Gary Sikes on the phone," Harris said casually, his finger pointing at the phone as he mouthed *Gary Sikes* like the Divine himself was on the other end.

And maybe he was. Gary Sikes was a smokejumper for the ranger department. Ty and Harris had both worked with him on a few task forces. The kid had skills. He busted his ass all summer fighting forest fires, then spent his winters rotating between teaching surfing in Mexico and skiing in Tahoe. He was the exact kind of guy the lodge could use.

"He's between gigs right now and coming through town Sunday with some buddies. Said he wants to take them to the north face of Cedar Rim. I can chopper you guys in if you want." Harris covered the mouthpiece with his hand and whispered, "He's looking for seasonal work."

"With Brody gone, there isn't anyone qualified to take them out," Avery said.

"Says the girl who had me staring down Canyon Ridge." Ty turned to Harris. "What time?"

Harris repeated the question, then said, "He says oh-seven-hundred works."

Ty opened his phone calendar, scrolled to Sunday, and groaned. "I blocked off the morning to scout out trails and possible staging areas for SAREX. I don't even know where each class will be held, and I have a call with Lance from Cal-SAR Monday to check in. Can he push it until eleven?"

"Um, Ty," Avery said, critically eyeing her monitor. "At eleven you're taking Mr. Lismore out on the lake, bass fishing, remember? The hike tomorrow, moved fishing to Sunday?"

He reached out to turn her monitor so he could see it better, and she smacked his hand. "No one touches my computer or my spreadsheets. Otherwise it would end up looking like that." She pointed to the giant paper calendar on the wall that had an array of colored Post-its stuck all over it.

"Noted," he said, a consistent throbbing growing behind his frontal lobe. "Now, can you help a guy out?"

She opened her mouth to say yes, then snapped her mouth shut and folded her hands on the desktop. "Which guy needs help? The one who kissed me or my coworker? Because if it's my coworker, I can move some things around, but . . ."

If she was still fired, he was out of luck. Got it.

Ty rubbed his forehead and glanced at Harris, who was mouthing, *Gary fucking Sikes, man*, then to Avery Adams, adventure coordinator, while she fiddled with her mouse. But Avery Adams, aspiring adventure guide, was taking her sweet ass time and batting her lashes his way.

"Fix this mess and you can go back to being Avery Adams, adventure coordinator."

He stuck out his hand, but she just stared at it, as if weighing her options. Ty gave her a charming smile, but she didn't appear charmed. Stubbornness did that to a person, made them un-charmable, and often uncharming. However, Avery managed to pull off both in a way that was beyond impressive.

"No," she said firmly. "I'll take care of all of the paperwork for SAREX, help you scout trails, run this office like it's the West Wing, and run interference with Dale. In return, I want to be trained to be a guide. Nothing huge"—he could almost see her mouth the word *yet*—"enough so I'm qualified to take over some of the senior trips and beginner classes."

"Deal," Harris said.

Ty set him a look.

"What? You need the help, she needs a trainer, and she's too pretty for Dale to snap at."

Excellent point.

"And you have six senior trips booked for next week alone," she said. "If Brody isn't back and you have to take over his schedule, there's no way you can handle it all. Plus, it's the last Wednesday of March."

Avery held up a flyer advertising Senior Spring Training sign-ups— a series of discounted classes and trips the lodge offered to the over-fifty-five residents. And it started today.

As if on cue, the phone lit up.

Ty groaned.

Avery put her hand on the receiver, finger on the blinking red button, ready to answer. "It's probably Ms. Lebowski. She told me she was going to call first thing to be sure and get the Sunshine League's annual Spring Bunny Poppy Hop booked before the schedule fills." She paused. "Do I answer it, or would you rather take the call? I know she'd love to tell you about how successfully her bunion surgery went." She held out the phone. "What do you say?"

That he was in for a world of trouble, and he'd never been so turned on. "Fine, you can assist me on Mr. Lismore's walk, but if you show up wearing designer shoes, the deal is off."

CHAPTER 7

If Avery thought her first day as an official adventure guide would bring on excited jitters, then working alongside Ty felt like scaling the fault line.

Now that she'd gotten a chance to watch him work, she'd figured out that he wasn't just skilled, he was a master explorer. He was great with the clients, keeping a casual feel to the hike while constantly assessing the terrain. *Effortless perfectionist* came to mind.

He showed up in a beanie, mirrored aviator glasses, and dark cargo pants that hugged his muscular thighs and perfect butt. A view she'd spent the past twenty minutes staring at, as he'd smoked her the second they'd hit the trail.

Partly because he was the guide and his place was up front. But mostly because of the stupid pack. Not his, hers. While she'd shown up prepared for every situation, Mountain Man had shown up with a giant travel mug of piping hot coffee—and nothing more. No pack, no picnic basket, nothing beyond the coffee and whatever MacGyver tricks he'd stashed in all of his hundred and one pockets—yet she'd walk into a blizzard with him in a heartbeat, he was that capable.

So halfway down the trail when he turned around to reach for Avery's pack, she waved him off.

"I've got it," she said, squaring her shoulders to make herself appear stronger than she felt. "It's not very heavy."

"Then why do you keep weaving into me?"

"I'm not weaving." She was being drawn in, his big bad body and rugged alpha prowess acting like a magnetic field. "I'm merely checking out the seasonal flora."

He took a leisurely sip. "And here I thought you were checking out my butt."

She snorted. "My focus is right where it should be—on the hike and the client. They call it laser focus."

"Laser focus, huh?"

She pinned her eyes with two fingers, then pointed them at Mr. L and Helga, who stood a few feet ahead looking up at a giant redwood. "It's the level of attention to the surroundings and client that separates a good guide from a great one."

One minute he was sipping his coffee, and then he was stepping into her, his free hand reaching around to cage her against the rocks behind them. "And what is it telling you?"

Avery's breath caught and her thighs hummed, because his face was so close to hers all she had to do was lean forward a whisper and they'd be kissing. "That she's into him."

His gaze dropped to her lips, and it dawned on her that he might think Avery was talking about herself. She backed up even farther into the rock wall, the damp stone pressing into her back, the dew seeping through the top of her jeans.

"Helga, I mean." She swallowed. "She's giving off all the right signals."

His lips curled up into a slow grin that had a ripple of awareness trembling through her. "What signals would those be? I'm just asking so I can cross-reference it with that guidebook you tote around."

Avery poked him in the pec, but he didn't move, so she looked to the side, and her heart warmed as she watched the older couple dance around each other. "Look, right there. Whenever she laughs she plays with her hair, which means she really likes him. She was impressed with the champagne and picnic basket, and based on how often she touches his hand or brushes his arm, if Mr. L plays his day right he'll get a kiss goodbye for sure."

Right then, as if in sync with the rhythm of falling in love, Mr. Lismore leaned in and whispered something that had Helga blushing.

"Isn't that amazing?" she said. "Two people who found true love once and then lost it, yet they're willing to risk being vulnerable in hopes of finding it again."

They were giddy with hope, Avery could tell. She knew those signs by heart.

"Amazing," Ty agreed, but when she looked back she found him staring at her—an odd expression on his face. "I called your former boss at the bank."

Now feeling the opposite of giddiness—and praying that he didn't get Carson when he called—she casually inquired, "You did? What did they say?"

"That you were one of the best employees they'd ever had and were hoping you'd come back," he said, studying her carefully. "It got me thinking, why would someone leave a stable job after five years to work for a boss who is crabby and stubborn and notoriously cheap when it comes to hiring office help?"

"You're not cheap," she joked, even though she knew he was talking about his dad, who was so tight he squeaked when he walked. But what Dale lacked in wages he made up for in bonus adventures. It would cost Avery a fortune to get the training she'd need to climb Sierra Point. Then again, she'd been there three months and this was her first hands-on training.

"Seriously, why did you leave?"

"*Stable* is as overrated as *the same*." And she already knew what that life held—long hours, paperwork, and a false sense of security. She wanted more. She wanted to live a life that made a difference—a life that made her happy. And she wanted to live it with people who loved and supported her.

Ty seemed to have that love and support in spades, yet he was intent on keeping his family at a distance. "Why weren't you here for Christmas?"

He hesitated. With his words and his reaction. He was trying to appear unaffected, and he was good, she'd give him that, but after a lifetime of reading between the lines with lab techs and doctors, Avery knew when she'd hit a sensitive spot. She also knew what it felt like to have no sense of privacy. "It's okay, it's really none of my business."

But she wanted to make it her business. For a guy who liked to portray such an easygoing persona, he rarely smiled. Life was uncertain at best, so living it surrounded by happiness but never embracing it was heartbreaking.

Avery wanted to blame the depleted oxygen zone for her shortness of breath, but she feared it had more to do with how long they stared at each other. Her silently offering to listen, and him deciding how much he wanted to say.

"I'm based out of Monterey," he said, and a loud alarm beeped in his pocket.

"Do you need to get that?"

Eyes back on her lips, he said, "No."

It beeped again.

"You sure?"

"Your thirty minutes are up, angel." He reached in his pocket and turned it off but didn't back away.

"And here I thought you were taking your time so I could check out your butt," she said, trying to hide her disappointment that the moment was lost. "If you need to go, I can take it from here."

"Of that I have no doubt," he said, and she couldn't tell if he was joking or not. "However, since you're still in training, and I'm supposed to be training you, why don't you tell me more than their SeniorDate. com compatibility ranking? You know, maybe touch on some observation that might be more guide related?"

"Guide stuff, right." Avery smiled. "Helga is having a hard time with the uneven trail and her cane, so when we hit the next bend we should opt for the lower trail—it's a little longer but flat. And Mr. L, poor guy, he's so nervous he can't stop talking about things he thinks Helga might find interesting, which explains why he's a little winded. Normally this trail wouldn't faze him, but between impressing his date and demanding to carry the picnic basket, he's getting tired and might run out of wind before we make it to the final stop. Which is why you suggested a brief break to look at the trees."

"Not bad, angel." His gaze slipped to the pulse pounding at the base of her throat. "You're breathing a little heavy too. Any particular reason?"

His proximity for one. Flirting with Ty was like standing in the middle of a lightning storm while holding a metal pole. The idea of getting to know him? The anticipation alone was like being struck with a zillion volts of electricity.

Secondly, she'd been so excited about taking such a big step toward hiking Sierra Point that she'd barely slept last night. Like any recent transplant patient, her immune system already struggled to keep balance, and a bad night usually led to a bad body, so a little jolt of electricity was welcomed. Which was why she scooted a little closer to the sparks.

"I knew that appearing young and strong was important to Mr. L, which is why I let him carry the basket, even though it was way too heavy." She jiggled her pack, and the clanking of silverware and glasses sounded. "And why I put all of the heavy things in my pack."

He didn't break a smile, but she could tell he wanted to. She'd impressed him.

"As for my weaving body and wandering gaze," she said, and this time he did smile, smug and sexy, "I was seeing if I could scout out some poppies for Mr. Lismore to pick for Helga. Orange is Helga's favorite color."

"Poppies, huh?"

"Not only are we on Poppy Alley, but a man picking a woman flowers is wildly romantic."

He studied her for a heart-pounding moment, and then ever so slowly, he tucked a stray hair behind her ear, his finger lingering on her lobe. "My mistake."

With a parting smile, he pushed off the wall and continued on the trail. Avery took a moment to collect her breath—stupid sexy smile—and make sure her pants weren't blazing from that lie. Confident that she had it together, she started walking and felt something tickle her ear. She reached up and found a flower tucked there—a California poppy.

She glanced up to see if Ty was laughing at her, but he'd already disappeared around the bend—with her pack.

And maybe a little piece of her heart.

By the time they'd made it to the lakeside picnic spot, Ty had a chance to think about all of the mistakes he'd made that had gotten him to this point. Agreeing to train Avery was on the list. Sticking a flower in her hair was definitely on the list. Yet neither ranked as high as almost opening up to her.

She'd looked up at him, those big expressive eyes filled with understanding and compassion, and he'd wanted to fall in. Even more powerful was the disappointed look on her face when he'd closed right up. That bothered him, more than it should have.

Which was why he needed to wish Mr. L and his lady friend a nice day and get back to the lodge, where he had enough work to keep him busy for two weeks solid. Perfect timing, since that was the end of his vacation time.

Only, his trainee wasn't on the same page. She helped set up the picnic, even laying out a handmade quilt she had in her gypsy camp and pouring the champagne, but then instead of wishing them well and heading toward the lodge, she wished them well and headed behind an outcropping of boulders—where she carefully selected the perfect little spot for her own picnic.

Fitting, since she'd packed enough food for a family in her sack. Fried chicken, fruit salad, and—

He squinted as she pulled out a container of . . . *Mom's pie?*

Son of a . . . she was planning to stay for a while. A long while by the looks of it.

Taking his hat off, Ty hiked up the small embankment and stood over her, purposefully looming. "What are you doing?"

Eyes closed, she took in a deep breath while the breeze blew a few stray hairs that had escaped. Her nose was pink from the chill and her cheeks flush from the hike. "Breathing it all in."

"Well, breathe fast, because I have to get back," he said.

She slowly blinked up at him. "You go on ahead. I'm going to wait until they're done so I can help Mr. L carry everything back."

"That wasn't the deal," he pointed out, sounding an awful lot like his dad. "The deal was a one-way hike, where you assist me, then you help me organize the office while the guests walk home. Alone."

She scanned the trail leading back to the lodge, the trail so clear it could be seen winding all the way around the lake. A concerned frown creased her brow. "It is an easy trail. You think they'll be okay?"

"Perfectly safe and they'll be fine." Or he wouldn't have left them there.

"Great. If it's safe, then you won't mind if I stay." He did mind, and that was a problem. She was fine sitting there, yet he had reservations about leaving her behind. Which was all kinds of crazy, since his goddaughter, Emma, could find her way home from there—blindfolded.

But Emma wouldn't be tempted to top off this romantic senior outing with a romantic view of the lake—from a higher elevation.

"There's a lot to do back at the lodge to prepare for SAREX. Equipment to catalogue, schedules to spreadsheet."

"Will we have time for lunch?"

"I'm not a total hard-ass."

"Great, then I'll take my lunch here and meet you back at the lodge." She crossed those sexy legs of hers to make a table for her pie while she dug through her pack—coming up with a fork. "Unless you want to share." She held up the pie. "I brought plenty if you want a bite."

Watching her sit there, the sun shining down on her, glistening off her curls and casting a warm glow over her body, he wanted a bite all right.

Pie would be nice too.

Almost as nice as it felt to make her smile earlier with the flower. A total wuss move that his guys would ream him for, but nice all the same.

His phone pinged again, echoing off the rocks and onto the lake.

"Guides are supposed to have their phones on silent during treks, emergency use only, so as not to disrupt the client's time in nature," she said sweetly.

"It's not a personal call, it's business." He pulled out his phone and checked the screen. He saw he'd missed several calls and a text from Harris.

The mechanic called back. He'll meet U @ the
boathouse @ noon. Unless you're too busy
picking posies.

Prick. He dashed off a quick text that he'd be there, and Harris
texted back immediately.

Stop flirting with the cute Adventure Girl and
call your mom.

He'd no sooner checked his phone to find five missed calls from his
mom, when his phone rang again. He blew out a breath.

"I have to take this." He pointed to the spot on the ground where
she sat. "Don't move."

She mimed cuffing herself to the rock—*smart-ass*—and then leaned
back, presumably settling in for the duration of Mr. L's courting, even
stretching out her legs and taking a big bite of pie.

Walking a few feet away, Ty answered. "Hey, Mom, I'm on a trek
with some guests. What's up?" he asked, ignoring the way Avery smirked
when he admitted it was his mom calling.

"Poppy Alley with Art Lismore and Helga, I heard. How very sweet
of you to accommodate him—and smart considering Art is the new
board chair of Jeepers Run."

"He is?" He eyed Avery, sitting back and soaking up the sun. Then
he remembered all of the attributes about the lodge she'd casually
thrown Art's way during the hike, and smiled. She was good, better
than he'd originally given her credit for.

Jeepers Run was the largest jeeping club and association in the
country. An account Dale had been trying to land for over a decade.
And based on Art's schoolboy grin, the man liked what he'd seen so far.

"Which is why Avery thought to pack some of my pie. Show him some home-baked hospitality," she said. "Did you get your piece?"

"My piece?" He looked at Avery, who made a big deal of shoving an enormous bite into her mouth and smacking her lips.

"I sent enough for the whole party with Avery, but I explained that the biggest slice was yours."

"Thanks, Mom, but if you knew I was with a client, why'd you call?"

Irene fell uncharacteristically quiet, and Ty leaned against a giant sequoia for the added support he knew he'd need. When it came to his mom, silence was never a sign of peace. "Mom, what's wrong?"

"Have you talked to your dad today?"

"No," he admitted. Ty hadn't talked to him since their lovely welcome home dinner a few nights ago. It had been a deliberate avoidance. Dale hadn't gone out of his way to connect either, so Ty had gone with it. Only now his mom was involved, so he needed to fix it. "I'll find him later and smooth things over."

"That would be lovely. It breaks my heart to see you two argue." He heard his mom worrying through the phone, which started a little worry knot forming behind his right eye. "But maybe you could find him now?"

He looked at his watch. "I have to get back to the lodge and meet a potential mechanic in a few minutes, and I have to put together an order for the new climbing equipment."

"I know you're busy, and I appreciate everything you're doing, but . . . it's just that he walked out of here early this morning and I haven't seen him since."

For as long as Ty had been alive, Dale ate with the sun, was at work before the night's frost could melt, and didn't come home until dinner was served. So his being gone was not a reason for concern, but ever since Ty had come home something had been off with his old man. From the condition of the lodge to not taking on as many treks.

Then there was his behavior the other night. Sure, Dale was ornery as hell, but he never raised his voice at the dinner table.

"Is there more going on with Dad I should know about?"

"Everything's okay," she said, too brightly.

"Define okay." There was another lengthy pause, long enough to allow that throbbing to encompass his entire frontal lobe. "Mom, I can't help unless I know what's going on."

In the background, a chair ground against the floor, and a heaviness settled at the back of his neck. This was obviously a talk she needed to have sitting down, and that didn't bode well for his timeline. He could picture her, staring down at the table settings, worrying the silver necklace she always wore while counting the seconds. Most folks only saw the courageous woman with the gentle smile, but Ty knew that she was a worrier. She could drive herself sick with worry. He'd seen it happen too many times to count.

"I don't know what's going on," she finally said, her voice thread thin. "He hasn't been himself lately, missing appointments, overbooking things, even snapping at the employees. Then today, we were supposed to have lunch together. Meatloaf sandwiches. Only he didn't show up or call, and he never misses my meatloaf sandwiches."

Dale also never missed a date with his wife. "It's not even noon."

"Lunch is at eleven thirty sharp. Has been for thirty-six years."

And Dale was as punctual as he was a hard-ass. To him, tardiness was a direct commentary on the lack of value someone placed on a person's time.

"I'll check on him after I meet with the mechanic," Ty promised.

"Thank you, honey," she said, and he could hear the relief in her voice. "And would you let me know where you find him?"

She disconnected, and Ty stared at the phone for a long moment. She wanted to know not *when* he found him, but *where* he found him.

As he pocketed the phone he looked up to find that Avery was no longer sitting on the lower boulder where he'd clearly told her to stay put. He scanned the area looking for her orange vest, which was so bright it glowed, but he didn't see her. He whipped out his phone to call her, and that was when he noticed her standing on one of the other boulders, staring out at the lake as if she were witnessing paradise.

Her arms were out to her sides, letting the breeze blow through them, her smile intoxicating, her breathing hard. She'd hauled ass up those rocks, no doubt taking advantage of his being distracted by his mom.

Ty took easily to the rocks, scaling them in a matter of seconds, only stopping when he reached her side. "What happened to staying put?"

Avery didn't turn to look at him, didn't even apologize for traipsing off. She just kept on smiling as if it were the best day of her life. "What happened to no business calls during a trek?"

He pointed to his clients. "They are toasting with champagne, so the trek is officially over."

She looked his way. "Great. Then I'll spend the rest of my lunch enjoying the views."

"You mean making sure that our special VIP guest, the new board chair for Jeepers, is enjoying his stay?"

That got her attention. "How did you know? Oh, wait, your mom."

"How did my dad finally get him to come and visit?" he asked, and the way her gaze skirted away told him everything he needed to know. "You brought him in?"

"His late wife and I met in Reno. She became a good friend of mine, so when I heard that he was having a hard time moving on, I invited him for a visit," she said, her voice thick with emotion. "I knew all he needed was a new view, a different perspective to jumpstart his life. If he came here and fell in love with the land enough to bring the Jeepers Run back, which I knew he would, then all the better. Only he came and met Helga." She looked down on the couple and sighed.

"And look, he's smiling." Her eyes met Ty's. "The last time he smiled was when he was with Ruth at the hospital."

Ty thought about that, about how open Avery had to be to read people so well. He didn't know if he would have the strength to do that, because in order to be open to others, she had to really put herself out there. And that was a place that, although Ty admired she could tap into, he'd never want to be again.

"Why didn't you tell me?" he asked quietly. "Had I known it was Art, I wouldn't have given you such a hard time when you booked the hike."

"Would it have mattered?" she asked quietly, looking back out at the water. And even though he couldn't make out her expression, he could tell that his answer was important to her.

Ty wanted to get it right, wanted to make her smile again, but he didn't know what that answer was. Sure, knowing now just how important it was to impress Mr. Lismore upped the stakes, had him rethinking every step he'd made and questioning how he could have made the hike better.

Only he'd bet his best skipping rock that for Avery, it didn't matter. She'd probably say that everyone deserved the same fabulous experience no matter the status. And she'd be right.

Ty stared out at the lake, watching pine needles skate across the water, while a strong breeze blew ripples across its wide surface. Perfect skipping ripples, he thought, remembering how he and Garrett used to spend their spring days on that lake, waiting for ripples like these. Then they'd spend hours picking the perfect rocks to go the distance.

The day they'd buried Garrett, Ty had come down to these very shores and stood for hours staring out at the water, holding his favorite skipping rock in his hand. He'd rolled it around in his palm, memorizing the smooth edges and the circular shape. It was Garrett's last wish, for Ty to skip it.

Just like that day, Ty's hand found its way into his pocket, his fingers moving back and forth over the edge, trying to soothe his emotions. He'd never skipped the rock, afraid that tossing it into the lake would be like tossing away his brother's memory with it. Because once it was gone, the wish would be over, and then what would Ty have to hold on to?

He'd been too damn selfish to grant his brother his last wish. And too damn scared to run for help. His chest tightened with anger, as it always did whenever he came home—which was why he valued his distance.

"I don't come home on the holidays because there are guys on my team who have wives and kids, a family who needs them around. So I take on extra hours so they can spend time with them," he heard himself saying.

A warm hand settled on his arm, soft and full of understanding. It was amazing how much Avery could convey in a single touch. He hadn't been this connected with someone since—

Garrett.

"You have a family too, and I know they miss you when you can't come home."

"If I was around all the time, they wouldn't miss me anymore." And then where would they all be? Thinking about Garrett and everything they'd lost. Nah, that was burden enough for Ty. He didn't want his family carrying that around too.

"I took a leave of absence from the bank because I was sick," she said. "And when I got better I found out that my fiancé, the guy I thought I'd marry, didn't feel like waiting. Since he was the senior loan officer and I worked at the desk next to him, going back was . . ."

He felt her shrug and glanced her way. The emotion he saw in her eyes was powerful enough to take him out at the knees. It wasn't just sadness she was feeling—the pain rolling off her went soul deep.

"I knew it would never be the same."

Ty studied her for what felt like an eternity, in awe about how open she was, how she wore every vulnerability and insecurity on her sleeve for the world to see and judge. Yet she wasn't embarrassed by it. It was as if she found strength in it—found her identity.

"He's an idiot," he said and meant it. Avery was beyond sweet, beyond beautiful, beyond perfect.

Avery was an angel. Sure she was impulsive and a dreamer and drove him a little crazy—in the best kind of way. Yet some pencil pusher had walked away from her, made her believe it was her fault. That she was the one lacking. Ty could see it in her eyes.

"He isn't an idiot," she said, but her smile said she appreciated the support. "He just wasn't as strong as I thought."

And wasn't that the heart of the problem, because Ty wasn't who she thought he was. If so, she wouldn't be looking at him as if he had single-handedly scaled Everest. He'd faced down that beast of a mountain and came out the victor, but only because it was less terrifying than facing his past.

"Enjoy your lunch, angel." With a final wink, Ty made his way down the rocks.

An odd sensation filled his chest as he descended. The more distance he put between them, the more acute the sensation became, until all he wanted to do was climb back up and share lunch with Avery.

Funny how the last thing he had time for was lunch with Avery, yet that was all he could think about. She had this magical calming ability about her that soothed his restlessness. Made him feel grounded.

He'd reached the bottom when she called out to him. "Your dad's probably down in the boathouse. He goes there when he's having a bad day because he knows your mom won't think to look there."

Ty looked up, his hand shielding his face from the sun. And man, she was beautiful. Her blonde curls hung long and free today, cascading down her back while the afternoon light cast a golden glow around her face and body.

"How do you know it's a bad day?" he asked.

Even from a distance he could see her face soften, watched her worry that lip, something he noticed she did when taking others' emotions into consideration before she answered. "Your mom called *you*."

Damn if that didn't sting. Then again, the truth usually did.

CHAPTER 8

"Wasn't sure you were coming. Was just finishing up with Brian here," Dale said, and Ty nearly groaned aloud as his dad patted the mechanic on the back and not so subtly steered him toward the exit to the boathouse.

Brian still had on his jacket, and his confused expression said he hadn't even opened his toolbox. Finishing up was not what Dale had in mind—he was brushing off.

Not the way Ty wanted this meeting to go. And definitely not how he wanted to broach the subject about hiring a new equipment manager. The only thing Dale hated more than change was being left out of the loop.

"I'm here now, and since Brian came all the way from Incline, why don't we at least let him check out the boats in question. Hear what he has to say," Ty suggested.

"It's your meeting." Dale put his hands behind his back tightly, as if they were shackled. "Don't mind me. I'll be over here, tinkering with my boat."

Of course he wanted to tinker with the boat that Ty had called Brian about. They hadn't seen each other, much less spoken, since the dinner, and his dad wanted to hide. Fine by Ty. So when Dale went to the back of the boat, Ty took Brian to the front.

"Sorry about that. A little miscommunication," Ty said, shaking the man's hand.

"Not a problem. My dad owns the largest machine shop in Reno. Which is why I went into boats."

After a shared a nod of understanding and a silent moment of male bonding over difficult dads, Brian looked over at Dale, who was staring out at the dock. Ty couldn't put his finger on it, but something was different.

He was wearing his usual uniform of pressed workpants and a fleece jacket, his hair the same slick style he'd worn since he was in the service, and his attitude was dialed to grumpy old man. Only he looked smaller, Ty thought. Maybe it was that his clothes hung a little looser than normal, or the way the landscape towered over him, but Ty really thought about what Avery had said, reflected on how frazzled his mom had sounded on the call.

He wasn't sure what a "bad day" entailed, but if he wanted to feel comfortable leaving in a few weeks, he needed to find out. Lighten his dad's load and delegate enough responsibility to qualified people so Dale could ease up a bit, and Irene wouldn't worry so much.

"This is the boat that we need to look at first," Ty said. "It has been chartered for three weeks from now. I need to know if it's safe to take out, and if not, can we get it running by that time."

"Understood." Brian hopped on the cruiser, gaining sea legs in a matter of seconds. He made his way into the cockpit and gave the dash an external once-over. Making sure everything was in its right position, he started her up. The engine sputtered against the cold temperature, the exhaust crystallizing in the air as it struggled to find its rhythm.

Letting loose a low whistle that had the same ominous ring as Harris's, he shut it down.

"That bad?" Ty asked.

"It's not good, I can tell you that. When I talked to Harris, he said it hadn't been serviced in a few months. It sounds like it was a lot longer than that, but I won't know what's going on until I get in there and look at it."

"It was serviced last month," Dale said from behind, the boat swaying with every step he took, giving away his impatience. And if that weren't enough, he squeezed up behind Brian to look over his shoulder, doing his best impression of a backseat mechanic. "And I know it was serviced because I serviced it right before I took a group from Sacramento trout fishing."

"Trout fishing?" Brian glanced over his shoulder. "You sure about that, Mr. Donovan?"

"Of course I'm sure. Took them around the lake to Crystal Bay and caught a thirty-one pounder. I got it in the log." Dale pulled open the cabinet above the console, rummaged around, and then rummaged around some more. "Mark must have misplaced the damn thing. He was always moving things around."

Ty and Brian exchanged a look.

"Dad, Mark left in November." Around the same time trout fishing went out of season. So either Dale was taking folks fishing illegally, or he was lying. And Dale might be a hard-ass, but he wasn't a liar, and he wouldn't risk the lodge's license over a trout, even if it was a thirty-one pounder.

"After everything I taught him, he left me high and dry right before the holidays." Dale was back to digging through the cabin for the log-book. When he couldn't locate it, he yanked open the lower drawer, and a bundle of maps fell to the ground. "Broke your mom's heart. You know how she takes people in like family, so when they leave she gets all emotional . . . Dammit, I know it's in here."

"It doesn't matter. Brian will be able to tell when he checks her out."

Dale slammed the drawer. "The hell it doesn't, because that log will prove it was serviced, and then Brian won't have to waste time checking things that don't need to be checked."

"Dad," Ty said, picking up the maps. "Mark left four months ago."

"I know that," Dale yelled, his temper spiking.

So much for hoping an audience would cause Dale to rein in his heavy-handed approach to change.

"Then the boat hasn't been used since November?" Brian asked Dale, but he was looking at Ty for direction on how to handle the situation. Ty had not a clue. He'd never seen his dad like this. Stubborn, yeah. Pigheaded, absolutely.

Losing his shit in front of company? Never.

Dale was unshakable—steady as they came. But he was shaken now, his body visibly stumbling as he straightened to scratch his head.

"I guess I don't know," Dale said, and just saying the words seemed to take the wind right out of him. He stepped back a few feet and looked up at Ty as if *he* had the answers. "I know Nelson came by once or twice to help me work on the boats before we put them away for the winter. And Nelson is the best in town, been working on our boats since my dad ran the place. We can give him a call, see if he remembers the date."

"That's okay, Mr. Donovan," Brian said. "How about I take her out and see how she handles? I won't charge you unless I find something wrong."

"Sounds good," Ty said as he hopped off the boat, wondering how many other logs were going to wind up missing. "Dad, you and I can hang back while Brian works his magic."

"It's your call," Dale said as he climbed off the boat.

With a confident nod at Ty, man-speak for *I'll run her until I find every problem*, Brian cleared the dock and pulled the boat out onto the lake. Ty watched the white wake slice through the flat surface and lop against the side of the dock, and he wondered what the hell had just happened.

His dad was lost in thought too, but his body language was hostile and agitated.

"Mom was looking for you," Ty said, going for neutral territory. Whenever they fought, it was always his mom who managed to smooth things over.

Dale walked toward the cluster of upturned kayaks on the dock instead of answering, and he took a seat on the one closest to the water. Pulling a cigar from his pocket, he rolled it between his fingers, something Ty had seen him do a thousand times before. Even though he hadn't lit it, a bitter cherry smell scented the air. It was almost as strong as the tension.

"She was worried," Ty added, his comment met by more silence.

Fine. If Dale was content to sit and smoke his damn cigar and watch the water lap, who was Ty to force him into a conversation—a conversation he sure as hell didn't want to have either. He thought about Avery, sitting up on that bluff and eating her pie, all by her lonesome. And wondered if he could still catch her. Only the first question that would come out of her pretty mouth would undoubtedly be about his dad.

Shit.

Ty took a seat. "Does she know you come out here to smoke?"

Dale ran the length of the cigar along his nose, smelling it. "Haven't smoked one of these in over a decade, not since your mom said if the cigar didn't kill me, then she would." A small chuckle escaped, and it was such a foreign sound Ty glanced at his dad. He was actually smiling.

Correction: it was as close to smiling as one could get without showing actual teeth—or joy. But Ty took that as a sign to keep talking. "If you don't smoke it, then why do you carry one around?"

Dale took one last sniff and tucked it back in his shirt pocket with a pat. "Same reason you carry around that rock. Habit I guess."

Ty's throat burned. Swallowing down years of remorse and disappointment hurt like hell. After the funeral, Dale had never once talked about Garrett with Ty. He remembered his dad standing here by the boathouse in his suit, looking out over the lake, his body so still Ty couldn't tell if he was even breathing.

It had been raining, so sheets of water spilled off the dock, but his dad hadn't bothered to change after the funeral. He'd left Irene to handle the guests and walked straight here, to stare out as a storm thrashed against the lake.

Ty had gone looking for Dale, and when he'd found him it was as if every step he'd taken to bring him closer tore them farther apart. By the time he had reached Dale's side, the shame and guilt was so heavy Ty could barely speak.

He'd prepared his apology, knew exactly what he was going to say, and was ready to take the blame—for sneaking out, for ignoring the rules, and for Garrett's death. All that he'd gotten out was "I'm sorry."

Ty remembered looking at his dad, waiting for him to look back, to say something, anything to make it better. Reassurance that he was still loved, even though he didn't deserve their love. But Dale never turned his head, never met Ty's desperate gaze. The only reassurance he offered were two words, spoken simply and without emotion. "Me too."

Ty had walked off the dock that day knowing that he wasn't forgiven. Fifteen years later and not much had changed. Except that Dale was the one who needed help, and Ty wasn't going to walk away.

"Brian seems like a good fit," Ty began, hoping to warm his dad up to the idea of hiring him on. "Avery said you liked him when he was a guest."

"Nice guy, good family man, but he's a bit young."

"I spoke to his boss this morning and the guy couldn't say enough. He's been working on a bigger fleet in Tahoe, mainly party barges, but I think he's ready to step up to equipment manager."

"He did some work for Jasper over at North Star, maintaining their lifts and snowmobiles. Jasper even claimed that for a young gun, he could sweet-talk anything with gears," Dale said.

Surprised by his dad's comment, Ty felt his shoulders relax. Maybe he wouldn't have to fight his dad on this. Maybe Dale would make it easy on everyone and welcome Brian with open arms.

Dale picked a pebble up off the ground and tossed it into the lake. "Doesn't make him a good manager."

Then again, maybe not.

"How long do we have until Sequoia Elite Mountain Rescue comes back for the inspection? Two weeks?"

Dale shifted with unease. "About that."

"Two weeks to get the boathouse in shape, the outdoor equipment catalogued and updated, the trails and staging areas finalized, and a new guide hired. And that doesn't include the lodging side of things or handling the schedule until Brody comes back." Not that Ty intended to hire him back—the guy had a lot of questionable sick days and took a very liberal approach to customer satisfaction—but that was a discussion for later. "We need someone overseeing the boathouse so that I can focus on the rest. I know Brian might not be your top pick, but the good news is he's skilled, reliable, and available."

"If it weren't for SAREX coming up, I wouldn't need anyone's help," Dale argued. "I've managed on my own this long. Had to since there was no one here to hold *my* hand."

Since arguing back would get him nowhere fast and would only add to Dale's stress, Ty swallowed down his frustration and took a deep breath. It didn't help.

He tried it again, this time watching the ripples slowly beat the shoreline.

Nope, still pissed. Dale had a way of doing that, spinning Ty right off the planet with one well-placed comment.

"I know, Dad. You don't need anyone. But you know what? You have people here willing to help. So unless you want to explain to Mom why SAREX is moving to Bear Valley, then step back and let us do our job. I promise when you pass the inspection I'll be gone and you can go back to handling things. Okay?"

"Great, you'll be gone and leave me with some young hipster running my boats." With a dismissive shake of the head, Dale stood, taking a little longer to straighten than normal, and headed back toward the lodge.

Ty watched him storm off, his feet pounding the pavement with intent, and even though a bitter sadness pushed at his chest, Ty found himself laughing. A deep, guttural laugh that hurt as much as it brought release.

Not only had he received permission to hire Brian, he'd been chewed out by a man wearing fucking house slippers.

CHAPTER 9

Tonight was the night, Avery thought, making her way toward the bar, her orange cowgirl boots echoing off the cobblestone sidewalk on Lake Street.

The sun was setting on what had turned out to be a pretty spectacular week, and riding the high she decided she wanted to pay tribute to one more special person in her life. So when Liv told her that some of the ladies from Living for Love were at the Backwoods Brewhouse for happy hour, it was clearly a sign to be bold.

And right now, Caroline Peters needed a little bold in her life. She was undergoing bone marrow transplant surgery next week, and Avery wanted nothing more than to put a crown on her head. So she'd told her friends she'd meet them there.

Only when she opened the front doors of the brewhouse, she was surprised to find not a few members, as Liv had said, but the entire group. They were gathered at the back of the bar, wearing orange Princess Caroline buttons with matching tiaras and boas.

"Perfect timing," Liv said from the head of the table. She wore a pair of trendy hip-huggers, a black pea coat, and red heels with a matching scarf and knit cap. If not for the fitted tee that said #LikeAMom, she'd look like a co-ed from the local campus. "Irene was finishing up passing out everyone's buttons."

"I've got yours right here." A portly woman with bottle-red hair and a perpetual smile separated herself from the group to pin Avery with a button when she reached the table.

"Irene, they are amazing." Avery greeted her with a big hug. Irene smelled like cookie dough and Christmas morning, and she hugged like she meant it. "When did you have time to make these?"

"I overheard Liv at the market talking about how you were going to ride Widow Maker tonight for Lola's granddaughter, so I asked Mavis to make these," Irene said, tapping the button with pride. Her grin was so big it was infectious. "Me and the girls thought we could pass them out around the hospital, so when Caroline shows up next week they'll all be wearing her buttons."

"This is . . ." Avery looked at the table full of women, spanning several sizes, backgrounds, and decades, and her voice cracked. At first glance they had nothing in common, yet it was their shared history with loss and the same desire to make a difference that drew them together. And together they were going to make a huge difference in this precious girl's life. "Really, truly amazing."

"A little ray of sunshine can cut through even the darkest of days," Irene said, and Avery closed her eyes against the building emotion. Those were the exact words she had said to Avery when she'd shown up at her hospital room a few years back, unannounced, with a freshly baked pie and two forks.

"Caroline will love it," Avery whispered.

"Almost as much as she's going to love you being rodeo princess for the night," Liv said, tipping an imaginary hat.

"I thought you could use these to decorate Caroline's page when you're done," Mavis said, then handed her a sheet of beautiful hand-painted princess stickers.

Mavis Bates owned Pins and Needles, the local craft store. She was north of seventy and a porcupine of a woman, with bright red spiky hair and a soft underbelly, and she wasn't big on hugs, but Avery pulled her in for one anyway. The old woman took it like a champ, her arms at her sides and lots of eye rolling until it was over, but she didn't pull away. So Avery held on until she felt the tears well up. "Thank you."

There was something magical about this group of women. When they got together there wasn't a single life they couldn't touch in a positive way.

"Last time I watched someone ride that bull, it was my Jonas," Wanda Mallory, retired librarian and Sequoia Lake's resident grandma, said. "We'd just seen that Nicholas Sparks movie about the bull rider, and Jonas wanted to prove he didn't have to be a young gun to last eight seconds." Wanda shook her head, but her eyes were glazed over with longing. "Silly man ended up leaving here with a bag of frozen peas on his parts."

"Did he last the eight seconds?" Mavis asked with the seriousness of discussing world politics. All of the ladies leaned forward in one collective movement.

Wanda gave a bright smile, then waggled a suggestive brow. "Even went a second round when we got home."

"Earmuffs," Liv said, covering her ears. "You babysit my son with that mouth."

"Which reminds me, I'm free to sit Paxton next month for Spring Fling if you need me to." Wanda steepled her fingers beneath her chin. "With Jonas gone I wasn't going to go this year. So"—she dragged out the word—"if you wanted to go with Chuck—"

Liv's mouth gaped open in horror. "The guy who works the meat counter at Bunny Slope Super Market?"

"I heard he was thinking of asking you," Wanda sang. "Even set aside some nice lamb chops for when you do your usual Monday shopping."

"Lamb chops, now that's romantic." Irene sat back and let out a wistful sign. "Dale used to bring me pinecones."

"Pinecones?" Avery asked.

Irene's eyes lit, and for the first time in weeks she didn't look so tired. "Oh yes. One year I saw a picture of this table setting Martha Stewart did and mentioned how lovely it would look on our table. It was silver-and-red themed with wood accents and a candleholder in the middle of the table. Not just any candleholder, but one made from a giant Coulter cone. Without telling me why, Dale planned a trip with the boys to Bear Valley, and they brought me home three perfect Coulter cones, which I made into holders."

"That's sweet," Avery said, her heart melting a little. Dale had not only gone out of his way to make Irene feel special, but he'd brought her a present that took thought and deep understanding of his wife.

Most men would have sent flowers. Carson always sent flowers.

"Every year after, he's brought me a different kind of cone for the table."

"Sweet and romantic," Avery said, and Liv pinned Avery with a *you are so not helping right now* glare.

"Creative or not, Chuck is, like, fifty," Liv pointed out.

The silvered women at the table exchanged confused looks. But it was Mavis who spoke. "Free lamb chops, dear. Offers like that don't come along too often."

"He's fifty!" Liv repeated, and it was clear that the ladies didn't see the problem with a thirty-year age gap. "That would be like you dating someone who was ninety."

Mavis considered this. "Does he have his real teeth?"

Liv took on the same panicked expression she got when the idea of dating was broached. Avery knew that what started as a little gasping and uncomfortable sputtering could quickly turn to tears—or a breakout of hives.

"I don't think Liv is ready to start dating yet," Avery offered with a supportive wink.

A collective *ah* of understanding filled the room followed by several women saying, "We got you, honey." The ladies might not understand passing up free chops, but they could all empathize with not being ready to move on.

Liv blew Avery a grateful kiss across the table, and Avery felt that familiar warmth that came whenever she saw her friends moving forward. Liv might not be ready to date, but she didn't look devastated by the suggestion as she once would have.

"How about you?" Mavis's gaze locked onto Grace, who was doing her best to blend into the wallpaper in a pair of nondescript khakis, a baggy white button-up that swallowed her whole, and cream ballet flats—all of which were speckled with various colors of paint. "You could use some lamb chops. You've got plans for the Spring Fling?"

Grace flushed from neck to forehead, her gaze zeroing in on the exit, most likely running through every route she could use to flee. Grace was a private person by nature. Even when they were young, she'd shied away from the spotlight and would rather leave the state than invite someone into her home—even if they came baring lamb chops. And when she was cornered, she tended to shout ridiculous things.

So Avery wasn't surprised when Grace shouted, "I'm not looking to date right now either, but you know who is?" Grace's attention went from the exit to her decoy. "Avery."

Twelve sets of eyes ricocheted around the room, from one end of the table to her.

"Grace," Avery hissed.

"Sorry," she mumbled, appearing completely horrified by her outburst. "But it's true, she even kissed someone."

Avery felt her cheeks heat. "He was a stranger." Even though it was the truth, she avoided looking Irene's way because, sure, she hadn't known who Ty was when she'd kissed him at the bar, but she knew now, and she still dreamed about kissing him. "And I did it for Bella. It was the one thing she wished she'd had time to do, go back to Paris and kiss the man who gave her a rose."

The man who had made her friend feel beautiful and treasured with a single romantic gesture. Bella had held on to the rose, a keepsake from a memorable moment in her life, and now it was in Avery's journal, next to a Fearless Red lipstick kiss on a bar napkin from Backwoods Brewhouse.

"You take your first guests on a trek, and now we hear you kissed a *stranger*." Irene highlighted the last word in a way that had Avery swallowing hard. "Bella is probably up there right now bubbling over with joy. I imagine her wearing that pretty red dress of hers, looking . . . well . . ." Irene tilted her head to the side, studying Avery like a mother would study her son's new girlfriend. "Like you do right now."

Liv coughed something that sounded a lot like *awkward*, and Grace busted out laughing. Irene, however, kept her focus on Avery, her smile big and mischievous.

"If I had a wish, it would be to ride on a hog again," Mavis said. "One more night with the motor rumbling beneath me, the wind in my face, and a good-looking man pressed to my front as we burn rubber down the interstate, the moon lighting our way." She closed her eyes and sighed with delight. "To remember what it feels like to be young."

Avery saw more joy radiate off Mavis in that moment than she had in the entire two years since losing her ability to walk without a cane. Even talking about it, she looked younger, took on a lighter energy. Avery couldn't imagine how trapped a woman who cherished her freedom like Mavis would feel when facing a future confined to a wheelchair. She wasn't in her chair yet, but at the rate her MS was going, the doctors didn't think it would be much longer. And wasn't that a heartbreak of a reality.

Avery pulled out her memory journal from her purse and flipped to a blank page. Smiling, she wrote TAKE A WILD RIDE IN THE MOONLIGHT.

Mavis peeked over her shoulder. "What are you doing?"

"Making you a page," Avery explained. "This journal is a way for me to honor people I love. And I want to honor you, Mavis."

Mavis flushed. "You want to honor me?"

"Yes, I do. You're adventurous and loud, and you never give up fighting," Avery said gently. "You also brought me an endless supply of magazines and wild ideas for trips when I was in the hospital, and I want to honor those parts of you and put you in my book. If that's okay."

Mavis smoothed her hair down. "I'd be honored." And having reached her emotional capacity for the night, she punched Avery gently in the arm.

"Even though most of the people in her book have passed, a few are in a place where they can't fulfill their wishes. Look at Caroline," Irene pointed out. "They finally found a donor match, which means in a few months she will be back in school, playing dress up, and laughing with her friends like a normal little girl."

Normal, Avery thought, such a trivial thing for most people. But for someone fighting for her life, it was a powerful motivator. There were days that just a flash of normal, like going to a high school dance, was enough to pull Avery through the worst of it. So the thought of helping Caroline play dress up, her favorite pastime, made Avery's chest soar.

Mavis fluffed her hair. "While you are all honoring me, remember that in my day I was a real catch. Red hair, big boobs, pretty. Just like I am now, only lighter and fewer wrinkles. So the rider would have to be a daredevil with thighs of steel, a butt so tight it could bounce quarters into space, and a mustache."

Grace frowned. "A mustache?"

"This is my wish, freckles, so back off," Mavis snapped. "When it's your turn to dress the wish up, you can ask for whatever you like. Me? I like mustaches. Handlebar ones."

Wanda smacked a bony hand on the table. "Well, if Mavis gets to ride a motorcycle with a hot bad boy, what about you riding that bull in honor of my Jonas tonight? The crown is for Caroline, but the ride could be a way to celebrate how that man would do anything to make me laugh."

"As long as I don't have to ride home with a bag of frozen peas, I've got some cowboy stickers at home, just waiting for a page," Avery said right as the door opened and in walked a group of mountain-climbing wild men bearing chiseled bodies, wind-chapped faces, and enough alpha swagger to send Mavis into cardiac arrest.

Avery was having some palpitation problems of her own, because pulling up the back in butt-hugging pants, a look-at-my-pecs pullover, and a smile that was 100 percent *hey, girl,* was her stranger, looking rugged and—right her way.

"Look who just walked in," Irene cooed, walking over to give her son a hug. "Hey there, *stranger.*" The last word was said in a way that let Avery know the older woman was onto her and Ty.

She tried to roll her eyes, but they were too focused on the sweet way Ty pulled his mother into him, holding her in a protective manner that made swallowing difficult. Ty might play down how much he missed seeing his family, but it was clear in the way he held Irene, as if she were the most treasured thing in his life, that they were close.

Avery had seen it before, the kind of bond families shared when they lose a member too early. Irene had started Living for Love a few years after losing her son, which meant that Ty had left home after losing his brother. Which might explain why he rarely came back.

She didn't know the whole story surrounding Garrett's death, only that he'd been too young to go and his death had nearly ripped their family apart. But unlike Avery's family, Irene had managed to pull them back together. Watching the two of them cling to each other now, Avery could see the lingering scars and struggles—and the unconditional and unwavering support.

It was such an intimate moment, one she'd hoped to share with her own father when her mom passed, that she felt as if she was intruding, so she busied herself with grooming her boa.

Avery's dad had been there for her during her treatments, in every way that he could physically be, but emotionally he didn't have anything left to give. Years of fighting to save his soul mate only to lose her in the end had changed him. Made him withdraw into his work, focus on things he could control. Avery had understood his pain, his need to distract himself, but she still felt his absence.

"What are you doing here?" she heard Ty ask.

"We came to cheer on Avery as she claims her crown." She looked between the two of them, and Avery could see the light twinkle wildly in the woman's eyes. It was the same wild twinkle Irene got when she'd introduced Art to Helga. "You know Avery, right, honey?"

"You know I do, Mom."

"Of course! You two went on an adventure yesterday," Irene said, but that didn't stop her from taking Ty's hand and dragging him away from his group. A group of big badass men who were all grinning at her. Because they all knew what Avery knew.

Irene wasn't just being polite. As the town's resident matchmaker, she was looking to make a love connection. Only Ty wasn't sticking around long enough for that—and Avery had a bull to ride. She was looking to leave her mark. Make a difference.

Maybe after the crown was secure she wouldn't mind spending some time with her tall and handsome trainer. Find out how it went with Dale yesterday, see how he felt about her progress as a guide. But mainly she wanted to see if that buzz she felt whenever he looked her way had to do with extreme situations they found themselves in or extreme chemistry.

Something that couldn't be tested with Irene standing right there.

So when Irene turned to say something to Ty, Avery made a dash for the bar. She could hear Ty let out a loud clucking sound, which suited her fine. He could cluck all he wanted. If they found themselves in a romantic situation, it would be because he wanted it to happen, not because his mom invited her to Sunday dinner.

Reaching the bar, Avery took a seat and watched Harris navigate a keg of beer under the stainless-steel prep counter. "Is Widow Maker looking to make a new friend tonight?"

Harris hooked up the keg and turned. When he saw it was her he smiled. "Why, tiny? You looking to take a ride?"

"If it means having Ty whittle me a crown from twigs, you bet."

He glanced at his cousin, who stood across the room but was clearly glaring back, and laughed. "In that case, the ride is on me. Roland's not working tonight, but I know where he hides the keys."

Harris grabbed a ring of keys from behind the cash register and then hopped over the bar. Slinging his arm around Avery, he pulled her close and quietly asked, "Should you be riding so soon after . . . ?" He waved a finger at her side—and Avery's attention was brought to the tight skin around her scar.

"It's been nearly a year." She patted her scar with a confident smile. "I think I'm good."

Harris didn't look so convinced. Avery wasn't either, but her riding that bull was worth a few aches. Caroline going into surgery with a crown was worth it all.

She gestured for Harris to go ahead of her. He gave her a long, disapproving stare, then acquiesced. "At least with that much orange, he'll think you're here to hunt not ride."

"Maybe it will give me an edge," she said as she followed him across the room, giving high fives and exploding rocks to everyone she passed. Even Ty's buddies were cheering her on. Ty, however, didn't look all that happy.

The fear of having to make a crown in front of his friends could do that to even the manliest of men, she thought, then sent him a pinkie wave. He didn't wave back, pinkie or otherwise.

But her good humor quickly faded. The closer she got to Widow Maker, the louder the cheers got, and the bigger the bull looked. Then she was there, dressed in girly boots and an orange boa, looking up at a mountain of pounded steel that had taken down men twice her size.

She was crazy. This whole idea was crazy.

"You're going to need all the edge you can get," Harris said, putting the key into the machine. "Widow's saddle weighs more than you."

Now that she was here, ready to take the ride of her life, she wondered if she was making a mistake. Rushing things.

It had been nearly a year since her surgery, and she was getting stronger every day, even gaining back some of the weight she'd lost. But if she was thrown and landed wrong, her doctor would not be happy—and neither would her body.

"Second thoughts?" Harris asked.

Avery knew where her mom had stood on second thoughts. If she'd let fear rule her life, she never would have climbed Sierra Point when she did, which meant Lilian never would have had the chance to make that journey—create those memories that pulled her through to the end.

"No room for second thoughts when you get a second chance," she said. "But I wouldn't complain if you went easy on me."

He slid her a wink. "I don't set the bully meter, but I've never seen Widow Maker go hard on a pretty lady."

"The tin man was just metal without his heart," she said, mainly for her own ears. "And heart is my superpower."

Harris looked up from the machine and smiled. It wasn't smug or flirty, it was the kind of smile he got when talking about his daughter. It was such a sweet contrast, really—a big man in battered jeans, a leather jacket, and a smile that could go from walking, talking trouble to incredibly touching. It was a smile that had her thinking. Why not make everyone's wishes come true tonight?

"You own a motorcycle, right?"

"Roxy," he said, sounding as if he were talking about his second child. "She's a sixty-six Harley Electro Glide with the original shovelhead engine and chrome. I rebuilt her from the ground up with my dad. She looks like she just came off the lot but purrs like she's been around every block."

"She sounds wild," Avery said, not understanding a thing he said, other than Roxy was a motorcycle and Harris would look spectacular in leather chaps. "Would you be willing to take a lady on a ride sometime?" Avery asked, making sure to add in a little lash batting.

Harris tapped his chin with a finger and pretended contemplation. "I don't know, it might make for some weird family reunions since you had your tongue down my cousin's throat recently. Not that weird is bad. For you, tiny, I might be into weird."

Avery smacked him in the chest. "I'm not asking for me."

"Well, break my heart, why don't you." Charm dialed to swoonworthy, Harris scanned the table at the back. "Which lady are we talking about?"

"What happened to your broken heart?"

"What happened to my cousin?" When Avery flushed he said, "That's what I thought. Now, which lady is clamoring to ride my hog?"

"Which lady do you want it to be?" Based on the way he was staring, he already had his eye on a hopeful, and it wasn't Mavis. Harris sent Grace a wink, and she turned around in her chair so fast she nearly fell over.

"It isn't Grace. I'm riding it in honor of Mavis because with her MS, there's no way she could straddle the bike. But like I told you a dozen times before, I don't think Grace is ready to ride your hog," Avery said with a quiet steel to her voice. Harris was a great guy, but he was also great with the ladies. And Grace was still in a delicate place in her healing—stronger than she realized but still too fragile to play with a guy like Harris.

"She's ready, she just doesn't know it," Harris said, then looked back to Avery. "But the *touch her and I will cut off your balls* look you got going on isn't necessary. I'm not offering what she needs. As for the bike ride, I can do it Wednesday night after work."

"Really? Thank you." Avery reached up and gave Harris a hug. She went to pull back, and he tightened his arms.

"I thought you wanted to avoid the whole making-family-holidays-weird thing?" she mumbled into his chest.

"I gotta get you up on that bull somehow. Your legs won't do you much good." His hands went to her waist, tightening for a second, and then effortlessly he set her on the saddle. "Doesn't mean screwing with his head in the meantime isn't fun. Now before you grab that handle, lean in close, then throw your head back like I'm the funniest guy in the world."

Jesus, could Harris put his hand any higher on Avery's thigh?

Not without causing a scene, Ty thought, watching the two flirt and carry on like they were a couple of kids partying after playing chicken with a steam engine. Granted, Harris was an overgrown kid—it was why he got along so well with his five-year-old daughter. But there was nothing childlike about Avery.

No sir. In a pair of fitted jeans, one of those flimsy sweaters with holes big enough to make you think you were seeing skin, and a faint trace of red lace peeking out one shoulder, she was clearly all woman. And every man in the room knew it.

And those who weren't in the know wised up the second Widow Maker started bucking and Avery started swaying. She moved back and forth at first, her body getting used to the rhythm, one hand in the air like she was a pro.

"You got it, girl," one of the ladies hollered, igniting an explosion of whoops and cheers, and Avery let loose a genuine, contagious laugh that rolled down Ty's body like warm honey.

Then Widow started jerking, catching her off guard, taking her round and round until it was clear she was going to lose this battle. She grabbed her side like it was pinching, and her friends went eerily silent. Ty shot into savior mode, gauging the fastest possible route from his table to the pen in time to reach her before she hit the mat. But his worry was in vain. Avery did not disappoint.

Nope. He hadn't even taken a step when, chin squared, she dug deep, wrapping her arms and legs around the bull's neck, clinging to the steel machine as if she'd rather break every bone in her body than admit defeat. Ty had to admire her spunk. The woman was stubborn—and sexy as hell.

"Three. Two. One," the crowd counted down, and when the buzzer went off and Widow slowed to a stop, the place erupted in cheers. Orange boas swung in the air, and some lady climbed up on a chair and started clapping.

Not some lady, Ty realized with a chuckle—his mom.

Avery, though, she kept holding on. Cheek pressed to Widow's neck, limbs locked like a pretzel, and hair spilling over the side, she hung on tight until Harris opened the gate to the pen. Even then she only opened a single eye—and it locked on Ty.

Fifty people were gathered in that bar, and she found him. A small smile tugged her lips, growing until Harris carefully helped her off the bull. And when he took her hand to hold it up like a champion, she didn't fist pump the air or do some smug victory dance.

Avery didn't do smug. His angel gave her table a big wave like she was riding on a float in the Main Street parade, then looked back at him and shouted, "I rode Widow Maker and lived to tell the story! Did you see?"

Oh, he saw all right. Couldn't take his eyes off her. She was so alive he could feel her happiness from fifty feet away.

"She's cute," Gary Sikes said, pouring himself a beer from the pitcher. "She works at the lodge, right?"

"Dating among coworkers is frowned upon," Ty informed Sequoia Lake Lodge's newest seasonal employee.

Ty slid his friend a hard look and, in case he didn't read all of the *back the fuck off* signals Ty was throwing his direction, added, "She's not looking to hook up with a snowbro."

"Well, lucky thing then that I'm staying until summer." Gary set the pitcher down and grabbed his beer. "When all of the snow will be melted."

Ty snatched the mug from him and downed a long pull.

"Not cool, man," Gary said, getting a new mug. "I was just curious, and it's not like I would step on Harris's toes. Not my style."

Ty frowned. "They're just friends," Ty said, watching Avery giggle at something the prick said as he handed her the 8 Seconds Tough ball cap. At least he wasn't hanging all over her anymore.

"You sure about that?" Gary asked, and Ty leaned back, crowding the table and accidently knocking Gary's shoulder, spilling beer down the side of the mug.

"Hey!" Gary jerked back and then flicked the foam off his hand. "All I'm saying is that none of my friends look like her. And you're *fuck off and die* glare was the only reason guys weren't lined up and waiting for her to get bucked off so they could buy her a drink and offer to rub her boo-boos—Ow! Jesus." Gary rubbed his shoulder. "Do you treat all future employees this way?"

"Only the ones who piss me off," Ty said, half joking.

All week he'd been dreaming about being away from the lodge so he could pound some serious dirt, get a hit of adrenaline, and pretend he didn't have a pile of stuff still left to do. And it had worked. The climb had gone great—better than great. Ty not only worked out some aggression scaling Cedar Rim but also landed Sequoia Lake Lodge a new elite adventure guide.

And it was time to celebrate. So he'd come here to throw back a few and enjoy knowing there was one less thing to do before he could head back to his life down south.

Then he walked in here and saw Avery, and all he could think about was her. Naked. In his bed.

Only she was with his mom, hanging out like they were besties, a view that should have had him running. It didn't. In fact, seeing Avery with his mom, talking and laughing with a group of women he'd known his whole life, might have killed some of the immediate fantasy, but it did nothing to curb his interest. If anything it drew him in further.

And now she was chatting it up with Harris, wearing his stupid cap, while he reached out for her side to rub her fucking boo-boos. But she batted his hand away with a casual laugh.

"They didn't line up because she didn't fall off. She's too stubborn for that," Ty said, but he scanned the room anyway for these *other* guys. He located nine possibilities. All under thirty-five, all interested, and not a one Ty couldn't take.

"And she isn't with Harris." Ty polished off his beer and stood. "And she earned a crown, not a ball cap."

Eyes locked on the target, Ty made his way toward the bull pen. And Avery. She watched him approach, her eyes widening as he strode through the gathered crowd. She went a little pink in the cheeks but didn't look away, instead engaging him with a playfulness that fed right into his mood.

He might call her "angel," but she was a fireball of trouble.

And Ty loved him some trouble. Walked headfirst into it every day for work. But her kind of trouble left marks. Sure, she was pretty in that all-American way, and she had a quiet confidence that was as calming as it was enticing. But it was her strength that got him. She had a resilience that was intoxicating, an openness in those expressive blue pools that made him want to fall right in and never come out.

Ty's life was full of people who needed him—his job, his team, his subjects, even his family—though Dale would rather lose the lodge than admit it. Ty's world worked on a need-only basis. But the relationships in Avery's life seemed to exist on her desire to make connections, not a need to connect.

"Hey," he said, approaching the two of them. He spoke to Harris but watched Avery. "My mom was looking for you. Something about leaving your girlie magazines in her bathroom. She looked mad."

Avery laughed. "Girlie magazines?"

"I'll go find her," Harris deadpanned. "Explain that you asked to borrow my entire collection." He turned to Avery. "Good job, tiny."

"Thanks for taking it easy," she said.

With a wink for the lady and the finger for Ty, Harris left.

"That was mean," she said, but he noticed she wasn't calling his cousin back over.

"Well, we have something to talk about." He leaned a hip against the metal pin railing. "Something important. It couldn't wait."

She looked startled, then looked around and lowered her voice. "I know. I hope this doesn't make things awkward between us. We had a great day yesterday, and I feel like we're finally becoming friends, and"—she clasped her hands in front of her—"I should have told you the second you walked in."

Ty crossed his arms. "Told me what? I was talking about what kind of crown you wanted."

"I was talking about the crown, silly." She rolled her eyes, then smacked him in the chest. Only to jerk her hand back. "Quick, pretend you came over to congratulate me and talk about the crown."

"I did come to talk about the crown." Ty looked around and saw a punk sitting at the end of the bar with a boy band tattoo and frosted tips, making *hey, baby* eyes at Avery. Not that she noticed—she was too busy faking a laugh. "Since the Backstreet boy isn't your type and Harris is behind the bar, what's going on?"

Her hands went to her hips. "How do you know he's not my type?"

He matched her stance and watched as a hint of pink darkened her cheeks, then stretched to reach the tips of her ears.

"It's your mom," she whispered. "She was acting all weird, saying cryptic things, and, well, I think she knows we kissed."

Ty burst out laughing. "Correction. You mean she knows you kissed me. Because when I kissed you there was no one around but the squirrels. When you kissed me it was in front of a member of every founding family in the area."

"Can't we just leave it at we kissed?" she hissed. "And now your mom knows, and she's acting weird."

"We kissed twice," he corrected. "And my mom always acts weird. It's part of her charm—and what happens when some strange woman kisses her son without even asking his name."

"I asked you your name, and you said Ty. Just Ty, like you're too cool for a full name." She waved a dramatic hand, flipping her wrist for flair, then hesitated as a pinch shot through her side. Briefly holding her breath, she put her hand back on her hip and, stoic smile in place, she continued, "How was I to know Ty was short for 'the boss's son'?"

"I was too focused on you being an adventure *guide* to notice I left out the last name." He moved closer and rested his hand over hers. "You're hurt."

She tried to bat his hand away too, but unlike Harris he didn't back down. "I saw you whip back when Widow made that turn. He jerked you pretty good. Did you hurt something?"

"It's just a pull," she whispered, her eyes on their hands, which were suddenly intertwined. "But it's better now."

"You sure?" He looked up, savoring the warmth of the connection. "I could kiss it better?"

"You could, but I'd have to lift up my shirt, and that would definitely make your mom act weird."

Ty groaned at the image of what lay beneath that shirt. "I'm willing to risk it."

Avery seemed to contemplate this, but then good sense kicked. "Your mom has enough on her mind without having to worry about an employee going topless at the local watering hole." Her hand tightened in his. "How did things with your dad go?"

"It could have gone worse," Ty said, intending on leaving it at that. But the warm compassion in her eyes made her impossible to ignore. Her genuine interest deserved a genuine answer. "It could have gone better too. I don't know if it's me being home that has him so riled up, or if he's just in a mood, but he was in rare form."

"It isn't you," Avery said. "He's been like that for a while. There has been a lot of change in his life recently, and he's struggling to deal with it. It's why your mom hired me, to help get the place organized and back running smooth. I know he's thrilled that you're back."

"I don't know about thrilled," Ty said. "But he did give in to hiring Brian on full-time. He starts tomorrow."

"That's great," she said. "And just in time for your meeting with Cal-SAR."

"I still have a lot to do to prepare for my talk. There will be a ton of paperwork and legwork after my call, and Gary can't start until next weekend, but things are looking better." Every second he talked to Avery he felt a little better too. Lighter and not so stressed.

It was her smile, he decided—it had the power to cut through all of the BS.

"I have a solution for some extra manpower to help with the legwork," she said, resting her hands on the table, so close to his all he had to do was move his finger and they'd be touching. "As for Brian, he's a good guy who I know will work hard not to let you down. Plus, his wife seems set on moving here. I don't think they have family close by, but she is sweet and won't have a hard time finding friends."

If not, he was sure Avery would make it her personal mission to see Brian and his family settled. Not that Ty would be around to see much of it, since he was leaving.

"Thanks for the heads-up about my dad," he said. "Otherwise I would have walked into an even worse shit storm. I don't even know what set him off."

Her face puckered in confusion, quickly softening into what he interpreted to be sadness. Her hand lowered, and she took a small step back, breaking the connection. "It seems like you're handling things fine."

An awkward moment passed between them, and Ty couldn't say what had caused the shift, but he felt it. Maybe it was that his mom was ten feet away talking to Harris, who kept looking this way. Or maybe his cousin wasn't screwing with him, and there was something more there than friendship.

He stuck his hands in his pockets and rocked back. "What were you and Harris talking about?"

"Oh God." She covered her face and burst out laughing. "It's bad. I totally cornered the poor guy into taking me out on his motorcycle this week. Being a gentleman, he said yes."

Poor guy his ass. Any healthy male in the bar would jump at the chance to have Avery snuggled up to him while blasting through the mountains with her wrapped around his thighs.

He looked down at her orange cowgirl boots. "You don't seem like a biker babe. Then again, I didn't take you for a cowgirl either, and you rode Widow Maker into the ground."

"And I won a crown."

He smiled. "That you did." Resting his hand on her lower back, he guided her toward a booth at the back of the bar. "Because you're the rodeo queen of the night, I'm going to buy you the first round, then after we toast you can tell me the kind of crown you want."

She squealed. "It needs to be big, fancy, with lots of filigree. Oh, and bling. A queen needs regal bling."

"What happened to beer coasters and napkins?" he asked, but if he had to learn how to mold platinum, he'd do it if it meant she kept smiling up at him like that.

"Coasters and napkins are perfect," she conceded. "As for the drink, although I'd love a s'more-tini, I'll settle on ginger ale."

"We talking ginger ale?" He mimed bringing a big frothy mug to his mouth. "Or ginger ale?" He stuck out his pinkie.

With a wiggle of her little finger, she added, "With some of those dyed cherries in it."

"Of course," he said. "Wouldn't be a celebration without those dyed cherries. Be right back."

Her laugh reached him as he made his way toward the bar. Harris was standing by the bar, so Ty sidled up next to him.

"What's up with you taking Avery on a ride?"

"Well, hey, cuz, sure you can buy the first round since I took a half day off to taxi your ass all the way up Cedar Rim. And yes, my plan worked—we impressed the kid, and now you have a new guide. You're welcome."

"And what's up with the special treatment? You don't even run the bull—Roland does. Hell, you aren't even working tonight."

"I told Roland I'd *handle* this one personally," Harris said, making some kind of suggestive expression with his brows.

"Well, you've handled enough, so call off the ride."

Harris grinned. "Are you saying that my handling is bothering you?"

"I'm saying that she isn't one of your barflies—she's an employee of the lodge."

"An employee you fired and I rehired," Harris pointed out. "Now, if she were more than an employee to you, then any and all handling on my end would be off."

"Stop with the fucking handling, all right?"

Harris put up his hands in surrender, but the idiot was grinning. "You're into her, got it." Harris leaned in. "For the record, I didn't ask her, she asked me, and I only said yes because it's on her bucket list or whatever."

That fucking bucket list. It probably came right after kissing a stranger and before—well, he didn't want to even go there.

"Plus, you're leaving in a few weeks." Which was why Ty couldn't go there. "And like you said, she isn't your type. Unless something's changed I should know about."

Everything had changed, except the one thing that mattered. He was leaving, and Avery deserved more than a passing fling with a snowbro. Especially since he'd be passing through on rotating holidays. "Nothing's changed."

"You sure? Because the look you've been sending me all night tells me I should cover my nuts, because something's changed."

"I owe her a crown, and then I'm finished helping her check things off."

"Uh-huh." Harris believed Ty almost as much as Ty did. "Well, it looks like I'm up then." Harris pulled two frosty mugs out of the freezer and set them on the counter. "Did you see how she held on to Widow Maker? Imagine her on my bike." He held up a mug. "Something non-alcoholic for the lady and a beer for her friend?"

Ty looked over his shoulder at Avery, who was looking back with a smile that wouldn't quit. As if she was happy to spend her night right there in that dark booth with him, sipping ginger ale and talking about paper crowns—and his family. And not a single cell in his body was itching to leave.

Which was why he needed to end this now, before this chemistry grew legs and took them down the wrong path.

"Make mine a Flaming Pig's Ass."

Harris laughed. "I'll make it a double."

CHAPTER 10

A gentle spring breeze clung to the late-morning chill, awakening the flowers and melting the frost into drops of dew that sparkled in the sun. Taking in a fortifying breath, Avery shut the office window and settled back at her desk.

She had spent the first part of the week identifying tasks that needed to be accomplished before the inspection, and that morning dividing the tasks into three separate lists. One list covered the food and lodging details for the event, one covered equipment and supply status with details of numbers needed and who to order from if they came up short, and the final focused on the individual classes and staging locations.

The call with Cal-SAR, the California search and rescue organization, had gone great. Ty had convinced Lance that the lodge was more than capable of handling all of the needs for their yearly training, and he even managed to get a day for the second inspection on the calendar. Seven days from today.

Normally with that kind of timeline, she'd tell herself not to sweat the little details, but this event relied on executing all of the little details to perfection, so she was sweating.

She was also yawning. A side effect from spending her days lusting over Ty and her nights wondering when they were going to kiss again.

She was ready. He'd seemed game. They'd spent Sunday night talking and laughing, the connection growing until her heart was racing and the bar was clearing out. All of the signs had been there. The wandering eyes. The casual brushing of bodies. Even the not-so-casual touching of hands. So when he offered to walk her to her car, Avery had heard, "Let's go someplace private."

Only he'd walked her to her car, where they had more privacy than a grizzly during winter, and he'd leaned in slowly, her toes curling in anticipation, and he kissed her—on the cheek.

The cheek.

After three hours of verbal foreplay, the only heavy petting she'd received was a goodnight peck and him buckling her safety belt in place.

Sitting in her office chair, she stifled another yawn and reached for her cup, only to realize it was empty. She stuck her finger down to the bottom to get the last bit of hot cocoa and was licking it off when she felt a shift in the room.

"It helps if you actually put coffee in there," a gruff voice, thick with sleep, said from the doorway.

Avery looked up to find Ty, leaning against the doorjamb in a pair of loose cargo pants, a half-zipper pullover, and enough bed head to make her feel not so alone in the sleepless nights arena. He was also holding a paper bag and a steaming coffeepot—which was filled with hot cocoa.

"Who needs caffeine when there's chocolate and sugar," she said, holding out her cup for a refill. "You should try it. It might do something for the scowl you have going on."

"This isn't a scowl. This is what it looks like when Dad disappears to go work on boats at three in the morning and doesn't bother to tell my mom where he's going."

Avery could only imagine how scared Irene would have been—waking up to an empty bed and Dale gone. She could also imagine how hard that must have been on Ty. She wasn't sure how much Irene had told him about Dale, but Ty had been home long enough to be putting together the pieces and realizing things were worse than they were letting on.

Irene could only hide Dale's condition for so long, so it was good that Ty had come home when he had. Irene needed help and support, but right now it looked as if Ty needed some support of his own.

"Sit," she said, taking the pot and disappearing into the break room. She poured two steaming mugs of hot cocoa, one topped off with whipped cream and a cinnamon stir stick. When she came back, Ty was still holding up the wall.

"You're cute when you're grumpy," she said, opening his hand to slip the mug between his fingers. "Take a sip and I promise everything will look different. You might even smile."

When he didn't move to sip it, she took a sip of her own and then made a big deal over how good it was. He didn't laugh like she'd hoped, no smile either, but he finally took a tentative sip.

"Well?" she asked, holding her hand out for him to sit in her seat.

"Not bad," he said, setting the paper bag on the edge of the desk and taking a seat.

He went in for another sip, and Avery's focus went to the bag, which was big enough to hold a dozen mysteries. A few came to mind: doughnuts, cookies, muffins from the bakery down the street. Oh, a slice of Irene's pie. Maybe even a silver compass to celebrate her officially making it as an adventure guide?

Ty caught her staring at the bag, and she saw his eyes twinkle over the rim. When he pulled back he had a dot of whipped cream on his upper lip. His eyes never left her as he licked it off and then smiled. Something heated and real simmered between them.

"Told you it had smiling powers."

"Yeah, pretty powerful stuff," he said, all gruff and full of male appreciation. A tingling started in her belly and dipped straight to her toes.

"It's even better snuggled under the covers watching the sun come up." She held up her hands as if swearing on the Bible. "True story."

He looked at her as if he'd like to be a part of that story, his gaze touching every inch of her mouth before returning to her eyes. "Maybe I'll try it."

"The morning cocoa or the view from my bed?" she asked coyly.

"I'd like to say both, but the second would end bad."

"Everything ends—that doesn't mean it will end badly," she said.

He laughed. "Angel, you dig in and sink your teeth into everyone and everything that comes within your reach. I would bet you'd never let go of a single thing you didn't want to in your life."

"You'd be surprised," she said and let that settle. Only, the silence allowed for a hollow feeling to build in her chest. She hated that feeling. It was cold and achy and, if given time, had roots, so she pushed it back where it belonged—behind the gratefulness of being alive.

"I'm not all that big on surprises, angel. And I don't want to complicate everything," he said quietly, then looked at the stack of files on her desk. He opened the first file and scanned the map she'd stapled to the flap. "What's this?"

Jarred by the quick shift in topic, she sat back to collect her thoughts. She could give in and let him have this one, or she could ask him what she'd been dying to know for the past few days. "Is that why you didn't kiss me the other night?"

He laughed. "You don't do subtle, do you?"

"Waste of time, and I would rather know where I stand than sit around wondering and second-guessing."

He thought about that for a moment then nodded. "Do you still want to be trained?"

"More than anything." It was how she was going to make it to the top of Sierra Point when the weather changed.

"Then that's your answer, because I don't sleep with my trainees. Ever. It clouds judgments and makes what should be easy decisions complicated. Complicated doesn't work from two thousand feet up."

"Things can only get as complicated as you allow them to get," she said. "And complicated doesn't scare me—it's what makes living so exciting."

He laughed. "Training you is enough excitement for any one man." He lowered his voice. "And lady, that one chance kiss spun my world right off the map."

There were several ways to take that comment, but Avery decided to focus on the positive. She'd never spun a man before, and knowing she'd spun someone as unflappable as Ty made her giddy. "Thank you."

He shook his head, but he was grinning. "Who do I have on my schedule today?"

"That's why I texted you to come in," she said, grabbing an extra chair and sliding it next to Ty. "Gary came in today, said he cut his trip short because everything was slush."

"More like Gary blew his slush fund on a game of craps and is broke."

"He didn't say that."

"Didn't have to. Guy lives his life fast and loose and lives to snowboard. If he's back it's because he's broke. So it was either the tables or a woman."

Avery stared at Ty. "Huh, he seemed so nice."

Ty narrowed his eyes. "How nice?"

"Nice enough to bring me something from the Bear Claw Bakery. He brought me one of those sticky buns that are as big as your face and coated with a vat of icing. I was still licking my fingers when you came in. Said he'd bring me an apple fritter tomorrow."

"Yeah, well, don't get too attached to your morning fix. He's a temporary solution and will be gone before you know it."

"Like you?" she asked.

"Like me," he said. "But I'm happy he's here today. Harris offered to help me scout a place for the choppers to land for the hoist training, and today is his only day off."

"It also frees up your schedule to meet with Brian. He called yesterday when I was closing up and said . . . um, it's on a Post-it, right there on the monitor." She reached across the desk to get the note, but they were seated so close her upper body brushed his upper body, and all kinds of sparks ignited.

A burst of heat rushed through her, and Ty plucked the note off the monitor and handed it to her, all business.

"Right. Thanks." She took the note, noticing her hands were shaking. "He said the parts for the Coast Guard Delta were ordered and won't be here for the inspection, but he promised it would be ready to go for SAREX."

"That's great."

"He also said he was starting to check out the rest of the boats and should have a report for you tomorrow on exactly what is working and what it will take to get the rest in running order. And when he gets you the list of what needs to be ordered, you can add it to the spreadsheet I made. You want to see it?"

"Yeah."

"It's on my computer, so I need to—"

Ty leaned back. He didn't move or switch seats, merely leaned back and gave her zero space to work the keyboard.

"Okay." She reached across to move the mouse to awaken her monitor, and she awakened something much more dangerous. The only way to reach the mouse was to reach across his body, which made for some tight quarters. "I made a spreadsheet that allows everyone to track what needs to be ordered, what has been ordered, and what projects are completed. I broke it up by terrain, then class, then how many anticipated participants. This way nothing slips through the cracks and we don't fall short."

She scrolled down to find the rappelling gear section. "You went through the harnesses and emergency equipment, right?"

"Yeah, I have everything right here." He lifted up his hips to pull a notebook out of his pocket, and when he settled back their thighs pressed together, and all of the oxygen in the room seemed to evaporate.

He flipped to a page in the middle and handed her his notebook. "This is the column to track rock rappelling harnesses, and this one tracks the air rappelling harnesses." She filled in the spaces with the information, and it gave them an immediate tally of what was still needed.

"Wow, it even tells me who to call to order that particular item," Ty said.

"I also included a few names of the first responders who are free to play a lost hiker for the K-9 teams. See? There aren't many due to the short notice, but I'm getting creative to bump up the list total." She flipped to the next spreadsheet. "Here is who I have so far. They are separated by department and availability."

"Impressive. Beyond impressive," he said, and when Avery turned to look at him she found their lips a breath away. "You are impressive."

She felt herself blush. She'd received compliments before from her bosses, knew she was good at her job, but this was personal. He was commenting on her—as a person. She felt it. "Thank you."

His eyes dropped to her lips, and he held up the paper bag he'd brought in and gave it a shake. "Do you want to know what's in the bag?"

"Yes," she whispered, and maybe it was the way his eyes twinkled with challenge under the brim of his ball cap. Or the way his battered jeans and black tee clung to his body in that *real men get dirty* kind of way that fried her brain. But one look at him, sitting there with that easy smile, and all she could think about was kissing him. And the bulge in his pants told him she wasn't in this alone.

So she leaned even closer and said, "But I want you to kiss me more."

"Tempting."

"Like one of those sticky buns covered in icing tempting?"

"Even better," he said, and then his mouth was on hers—soft and inviting and so damn confident she felt her toes curl up right in her pink hiking boots.

"Complicated is hot," he whispered, upping the pressure. Avery had to agree—complicated had never tasted so good.

Kissing Ty was like chasing fire in a blizzard. One kiss and chills went down her spine while her body went up in flames. He tasted like chocolate, whipping cream, and the exciting start to a new chapter.

He somehow transported her back to what it was like before the diagnosis, before she knew life had limits and the world could fall apart in a heartbeat, before she knew how hard she'd have to fight for her happiness.

Only, right now she was beaming with happiness. Radiating it. She felt free and alive, like she wasn't an adventurer trapped inside a broken box. And then she felt his hand slip down her back to cup her butt, and suddenly she was being lifted off her chair and onto his lap.

His hand slid through her hair, angling her head so he could deepen the kiss, take what he wanted. And she wanted him to take, to kiss her like she wouldn't break in his arms. Like she was tough enough to withstand everything life could throw at her.

And more.

His hands were tugging at her shirt, and hers were pulling his hair, and it got her thinking—if this was his idea of complicated, she was ready to buy a ticket and jump on board. For as long as that train would take them.

Only just when his hands were getting some traction the phone rang. There was a brief pause, followed by more kissing, and more of that *more* she was dreaming about. She'd never considered herself greedy, and she knew she'd already had a sticky bun, but she wanted a cookie too.

A big warm cookie delivered by her back-to-nature Mountain Man. But the phone wouldn't stop ringing, and it wasn't the normal ring. In fact, three lines lit up all at the same time.

"I should get that," she said breathlessly. "It could be a guest."

"It could be a wrong number," he said, taking her lips yet again.

Another line lit up, and with a frustrated groan Ty leaned back in the chair. "You should get that," he said, but he didn't sound happy about the interruption. Which made her smile.

"Sequoia Lake Lodge, this is Avery. How can I help you?"

"Hi, hon, this is Sheila down at the Bear Claw. I was delivering some pastries earlier at Sips and Splatters for Grace's morning watercolor class when I saw the ad you placed in the *Gazette*. It says you're looking for volunteers for SAREX this year. Is that true?"

"The ad ran? Today?" Avery asked, doing her best to appear calm and collected.

"What ad?" Ty whispered.

She shushed him and turned around to stand, which meant she had to leave the safe bubble of Ty's lap. Now that she was there she wanted more time. More kissing. More Ty.

But once again life interrupted her going after a life. And she didn't think he'd want to pick up where they left off after he heard about the ad. Which was a great idea, one she'd planned on running past him *before* the ad ran. Only he'd been avoiding her, and she'd thought it was going to run in next week's edition.

"It's all the talk around town," Sheila said, her voice so loud Avery pressed the handset to her ear to help contain the information from bouncing off the walls—and into Ty's ears. "Anyway, some of the girls were wondering—not me, seeing as I've been happily married for forty-two years this July—if when they were rescued their big, strong heroes would be wearing those harness things that show off their butts?"

She turned to look at Ty, and before she could ask he said, "No, we do not. And no, we are not taking volunteers."

"What was that, hon?" Shelia asked.

"Hand me the phone," Ty said, holding out his hand.

Avery stepped away so he couldn't grab it, then turned around so she didn't have to see him glaring. It didn't help she could feel his eyes boring into her back. "Hey, Sheila, let me put you on hold."

Avery pushed the mute button but didn't give up the handset.

"This is a great solution, Ty," she explained. "Finding the few firemen and forest rangers who were off duty *and* open to playing victim was hard. Which is why I said I was getting creative. First responders cost money that we need for the new supplies and parts. Volunteers are, well, free. And available."

"It is a great idea, and if you had asked me earlier I could have told you it's more time than it's worth," Ty said. "Volunteers take a lot of planning. There are release forms, insurance in case someone gets hurt, and extensive preparations to make sure that all the extra bodies don't stumble into places they aren't supposed to be. They might come free, but it's a logistical nightmare, trust me."

Avery opened the top drawer of her desk and snagged the bright orange folder and handed it over. "The top form is a release that the K-9 team uses for volunteers at their monthly training. I changed some of the verbiage to match our event. Also, I called the insurance company, and as long as they sign the release any volunteer will be covered under the lodge's policy. And finally, it may have been a nightmare in the past, but you didn't have me."

Ty took the file and flipped through it. When he reached the end, he said, "When did you do this?"

"Monday after you got off the phone with Lance from Cal-SAR. You said we needed first responders to play lost hikers, so I started calling around and found out that we needed to reach out months ago, but one of the fire captains said his department uses volunteers sometimes. I figured it was worth looking into." She sat on the end of the desk. "As for the ad, I was going to talk to you first, but I guess Frank at the *Gazette* got print happy."

"The guy is the worst journalist. He couldn't hold a secret if it were in a paper bag." Ty scrubbed a hand down his face.

"Think of how much more realistic it will be rescuing people who don't know protocol and won't listen when you tell them to stop pinching your backside."

"It's a lot of work, angel," he said, but she was getting through to him.

"I stared down a two-hundred-foot cliff—a little hard work doesn't scare me." To prove it she grabbed her No Fear hat off the desk and pulled it on her head.

At that he smiled, but it didn't reach his eyes, and that got to her. She'd never intended to add more to his plate. Quite the opposite, in fact—she'd been hoping to help with the weight he was carrying.

"I know this isn't what you wanted to deal with after last night. You're probably tired and frustrated, but I assure you I can handle this. The residents seem excited, and allowing them to participate in this will only make the lodge's connections in the community that much stronger."

Avery set her hand on his knee. "It will also give your dad something to do that day. He would be great at organizing the volunteers. It would give him a direction, put him in a place where he felt important, and keep him out of your hair."

"Whoa," Ty said. "You make it sound like I'm going to run SAREX."

"Do you think your dad can really handle an event that size?" Avery asked gently.

Ty went to argue, and Avery gave him a look. With a defeated breath he rested his head back and closed his eyes. She could see the moment the reality hit. The stress on his face returned, and the heaviness of the situation nearly swallowed him whole.

"Shit, I'm going to have to be here." He stood and paced the floor, his hands working the knots she was sure had sprouted in his neck. "Being here with him like this seems to be making everything worse. Me and Dale working the mountain together?" He shook his head. "The longer I stick around the more stressed out he seems to become . . ."

The amount of responsibility and blame he carried for his father's recent behavior was so raw and so misplaced her chest pinched. She knew this wasn't her family and, therefore, not her place, but someone had to tell Ty what was happening. And it was obvious Irene wasn't ready to accept the truth, let alone tell her son.

"From what I've seen the past few months, stress isn't the problem, Ty," she said cautiously, softening her voice even more. "What has your mom told you?"

"That he's been stressed out. Not sleeping right."

"Do you think it's stress?" she asked cautiously.

Ty's eyes met hers, serious and challenging, but she could tell that after last night he was still hoping it was stress, but wasn't counting on it. "You obviously don't, which means you're either keeping a secret *for* my mom or *from* my mom."

That he believed she'd been holding out on him went unsaid, but bewildered hurt was there in his expression.

Indecision about how much to share weighed heavily on Avery, almost as suffocating as the guilt of knowing that she had been holding back with him. It was true that Irene had trusted Avery to be discreet about Dale's condition, but she never imagined Irene keeping information so important from her son.

She was crossing the line, but she wanted nothing more than to help Dale. Help Ty. Help this family find their way. And for that to happen there needed to be honesty.

"I don't know if it's the early stages of dementia or Alzheimer's or something else, but whatever is going on with Dale, it isn't stress."

Ty stopped dead. The only part of him moving was his chest, which was laboring from the news. She could almost hear him struggle to take in air, feel the moment he recognized that he'd known the truth all along and had chosen to look past the signs.

"Jesus." He was quiet for a long moment, then walked to the window to stare out at the lake. Even from a distance she could feel the emotions building and turning inside him. He looked lost and ready to run, and she almost offered him the out. Told him that if he needed to regroup, get some distance, she could handle SAREX. She could hold it together until he knew how he wanted to handle things.

But she knew from experience that running didn't solve anything. And time only made the pain more intense, harder to cope. And if she was right about Dale's issues, which she was sure she was, then time was one thing they didn't have.

"The other day you said he had bad days—I assumed you were talking about his temper," he said, staring blindly out the window. "How bad is it?"

"I don't know," she said honestly. "He does a good job of covering it, and your mom plays into it, but in the past few months it has gotten worse. At first he was forgetting meetings, misplacing schedules, little things, which is why your mom hired me. But lately he's been moody, agitated, forgetting important things."

"Like the inspection?"

She wished it were that simple. "Last month he came out of the supply closet and told me to find Garrett and have him restock the emergency supplies," she said, joining him at the window. "Said he'd asked him to do it a week ago and wasn't about to wait for an emergency to happen."

Ty's throat worked hard, and Avery ached to reach out and comfort him, but he had a distinct hands-off vibe going on. "What did my mom say?"

"She asked me if I would quietly restock the supplies," Avery admitted, her stomach knotting at the admission. "I told her I would, then encouraged her to take Dale to the doctor."

Ty finally looked at her, the lines on his face giving away just how hard he was struggling to maintain composure. "But she didn't."

"I don't think so. I think she's too scared to find out the truth, but someone needs to. If anything, for the safety of the lodge and its guests."

Ty looked back out the window, his eyes heavy with pain, his shoulders tight with the weight of the world. "He can't handle SAREX."

Even though it was a statement, she answered, "Not on his own."

Ty's eyes slid closed with pain, and a wealth of empathy rose up inside of her. "I can't do this."

"Yes, you can," she assured him. There was clearly a lot of love in this family, only it was tainted by what she was coming to understand was misunderstanding and a history of deep loss. And Avery liked to believe that history was only important when it guided the way to a happy future. And she didn't think Ty or his dad had been happy in a really long time. "You'll have me on your team."

He just looked at her.

"Let me help, Ty."

She held her breath, expecting him to either fire her for sending out the ad without asking permission, or tell her she was office-bound for eternity. To her surprise he did neither.

"You can help me scout new trails tomorrow," he said.

Unable to resist, Avery placed a hand on his arm. It was tense and coiled—like the man. "I wasn't just talking about SAREX."

He slid her a look that sat somewhere between grateful and sorrowful, and it made her hand squeeze tighter. "I know, angel, but right now I need to tackle something that I understand."

"Are you at least going to talk to your mom?"

He cleared the emotion from his throat. "Yeah, but can we talk about something else for a bit?"

"You bet," she said, letting him know that he had her full support. Finding out something that had the capacity to change everything was overwhelming, and it was natural that he needed to focus on something that was actionable. "Scouting new trails it is."

With an appreciative brush of his hand over hers, he said, "It'd be good to see how long it will take a local to make the hikes versus an experienced hiker."

"Really?" She paused. "Wait, are you saying I'm out of shape?"

He smiled. It didn't reach his eyes, but it was better than the remorse he'd worn a moment ago. "I'm saying that I'd enjoy the help. And the company."

Avery warmed at the thought of spending tomorrow morning out exploring nature with a sexy mountain man. Actually, she was looking forward to seeing him in his element, where he felt strong and in control. Where his smile reached his eyes—and her heart.

"I'll bring the hot cocoa," she said.

"Make sure mine has a shot or two of caffeine in it," he said with a wink and headed toward the door. At the entryway he stopped. "Oh, and check out the paper bag. It's way better than a sticky bun."

Avery watched him go, then raced over to her desk. Too impatient to wait, she picked up the bag and opened it, and her heart rolled over.

It was a crown. Not fashioned from bar napkins and coasters like they'd agreed. But made from dried poppies and woven bark.

It was breathtaking—and proof that Tyson Donovan was beyond impressive.

CHAPTER 11

"Well aren't you a welcome surprise," Irene said to Ty as he hung his coat by the door.

He wasn't so sure about how welcome he'd be after they had a much-needed talk, but he pulled her in for a hug. "Hey, Mom."

"You're in time for tea."

"I think I might need something stronger," he admitted.

Irene pulled back and studied him, like she had when he'd been a boy and she had the power to love away even the biggest of problems. "Rough day, huh? Well, how about some milk and cookies then? I have chocolate chunk peanut butter."

And like when he'd been a boy, Ty wanted nothing more than to sit at that kitchen counter, eat some cookies, and watch the worry disappear. But he wasn't that kid anymore, and this wasn't the kind of problem that was going to disappear.

Finding Dale in the boathouse last night in nothing but a bathrobe and slippers while he searched for his tackle box had knocked some of the spite out of Ty. Watching his dad struggle to remember why he'd gone out there in the first place nearly knocked him to his knees.

Dale Donovan was as tough as they came. Mentally, physically, and spiritually he was untouchable. There wasn't anything that could break him. The man had buried his son without shedding a tear and disowned his other without a second thought. Garrett's death had seemed to make him harder, more rigid and remote. Dale was a tough son of a bitch who had become an island unto himself.

That wasn't the man Ty had seen last night in the boathouse. That man had been lost and vulnerable. Two emotions he never thought to witness in his father. Then he'd become flustered and agitated, and Ty was the closest target.

Not that *that* was new. Ty had become used to being the focus of his father's disappointment for years. But this was different, and after his talk with Avery, Ty couldn't ignore that anymore.

He had hiked a few of the more challenging trails, racking up six miles of brutal terrain in under two hours, hoping to clear his head. Get a better perspective on the situation. Epic fail.

He came back sweaty, exhausted, and no closer to a solution than he had been when he'd first returned home. If anything, the situation with Dale left him feeling even more inadequate than ever. He'd come home to help his parents, something he couldn't do until he understood the extent of the problem. Which meant pushing his mom for answers it didn't sound like she was ready to admit yet.

"Make it a plateful of cookies and a tall glass of milk," Ty said as he walked into the kitchen and sat at the counter. He looked at the stool next to him and, for the thousandth time since Garrett's death, wondered if the emptiness would ever subside. When he'd been a teen the loss had been consuming, and the only way to survive it, he felt, was to run.

Now, experiencing it as an adult, he felt the crushing weight of the guilt, but there was something new stirring inside of him—a deep desire to make it right. And that required a painful but truthful conversation.

Irene slid a plate of three cookies—arranged like eyes and a nose—across the table and went to the fridge for the milk. When she returned, Ty decided the best thing was to face it head-on. "What's going on with Dad?"

Irene froze, her smile wavering at the corners. "Did you two have another argument?"

"That's not what I'm talking about, Mom. And you know it," he said with gentle steel.

Irene busied herself with pouring Ty's milk. "It's just stress, I told you."

Ty rested a hand on hers, stilling her actions. "One or two of the things could be explained away by stress, but the schedule, forgetting clients, the inspection, meeting a potential employee is his slippers, Mom. His freaking slippers. That isn't stress—that sounds more like memory problems. Maybe even some kind of dementia."

Irene didn't answer right away. She looked at the counter, her hands, anything to keep her from meeting his gaze.

Ty stretched his neck to the side until he felt it crack. "If I'm way off base, then please tell me. But I can't help unless I know what's going on."

"I told you all that I know," she admitted. "The eye doctor said it wasn't night blindness, and that maybe it was stress and we should have it investigated more."

"Then why is he refusing to go to another doctor?"

"Why do you think?" she snapped, and it was the first time Ty had seen his mother this close to frustrated helplessness since Garrett died. "I'm sorry, I didn't mean to take it out on you."

Ty rounded the counter and pulled his mom into his arms. "That's okay. I know this is hard. I just need you to be honest with me about what's really going on."

"That's the problem," she said, resting her cheek against his chest. "Your father—oh, how I love him dearly—is the most pigheaded, stubborn man I know. He won't go to the doctor. I've made three separate appointments, even used getting his driving privileges back as incentive, but every time the appointment arrives he's too busy or tired to go. And between trying to keep this business running and the guests happy, I don't have the extra energy to push right now."

"Let me talk to him, see what I can do," Ty offered.

"No." Irene stepped back, her head shaking in a definitive way that left no room for argument. "You'll talk to him, an argument will ensue, and I won't see you for another six months, or maybe a year this time. No. I won't lose you too."

"You haven't lost me, Mom," Ty said, his stomach knotting to the point of pain. Was that how she'd viewed what had gone down? That she'd lost Ty too? "You haven't lost me. My job just requires me to be near the ocean."

Irene looked at him with knowing eyes. "It's not your job that keeps you away, which is why I want you to let me handle your dad, my way and in my time."

"We might be running out of time, and your way is nothing more than covering for him," Ty pointed out. "Hiding his illness from people. Including me." Ty was shocked at the anger and betrayal he felt when he said that. "Dad's only going to get worse, and one day your covering will get him hurt. Or, even worse, get someone else hurt. And trust me, that isn't a weight you want to carry, Mom."

There was a tense silence that filled the room. Irene's face crumpled as she took in the truth behind Ty's words and the importance of his last admission. Ty wished he could take it back, hated seeing his mom so close to tears, but someone had to say something before it was too late.

"You all make it sound like I need a goddamn keeper," Dale said from the threshold.

"That's not what we mean," Irene said, love in her eyes, taking a step toward Dale. "We're just worried about you."

Dale put a hand out, halting his wife from coming any closer, and Ty heard Irene let out a small sob. He'd never seen his dad wave off Irene's offer of love and comfort. Ever. He might be a cold son of a bitch when it came to his son, but never to his wife.

Dale's eyes went glassy as he realized what he'd done, but he stood firm. "I might not be in my prime, but I'm still the best guide on this mountain." Then his gaze went to Ty, angry and challenging. "So unless you're ready to come home and take that title from me, then you best keep your concerns to yourself. This lodge can't take any more criticism right now, and I might not be perfect but I get things done. And that's better than what you're doing."

It was past five, and Avery's cheeks hurt from smiling so big. She'd smiled all the way through the morning calls, when the phones were lit nonstop with locals wanting to volunteer, during the two-hour explanation to the Senior X-Treme Team about why there would not be a polar bear plunge this weekend, even lasting through her one-year checkup with her specialists. Which included several jabs and a few needles.

Now she was back at the office, checking her watch and counting down the minutes until she got to clock out and go for her ride. Mavis and the ladies were meeting her out front at six-thirt to send her off on her moonlit ride. Avery was in her baddest jeans, faded with strategically placed tears to give them a dash of vintage attitude, and Mavis's old riding jacket. It was butter-soft, candy-apple red, and so tight when zipped that it brought Avery from a respectable C to an impressive D cup. She'd even borrowed a pair of kick-ass boots from Grace. Not that they'd ever kicked any ass—Grace was a pacifist by nature—but they looked tough.

And Avery felt tough.

A sentiment she carried with her as she double-tapped her mouse and opened one of her impressive spreadsheets, then entered some figures like a ninja. She already had enough volunteers for the entire week of SAREX, and she was getting ready to shut it down when her twelve o'clock appointment waltzed in—almost five hours late.

Squaring her shoulders, she said, "You made it."

Brody plopped down on the chair across from her desk and sprawled out as if he owned the place. "You wanted to meet for lunch. I never stand up a beautiful lady."

"It's almost dinnertime."

He looked at his watch and shrugged. "My bad. I had a checkup on my ankle, and it took longer than expected."

The finger-combed hair and faint hint of lip gloss told her that it had been a home visit.

"Well, you're here now," she said in her most professional tone. "And, I have to say, for a sprain as bad as the note implied, you look good."

Way too good for someone who was in his second week of a mandatory three-week recovery, which happened to coincide with the last fall of powder for the season. He was in baggy sweats, a SLICED UP MY HOOD T-shirt that was from Oregon and looked right out of the package, and a foot bootie.

"Nice bootie," Avery said. It was light blue, looked a little small for his foot, and removable.

Brody gave it a pat. "Another week with this baby, then the doc said I'm good to return to work. Then it's all wilderness, all the time. It's getting a little lonely at home, resting in bed all day long." He winked. "You should come over, keep me company."

Avery stood and walked around the desk. "I have a better idea."

"Yeah?" Brody leaned back and rested his hands behind his head, striking a pose that had Avery rolling her eyes.

"Oh yeah." She picked up a stack of files she'd created. Thirty-six in all. Each one represented a class Cal-SAR intended to offer at this year's training. Inside she had detailed all of the necessities each class required. She dropped them in his lap.

"Oufffff," he said, jerking forward as the breath left his body. He glanced at a file, opened it, and then gave a broody frown. "What is all of this?"

"*That* is adulthood," Avery said with a smile. "It's time you paid it a visit. You can get your feet wet by reading the requirements of each class, then filling out a location request for where you think each class should be staged and held. Many of the classes need the same type of terrain and are taught by the same instructors, so be sure to cross-check and cross-reference so you don't book two classes on the same trail or an instructor in two classes at the same time."

Brody set the files back on her desk. "No can do, babe. Doctor said he can't clear me for another week."

Avery sat on the corner of her desk. "That means you can't help with any of the prep for the event, but you'll be healed in time to benefit from the free admission you get as a lodge employee."

Brody shrugged his shoulder as if he'd just realized that. "Guess I'm lucky it was only a sprain."

"Me too," Avery said. "Because had it been a break you wouldn't have been able do anything but lounge around watching Comedy Central all day in bed."

"If I was in bed, I wouldn't be watching television." He winked.

Avery ignored him. "According to this doctor's note, though, a sprain exempts you from field work but not office work."

He sat up. "But I'm not a coordinator, I'm a guide."

"Right." Avery picked up the handbook and flipped to the section that covered training and special events at the lodge. "But during big training events, every member of the team is required to pitch in and help prepare in the weeks prior. It's why you get free admission into the events. And since you aren't cleared to help scout trails and test rappelling gear with the chopper runs tomorrow, you get to stay here, in the warm office." Avery picked up the files and plopped them on her desk.

"I didn't read that part," Brody said, as if his laziness was a viable excuse.

"Funny, because there's a box you initialed in your contract that said you read and understood the entire handbook," Avery informed him. "If you want, I can call Dale since he did your interview and ask him how to proceed?"

She couldn't tell if he was pouting or going to cry, but finally he shook his head. "Nah, guy wouldn't remember what we talked about anyway."

Avery considered putting her kick-ass boots to work but decided that nothing was going to ruin her night. Not even Brody. "Great, then you can start with these, and whatever you don't finish tonight you can work on tomorrow, but they'll need to be complete before I come in tomorrow at eleven."

"Eleven." He stood. "No way am I going to bust my ass to do your work so you can sleep in."

"Oh, my day starts with the sun tomorrow. Since you're injured, I'm going out to scout trails for SAREX, which is why we need a list of places to start," she said, grabbing the jacket off the back of her chair, zipping it until she reached maximum cleavage, and heading for the door. "Be sure to lock up when you're done."

"Wait, what if I have a question about something?"

"Put on a harness. It might get you in the zone."

Avery played it cool until she pushed through the side door of the lodge, which led to the parking lot. Once those doors closed behind her, though, she did a little victory dance, complete with some fist pumping and booty shaking. She hadn't walked softly, nor had she swung a big stick. Nope, a little gentle confidence was all she'd needed to make her mark.

"Are you going to do the chicken dance next? If so I want to get my phone out and record it."

Avery spun around and found Ty wearing mirrored aviator glasses, a black leather jacket, and boots that were so battered they only added to the bad-boy vibe that he had going on. He was also straddling a motorcycle and wearing a smile that said he was looking for trouble.

CHAPTER 12

Avery knew that smile well. Was so affected by its power that one flash and her body sighed a breathless *Oh my*.

"What are you doing here?" she asked.

He looked down at his bike and lifted a single brow, which in itself wasn't a sexy gesture, but everything Ty did sent her hormones into a frenzy. "Going for a ride. You?"

"Oh, just waiting for Harris."

"You might be waiting awhile." He leaned forward, resting his arms on the handlebars in a move that was all male grace and swagger. "He got a call-out. Something about hikers in a snowstorm."

"How sad for him." Avery tilted her head and studied the sky. The sun was setting as a gentle evening breeze blew the scent of poppies and pine across the lake, and there wasn't a single cloud in sight. "A snowstorm on a perfectly beautiful spring night?"

"Some freak blizzard or something."

She walked over and stopped short of the front tire. "Shouldn't you go help then?"

"Nope. I'm on vacation for another week, so I figured I'd start enjoying myself." His gaze dropped to her cleavage. "Nice jacket."

She ran her hands down the front. "It's Mavis's. And the kick-ass boots are Grace's." She looked around the parking lot, surprised to find it empty. "Where are Mavis and the girls? They're supposed to be here."

"Mavis stopped by my mom's earlier while I was there. She said she has a big date tonight, and the ladies are helping her get ready. I guess she went to a funeral yesterday and met some retired football player who's helping her improve her passes."

"I don't think she needs any help in that department."

"Me either," Ty said. "I'm pretty sure she goosed me the other night at the brewhouse. She feigned innocence, but I wasn't buying it."

"She's fast."

"Not as fast as this bike." The cool timbre of his voice rolled down her spine and liquefied her entire body.

"So you met with your mom?" she asked, and the way his mouth tightened told her it hadn't been a good chat. She took a step forward and placed her hands on his. "Do you want to talk about it?"

"I want to talk, but not about that," he said, flipping his hands over so that he could lace their fingers. "I heard you were looking to check some more things off that list of yours, and I figured we worked so well together last time, we should give it a second go round."

Understanding and respecting his need for a distraction, Avery said, "We already had a second go round on Cedar Rim." She bit her lower lip. "Then we had a third go round—oh, a few hours ago in my office. So, to be clear, what kind of go round are you offering?"

Avery prepared herself for some witty comeback or charming line, but she welcomed the warm surprise when instead he said, "The kind where we talk and laugh and maybe do some kissing by a campfire. Okay, we'll definitely do some kissing. Lots of kissing by a big fire." He grabbed her by the hips and steered her around to his side. "And touching too."

"I like touching," she breathed. To demonstrate how much, she ran her hands up his chest to his shoulders, the leather softening as she went.

"Me too," he said with a voice as rough as tossed gravel.

"What happens when the fire burns out?"

"I don't think that's our problem, angel."

A flutter ignited and settled right beneath her belly button. No, burnout wasn't going to be a problem. If anything, their chemistry increased with every look, every touch, every single sexy grin he threw her way.

"Remember, the fire's big so it will take a long time to burn, maybe all night. But I promise when it finally does we'll both come home feeling a hell of a lot lighter than when we left." His thumbs dipped under the hem of her jacket and rubbed the naked skin beneath. "What do you say?"

Avery didn't know what to say. It was quite possibly the most romantic thing anyone had ever said to her, and her head was trying to catch up to her heart.

"I guess I want to know if you know how to drive this thing fast. Like *burn rubber down the interstate with only the moon lighting our way* fast?" she asked, because according to Mavis this was important stuff.

"I was born fast." He lowered his voice to the panty-melting level that she loved. "That's not to say I don't appreciate a little slow action now and again. So what do you say? You, me, and the stars?"

Maybe it was the boots, or perhaps the jacket, or maybe she was too excited over the possibilities of what the next few hours could hold. Because even though Mavis wasn't there to see her ride off into the sunset, Avery still felt like tonight was a success, so she took the helmet and said, "I want to fly."

"That's my specialty," he whispered.

Without another word, Avery climbed on, wrapped her arms tight around his torso, and—*whoosh!*

Ty gave it gas and they tore up the windy mountain road, gaining so much speed the pine trees blurred by and their bodies pressed tighter and tighter together until there wasn't an inch of space between them. Her front was so plastered against his back that she could feel every curve, every hard-won muscle moving and shifting with the bike. And she could feel all of the rules and expectations and pressing history fade into the night sky as the sun dipped behind the mountain range.

Most importantly she could feel thighs of steel and that butt—definitely tight enough to bounce quarters off.

Within moments a million stars began to shine through the inky sky, lighting the road and dancing off the river to their side. She could hear the water rushing around the side of the mountain and over the rocks, stirring up an earthy smell of sprouting moss and moist clay.

A hand tightened on her thigh, and over the wind she heard, "You ready to fly?"

Avery had been born ready—it had just taken her body twenty-seven years to catch up. And she wasn't going to wait another minute.

"I'm ready." At the words, a heady mix of thrill and terror pumped through her body, causing her hands to lock around his waist so tightly she was sure he couldn't breathe.

As if sensing her unease, Ty placed his hand over hers and gave them a comforting squeeze. "I got you, Avery."

Avery wanted to believe him. Wanted to know what it felt like for someone to carry her burden, the weight of not knowing what tomorrow held. But life had taught her better. Her mother, her father, even Carson had promised to love her forever, but love wasn't enough to go the distance.

Ty was different, though. He wasn't asking for her love, wasn't even asking for more than a night out under the stars. He just wanted her to take this ride—with him. And something about the capable way he handled his world made giving herself over to this moment feel easy. Right.

"I'm glad someone does," she said, loosening her grip slightly.

His hand came to cover hers, as if saying, *Don't let go.*

His chuckle carried on the wind as they crested the top of a ridge and then started to circle down, hugging the mountain as they drove toward the glowing moon.

It feels like flying, she thought, closing her eyes and letting her head tilt back. Every cell in her body seemed to hum to life at the same exact moment. Her chest tingled, her hands shook, her stomach went into a free fall—and Avery felt as if she'd earned a set of wings.

Being young and carefree was a foreign concept. Avery had spent her childhood caring for her mother and until recently waiting for the green light to start living. But Mavis was right, straddling a motorcycle with a good-looking man pressed to her front made Avery feel invincible.

"Where are we headed?" she asked, but it didn't matter. Wherever they ended up would be the start of her biggest adventure yet.

To hell, Ty thought as he dismounted the bike, took Avery's hand, and led her down to the river's edge. He was as aware of how good she felt by his side as he was that his time here was winding down.

He should have run in the opposite direction the second Harris showed up with his bike and this ridiculous plan. Only the opposite direction led to dinner at his parents', and Ty couldn't stomach another argument with his dad.

Not after today.

He didn't have it in him.

Fighting his dad, the guilt, the uncertainty—the overwhelming itch to pack up and head back to his beach and the simple existence he'd created. He didn't have the energy for it. Not when he had the possibility to lose himself in the one person who always managed to make him smile.

And man oh man, when he'd seen Avery in the parking lot, dancing as if no one was watching—her life's motto it seemed—he'd been unable to tear his gaze away. Her hair had been loose, her jeans snug, and she'd had on this red jacket that was designed to make a man think about taking it off.

Slowly.

But it was how she approached life, as if every day had the potential to be amazing, that fascinated him—calmed him. Made him feel connected to something pure.

"You seem to know exactly where we're going. Do you come here a lot?" she asked, their hands swinging as they walked.

Ty never considered himself a hand swinger, but tonight it felt good. "I know nearly every inch of these mountains. But yes, I've spent more time here than other places."

"Ah, the secret high school hangout," she said when they reached a circle made from felled trees enclosing a makeshift fire pit. "Did you and Harris used to bring girls up here? Sweet-talk them into skinny-dipping?"

"My brother and I used to come here to camp, fish, get away from Dad. Sometimes Harris would come along," he said. "But no, you're the first girl I've brought here. As for the skinny-dipping part, that depends if it's on your list."

"It's not on the list," she said, sounding as disappointed as he felt.

"We can add it."

"The list doesn't work that way," she said, disappearing behind a tree to pick up some twigs.

"Your list has rules?" Ty set his pack next to one of the logs and went about gathering some dry kindling. "What am I saying? Of course it has rules. You probably read some handbook on how to make a bucket list."

"It's not a bucket list. It's a memory journal." She appeared from behind an outcropping of trees holding a pile of dried needles. "And tonight we'll both benefit from my need to read handbooks, because I'm going to make fire."

She made a flint rock and a tiny pocketknife appear out of nowhere. Where she'd been hiding it Ty could only guess. He eyed her jacket, which barely had enough room for her cleavage, and decided she must have stashed it in her jeans.

"Stand back and be amazed."

Ty considered keeping quiet, letting her have her fun, but he knew that in the mountains it didn't take long after the sun went down to drop from chilly to butt-ass cold.

"Or you could use this." Ty pulled out a lighter and held it in the air.

She contemplated her options, then smiled. "Lighter tonight, tomorrow I'll make fire from the batteries and wires in my flashlight."

"Your call," he said, but she already had the lighter in hand and the tinder smoking. Within minutes the soothing crackling of the fire filled the air, and they were seated next to each other on the ground, using the log as a support. They weren't touching, but she was close enough that he could smell the heat of the fire mixing with the sweetness of her perfume. It was a heady combination.

Ty dug into his bag and pulled out a bag of marshmallows.

"Are we making s'mores?" she asked, her smile so bright it was contagious.

"Better." Ty stuck two marshmallows on the end of a pointed stick and handed it to her. "Put that over the fire until they get golden and your hands get warm." Currently, they were a degree above frozen.

He dug through his bag and pulled out a thermos, two camping mugs, and an emergency blanket. Draping the blanket over her legs and tucking her in, he turned his attention to the thermos, which he shook and poured into the mugs.

"What is that?"

"A surprise." She tried to peek over his shoulder to see what was in the mugs, but he waved her off.

"You know what I like better than surprises?"

He slid her a glance. "Skinny-dipping?"

"Being in on the surprise. So how about you tell me what you're doing, and I promise not to tell anyone."

He held out his hand. "Marshmallows ready?"

With an adorable huff, she pulled the stick out of the fire and handed him a perfectly toasted one, then made a big show of slowly licking her fingers clean.

Focused on the task at hand and not getting his hands on her, Ty stuck the toasted marshmallow on the rim of the mug like a garnish in a cocktail, then handed it to her.

Lit by the fire, Avery's eyes sparkled when she looked up from her mug. "Did you make me a campfire s'more-tini?"

"Not just any campfire s'more-tini, but the current Girl Scout leader's special s'more-tini. She said the secret was in the toasted marshmallow. You're supposed to take a bite with each sip."

"In that case . . ." She plucked the last marshmallow off the stick and held it out to him. "Take a bite."

Never one to say no to a pretty lady, Ty did just that, making sure to snag her fingertip in the process, making her laugh. She had such a cute laugh, so he did it again, this time kissing the tip when he was through, and making sure to lick off every piece of sticky treat.

Those baby blues took in his pack, then met his gaze. "This is a lot of equipment for a last-minute night ride. Some people might think this was a little more premeditated than you previously let on."

"Some people might think you should enjoy your surprise and drink up."

"Are you trying to get me drunk?"

"If it will up my chances of getting skinny-dipping added to your list, then bottoms up," he said and saluted.

She took a tiny sip, no more a thimbleful, then said, "I already told you, it's not a list, it's a journal, and that's not how it works. I can't just say, 'Oh, hey, I feel like kissing a sexy guy under the stars' and then add it."

"You sure have a lot of kissing in that journal." He paused. "And you think I'm sexy? Hey!" he said when she nudged her shoulder to his.

"Is that really all you heard?"

"A good guide focuses on the important details," he said with a teasing tone, then speared two more marshmallows and held them out over the flames. "So, I'm guessing sex under the stars with a sexy adventure guide isn't on the list?"

"Not last time I checked."

He shrugged. "That's okay. I'm not a first-date kind of guy anyway."

This time when she nudged him, she didn't pull back. Instead, she rested her head against his shoulder. "Thank you for making this night special. I know you have a lot going on. Between your dad and SAREX you probably feel like the world is pressing down on you, yet you took the time to bring me a pinecone."

"I promise if there's a pinecone in there, I got the recipe wrong."

She tilted her head up, her hand going to his chest, resting there as if it was at home. He could feel his heartbeat against her palm, slowing its rhythm with a simple touch. "No, a thoughtful gesture, like the pinecones you and your brother and dad would bring your mom for Christmas."

Ty found himself chuckling. "I'd forgotten about that. Every year we'd bring her home a different kind of pinecone to decorate the table with. I have no idea why she loved them so much, but she'd always tear up. Every year. Like she was surprised by another bag of pinecones."

He felt the weight of Avery's gaze, as if she was staring right through him. "It wasn't the pinecones, Ty. She was crying because it meant your dad took you boys out and made a beautiful memory."

Ty thought back on those trips as some of the best times he and Garrett had spent with their dad. There were no lectures, no regimented routes or schedule. Each one was a real father-and-sons-in-nature kind of trip, with the only goal to find the best pinecones of the season. They would cook over a campfire, bathe in the river, see who could come up with the dumbest joke.

They traveled as far as thirteen hours south one year to bring back the biggest type of pinecones in the country. And Ty remembered coming home happy, laughing while they retold all of their stories over dinner.

He wondered if his dad still remembered any of those times. Sometimes that man was as sharp as a tack and determined as a grizzly. Other moments, Ty barely even recognized him. Even worse, after some online research, he now understood there were probably days Dale barely recognized himself.

"I know coming home hasn't been easy," she said quietly, "and that Dale makes it even harder, but he's happy that you're here."

"I don't know about that."

"I do." She ran her hand down his chest. The motion was meant to soothe, but there was something intoxicating about the gentle steel in her touch, and his entire body felt the jolt. "You're a good son, Ty."

Ty didn't know how to respond to that, especially after today, so when she nuzzled into him, he wrapped his arm around her and held her tight. He told himself it was because he'd felt her shivering, but the truth was he liked touching her, felt like he was at peace when he held her.

The silence stretched until it became a comfortable and warm blanket that surrounded them both. Avery stuck a marshmallow on the stick, and he held it over the fire until it was good and golden, then she plucked it off and they shared it. They did this a few times while listening to the river ramble in the distance.

The night continued to grow, but in their cocoon by the fire it felt as if time had slowed enough to breathe. Slowed to where the hollow ache that had taken up residence in his chest a decade ago felt lighter, and his itch to run faded.

He didn't know how long they sat like that, toasting marshmallows, watching the embers float into the inky sky, and silently listening to the wind whistle through the pine trees, but it didn't matter.

Ty wasn't sure he'd known what true contentment felt like before tonight. In fact, he'd always thought the word had a negative connotation. Who wanted to be content when you could be pushing the limits?

But sitting there, staring at the fire with Avery curled into his chest, he was pretty sure he'd take this over jumping out of a chopper any day.

"Ty?"

"Yeah?" he said, and she shifted so she could see him.

He tried to meet her gaze, because he could tell by the tone she had an important question, but the angle was just right, the zipper on her jacket had given a little under the pressure, and he could see straight down. Bright blue lace and creamy cleavage.

Hot combo.

"Is this what you and your brother used to do?" she asked, and he was no longer wondering if the panties were a matching set.

"Cuddle by the fire?" Ty asked, then waited for his body to backfire at the mention of Garrett, waited for the dark memories to settle and the guilt to kick in. Only it never came. And he had a pretty good inkling it had something to do with the woman in his arms. "Nah, Garrett wasn't much of a cuddler."

"Too bad, he missed out." Then, not giving him the change of topic he was hoping for, she looked up at him through her lashes. "Is this where you came to talk, blow off steam, find your balance? I know your dad's dementia has made things worse, and that under all of the bluster he has a big heart, but I don't imagine he was an easy father."

"I wasn't all that easy to raise," Ty heard himself saying. And then because he couldn't shut up he added, "I was actually a pain in the ass, always looking for the line so I could cross it, see what would happen. I never met a rule I didn't want to break, my dad would say. And since he lived his life by the rules, it made for some heated moments."

Some frustrating moments too. What Ty had seen as genuine curiosity, his dad had taken as disobedient and willful. When he was little Ty tried to curb that itch, trying to make his dad happy. By the time he'd become a teen he realized his dad would never be pleased, so he stopped trying.

"Kids are supposed to test their parents—it's part of being a kid," she pointed out.

"When I was eleven my dad and I found this big ravine on the west side of the mountain. He said a hiker stranded without gear could never make it out alive. The next day I went back alone and scaled that two-hundred-foot cliff without any gear."

"Did your dad find out?" she asked.

"Oh yeah, I was so proud that I had figured it out, I went home to tell him. He took one look at my ripped jeans and bloody shin and he knew. The crazy part is I really thought he was going to be proud of me." Ty could still remember the frustration and disappointment burning in his gut. Frustration that he was in trouble, and disappointment that he hadn't managed to impress the most impressive man in the world to him. "He grounded me for the entire summer, which in my dad's world is the equivalent of being disowned."

At least that's what it had felt like. He had been cut off from his friends, the mountains, and any connection between him and his dad had become beyond strained—and Ty never knew how to close the gap. Where Dale was happy to walk the same trail day after day, Ty craved diversity. His mind liked to solve impossible problems—it was what made him the best at what he did. Yet, he'd never managed to solve the one problem that mattered the most—how to gain his dad's support.

"Not the homecoming you were looking for," she said, her arm tightening around his middle.

"He said that one day my curiosity was going to get someone killed." He threw the stick into the fire. "He just always assumed it would be me."

"Did he actually say that?" At his pain-filled expression, she sat up, hers turning fierce. "He had no right to put that on you!"

"Garrett and I got into some pretty squirrely situations growing up. Two boys living in a lodge with the Sierra Nevada as their back-yard, trouble was bound to ensue. Sometimes Garrett was the instigator, sometimes it was a collaboration, like the time we caught a bobcat in a coon trap and tried to leash train it. But usually it was me." He looked into the fire until the flame became a blur of bright reds and oranges. "That night. It was me."

"Oh, Ty," she said gently, taking his hand in hers.

Talking about that night never got easier, but reliving it through Avery's expressions would be painful. Knowing that she couldn't hide what she was feeling to save her life, Ty gave a gentle tug and pulled her back to his chest, then rested his cheek on the crown of her head.

"I was offered a spot to go with my uncle and the Sierra Mountain Team to climb the fourteens in Colorado. I would have been the young-est person on the team. I was so excited, I told everyone at school before asking my parents, because I was so sure they'd say yes. When I got home my dad didn't even listen. He just said no, that if I wasn't old enough to climb River Rock, I wasn't old enough to go backpacking all over the country." He could still feel the gut-wrenching humiliation that his dad wouldn't support him in this. Couldn't see the same potential in Ty that others did. "So I figured if I could prove to him that I'd tackled River Rock, then he'd have to let me go."

She nuzzled closer, her arm going across his waist. "So you snuck out?"

"The second the sun came up, Garrett was in my room ready to go. I told him he didn't have to suffer through being grounded with me—it was a two-day trip, so we were bound to get caught. He said he might be younger, but he wasn't weaker, and no way in hell was he going to let me hog all of the victory."

God, Garrett was a competitive son of a bitch.

"Did you make it to the top?"

"No, it started getting dark before we cleared the ridge. I wanted to sleep for the night, find shelter, and pick up in the morning. Garrett wanted to get to the top before nightfall. The hardest part was out of the way, and all that was left was a short hike. That way if Dad came looking for us and dragged us back we could say we made the climb." Prove he was special. "It had been a wet winter, so the river was wild and the ground was still saturated. Fatigue combined with limited light and loose soil made for poor conditions. Garret took a wrong step and slipped down a bank and right into the river." Ty shook off the memory. "I scrambled down as fast as I could and found him, but even when I got him to the shoreline I knew. He was bleeding pretty bad, his body was going into hypothermia, and . . ."

The helplessness of watching his brother slowly slipping away, knowing that he didn't have the skills to save him, still haunted Ty.

"I thought for sure my dad would come looking for us, but the search team didn't show up until the next morning, and by then he was gone."

They found Ty on the ground, holding Garrett to him and rocking him back and forth. It took three men to pry him away, and even then Ty's arms circled around his own middle as if he was still holding Garrett.

Ty didn't remember the chopper ride home, or much of the days that followed, only the overwhelming numbness that settled in his soul and never left. Without Garrett, Sequoia Lake was no longer home, and as long as he stayed there his family could never move on.

"That's why you went into swift water rescue," she said softly, resting up on her elbow to study him.

She looked so long, Ty was scared of what she'd see. What kind of conclusions she'd come to about his character—about him. He knew what other people thought, what his dad thought, but for some reason Avery's opinion was the only one that seemed to matter in that moment.

"What a beautiful way to honor his life," she said, and Ty felt his throat close. And that was it, the moment that Ty knew he was in serious trouble. What others saw as him running away from his past, Ty did to make sure the past never had to happen to another family. "He'd be proud of the man you became."

"Don't make me out to be more than I am, angel." She was starting to get that hero worship in her eyes, which could only lead to disappointment—for both of them. "Rescuing people is different than being a hero."

"I'm not looking for a hero," she said with a conviction so strong he had no choice but to believe her. "And I know exactly who you are, Ty. You're the kind of guy who, after a trying day, went out of his way to make my night special. First with a moonlit ride, then a campfire and s'more-tinis."

"Don't forget the marshmallows," he whispered.

"I haven't forgotten anything," she said, her eyes big and luminous. Her heart was right there on her sleeve, and she radiated so much warmth all he had to do was reach out and grab tight.

Only he was afraid he'd never want to let go.

CHAPTER 13

Ty was a goner.

He saw the kiss coming, watched as she moved in, licking her lips in the process, but he still wasn't prepared for how hard she rocked his world. It felt like he took a freight train to the chest.

In his defense, it wasn't just a kiss, it was a high-octane, zero-to-a-million meeting of the lips that left no room for questions.

Avery was an all-in kind of woman, so it shouldn't have been a surprise that she'd be an all-in kind of kisser. Hell, they'd kissed before. But this was different, it was more, and she was making it clear that it was more. She wasn't shy about what she wanted, and lucky son of a bitch that he was, right then she was making it crystal fucking clear that she wanted just one thing.

Him.

Again with the lucky, because he wanted her too. Bad. So when she placed her palms flat against his chest for leverage and scooted up on her knees, he ran his down to her hips to help steady her—he was a gentleman, after all. And when that wasn't enough he slid them lower, to that denim-clad ass, to let her know that he was there for her.

She seemed to appreciate his efforts, even making this sexy little purring sound as she crawled up his chest until she was straddling his lap, as if afraid he had somewhere else he'd rather be.

Fat chance. He'd meant what he'd said earlier—he wanted to kiss her all night. Long, open-mouthed kisses that blurred into one another until the sun rose or they passed out. He didn't care, as long as he woke up with her in his arms.

Avery seemed to be on the same crazy train with him, only she was in the driver's seat, taking her sweet ass and making his lap into her own personal chair. Which was A-okay with him. She could make him anything she wanted as long as she didn't stop kissing him.

So when she gently tugged his lower lip between her teeth, he let himself fall into her sweetness. Or maybe he'd fallen when he'd caught her scribbling obscene offers on his truck. Either way she got to him.

In the best possible way. At the worst possible time.

His instincts were screaming for him to pull the cord. Reminding him that she was a *from this day forward* kind of girl. He was leaving in a week and needed to leave this well alone.

But he'd spent his entire vacation leaving things alone—the past, his dad, the relentless guilt—and look where that had gotten him. Spending his days saving a lodge that was one frayed rappelling rope from snapping and his nights playing Marco Polo with a man who didn't comprehend that he was lost.

So for just a moment, Ty wanted to be the one who was lost, because he was certain that Avery would find him. Bring him back. To where and from what he didn't know, but when he was with her he felt his world turn right.

"You taste like s'more-tini," she said, her face flush and her lips swollen.

"You taste like . . . hmmmm. I'm not sure." Framing her face with his hands he took another taste, long and languid, and when he pulled back they were both breathing heavy.

"Still not sure?" she whispered into the silence.

"I might need another sample."

She wrapped her arms around his neck and her legs around his back. "Sample away."

Ty groaned, and she was laughing as he kissed her, and man she had a great laugh. It filled the air and lit him up from the inside out until he couldn't feel anything but her.

Her joy, her passion, her zest for life. It was intoxicating.

She was intoxicating.

She tasted like campfire and wild nights, but she kissed like lazy mornings in tangled sheets and—*man oh man*—she locked those boots of hers low on his hips, encasing him between her thighs and bringing all of their good parts into mind-blowing contact.

With a low growl, he took over, delivering a kiss that burned hotter than the fire roaring behind them. She must have felt the heat too because her hands fisted in his hair and she purred into his mouth.

And holy hell, her mouth was a little slice of heaven.

Everything inside him stilled, and a smile tugged in his chest. "Heaven. You taste like heaven."

Those eyes of hers slayed him. "I feel even better."

She reached for the zipper of her jacket, and Ty stopped her. "I've been wanting to do this all night. In fact, if I had a wish list, me getting you out of that jacket would be on it."

"Oh." She leaned back, resting her hands behind her on his knees. The position caused her thighs to widen and her hair to slide across his legs. "What else is on your wish list?"

Ty took her in. Hair loose and wild from the ride, she was flushed from heat, and her breasts—a place he'd spent hours fantasizing about getting up close and personal with—pushed provocatively against her jacket. So tight he could see the zipper straining under the pressure. Which caused some straining of his own—right below his belt buckle and a breath away from the promised land.

Damn, Avery was sexy and sweet and so damn primed he could feel her body hum.

"I'm more of a doer than a talker," he said.

"I like both," she said, and he could see a hint of shyness tint her cheeks. "The talking and the doing."

"I'll remember that." Taking the smooth metal pull of the zipper between his fingers, he gave a gentle tug, parting it down the middle enough to see that she was indeed wearing a very pretty blue bra—and not much else.

No amount of fantasizing could have prepared him for the up-close-and-personal. She was firm and high, with a perfect set of tens in a barely there bra that were *from this day forward* his personal favorites.

"Angel, had I known there was nothing but lace under there, I would have had this off back in the parking lot."

"It would have made for a nippy ride," she said with a grin. "And I had to leave the shirt at home. There wasn't enough room in this jacket."

"So nothing beneath this? At all?" he asked, sliding his hands from her hips, over the bottom of the leather jacket, and slowly up to the underside of her bra—then higher. He heard her breath catch, and his chest did some sputtering of its own. "As for the next thing on my list . . ."

Cupping her ass, he scooped her up and carefully laid her back on the blanket. She looked so ethereal lying there with her hair around her, the fire flickering off her silky skin. Unable to stop himself, Ty leaned and gave her a lingering kiss. Then another. And when she was panting again, straining to get closer, he made good on his word that he was a doer.

He placed a kiss, wet and openmouthed, at the base of her neck, and she arched into him. Just like that, one touch and she was vibrating. Taking that as the best green light on the planet, Ty trailed little kisses down her throat to the creamy cleavage he'd been dreaming about.

She smelled good. Like turned-on woman and toasted marshmallows good.

Ty pulled the zipper down, nipping and teasing the thin patch of silky skin he'd exposed, until the jacket parted, leaving her in nothing but lace, moonlight, and—

"Avery," he said, his hand going to an angry scar that started below her sternum and ended by her hip. He lightly traced it, wondering if it hurt, then remembering the way she'd clutched her side at the bar, on their first hike, and this overwhelming protective urge roared in his head. "What happened?"

"I had a surgery last year when I was sick. But I'm fine now."

He didn't know how she could be fine because nothing about seeing that scar on her fragile body made him feel anywhere near fine. He knew enough about injuries and healing to make a calculated guess at the level of pain and recovery she must have gone through. The thought of it brought on a sense of panic and helplessness—mixed with a good dose of respect.

Through his career he'd seen some hairy stuff, and nothing ever really affected him. Not like this.

"I'm okay," she assured him, but he heard something different in her tone. Uncertainty.

She pulled the lapels of her jacket closed and tried to sit up. "But if you're not okay with it, I understand. Some people might find it kind of shocking. At first I did too, but then I got used to it, but that doesn't mean everyone will."

Ty had a bad feeling in the pit of his stomach that she'd heard it all before, in this kind of situation, and that more than anything tugged at his heart.

"You're beautiful," he said, looking her right in the eyes to be sure she understood what he was saying. "Everything about you is beautiful, so beautiful I can't think straight from wanting you." He pressed into her to show her the severity of his affliction. "You're everywhere, lighting up my mornings, helping me through the day. I dream about you at night. You and that smile."

He kissed her lips.

"And your eyes? They're bright and warm and slay me at every turn. Plus, you have just the right amount of curves, so when I hold you it's like you were made perfectly."

He unclasped her bra and slid it down her arms. Not letting her cover herself, he pinned her hand to his chest and took in the glorious sight. "Perfectly made. For me."

When he heard the telltale sniffle that announced the impending appearance of tears, he lightened the mood. He'd promised her a fun night, and he was going to deliver.

"And that ass of yours, angel. Don't even get me started. It keeps me up all damn night." He slipped his hand beneath her and took a handful, and she laughed. It was watery but so damn beautiful.

"And your laugh lights me up. And this here . . ." He trailed a finger down her scar. "This is a symbol of your strength, and if anything, it makes me want you even more. So all that's left to ask is, do you want me back?"

With a small nod, she said, "I want all of you."

"Thank Christ," he said and lowered his head in a kiss that had nothing to do with a stupid challenge and everything to do with wanting to be inside of her since the first minute they'd met.

He held her with a tenderness that was guaranteed to erase any doubt she might have had. And hopefully any voices from the past whispering in her head. Avery had this way of making people feel accepted for their truth, and he wanted to give her the same gift.

He kissed her softly at first, wanting nothing more than to savor her all night. But before he knew what was happening, her hands were under his jacket and sliding it off his shoulders, hers hit the ground, and by the time she was tugging at his shirt, they weren't kissing softly at all.

The heat radiating off the fire was almost as intense as the big freaking hot ball of fire that raged between them.

"Ty," she said on a breath. "I hope 'make love under the stars' is on your list, because it's not in my journal, and I can't—"

"I know, yours doesn't work that way." He took in her half-naked state and gave a low whistle. "Good thing mine does."

Her hands locked around his neck, and his went for the top of her jeans. The second his fingers moved against the warm skin of her stomach as he undid the first button, the anticipation sizzled between them. With five more buttons to go, he got to work while she made short order of his shirt.

His fingers reached the last button, and he discovered that, indeed, the panties matched the bra. He traced the edge of the lace, and she sucked in a breath. So he did it again, and this time her hips pushed into his hand.

"Please tell me that's on your list," she moaned.

"You mean this?" He delved his finger beneath the lace band to the very tip of her heat and applied the right amount of pressure to have her eyes sliding shut.

"Yes," she cried out.

"Or this?" he asked, dipping even farther, and her hips flew off the blanket.

"God, yes!"

"I had to ask because I didn't know if you meant this instead."

Ty tugged the loops of her jeans, sliding them down her hips, her legs, and off. On his ascent, he paused to give her three very wet, very open-mouthed kisses. One on her inner thigh, one on her hip, and the last one right on her center.

"That!" she moaned. "Keep doing that!"

"This?" He sucked her through the moist silk.

"Please, yes!"

"Are you sure?"

"More than sure," she said, and he grinned at the impatience he heard in her voice.

He nipped at the silk, then pulled it to the side, giving himself complete access. "Because I can always do this if you want."

"Oh, I want, Ty," she pleaded. "I want so badly I feel like I'm going to explode. The only thing I don't want is to keep talking about it."

"Oh, but I thought you liked talking," he teased. "And, angel, you're not going to explode, you're going to fly."

And with that Ty proved over and over again just how much of a doer he was. He kissed and teased, nipping until her breath became nothing but choppy gasps and moans. And when her breathing stopped altogether, he slid a finger in, then two.

With a sweet cry, he felt her walls collapse around him, pressing so hard on his fingers he knew the second she let go, the second she couldn't hold back because the pain turned to pleasure and she soared. He rode it out with her, wave after wave as she slowly came back down.

But he didn't let her get comfortable. Oh no, Ty wanted her to fly so long she'd forget how it felt to walk. So even as her final spasm hit, Ty pulled the condom out of his back pocket. The one he kept there in case he rescued a team of playmates—or ran into a woman he couldn't walk away from.

Until he'd met Avery he figured he had a better shot at the first, but now that he'd met her he was glad he'd come prepared.

He pushed his jeans down as far as they'd go with boots on, then leaned over her, and when she opened her eyes, he asked, "Want to know what's the top item on my list?"

She nodded her head with a dazed smile.

"Making you scream my name."

Ty entered her in one long thrust that had Ty's eyes rolling to the back of his head. All of the flirting and buildup and tension had taken its toll, and all Ty could think of in that moment was, *Finally.*

No more denying himself, ignoring the connection, or wondering how great it would be. Because she was here, in his arms, connected in the most intimate way, and it was better than great.

It was amazing. The kind of amazing that happened once in a lifetime, where timing and anticipation, and maybe even the fucking stars, lined up to create a moment that couldn't be matched.

Careful of her scar, Ty slid one hand behind her head, and the other slid down the entire length of that gorgeous leg of hers, locking it behind her knee and pulling it up as he began moving, slowly to let her adjust to the pressure.

"You okay?" he asked, because he was completely aware that, aligning stars or not, this was as comfortable as it would get. At least lying on the ground in the woods. He didn't want to hurt her, but he didn't want to stop either.

"Yes, but I'm waiting for the me screaming your name part you promised." She laughed, then lifted her leg, resting it low on his back.

Slowly, she lifted her hips off the ground to lock her leg all the way around his back, so when she lay back down she brought him with her.

Pressing his mouth to her neck, he said, "I always make good on my promises," then slid all the way inside of her.

When she sighed with pleasure, he pulled back—all the way back—only to give a nice thrust that kicked up the friction and had her moaning. Not his name, but they were getting there.

She moved with him, faster and harder, and harder still as if she was reaching for more. And he wanted to be that guy who gave her more, he really did, but he also didn't want to hurt her.

"I won't break, I promise," she whispered, then captured his mouth. His hands were doing some capturing of their own as he braced her against him until they were so close their bodies could only move as one.

He kept the pace slow but upped the pressure to the breaking point, moving them from amazing straight into mind-blowing, and finally she did this twist of the hips that was off the charts and had him desperately close to blowing. The muscles in his arms strained from holding back, his sanity started to fray, and he was so close—so damn close to not just giving her more.

But giving her everything.

"Oh God," she moaned, her eyes squeezed shut as she bit her lower lip as if that was the only thing keeping her from shattering into a million stars.

"Look at me, angel," Ty coaxed. "Open those pretty eyes."

She did and that was all it took. Her breath caught and body coiled tight, matching his. And with one last thrust she threw her head back and shouted, "Oh God, Ty!"

Oh God indeed. Hearing his name rip from her lips was the biggest turn-on of his life. His body stiffened, his heart slammed against his ribcage, and he exploded. So hard the world spun and his arms buckled and he knew that once wasn't going to be enough.

Nope, he'd fallen for a woman who wanted all of him. And damn if he didn't want to give her everything he had.

CHAPTER 14

It was a perfect afternoon in the Sierras, Avery thought as she made her way down the stone pathway toward the boathouse, a special to-go lunch from Irene's kitchen in hand—prepared with love for one Dale Donovan. The lavender was in full bloom, casting a purple glow across the meadows and scenting the air with the first hint of spring.

Today was a day to celebrate. Caroline was getting prepped for tomorrow's surgery, Brody was busy fielding calls from senior volunteers—most of them ladies who wanted to know what Brody would be searching for—and Avery was still feeling the afterglow from the best night of her life.

Ty hadn't just given her an experience, he'd opened up and given her a part of himself. An important—and heartbreaking—piece to his life. She knew he was leaving and that this too would eventually end, but she wasn't going to let an expiration date stop her from experiencing everything she could.

And she had experienced a lot last night. She smiled every time she thought about it, which was so often her cheeks were sore. So was her body—but in the most delicious way.

Feeling relaxed and a bit giddy, Avery stepped onto the dock. The wood planks shifted under her feet as the water lapped against pylons and shoreline below. A few feet from the boathouse she heard voices.

Loud, angry Donovan voices.

She couldn't make out what they were saying, but their tone was enough to have her sneaking behind a stack of kayaks for a better view. She still couldn't hear what they were saying, but their body language was enough to tell her this wasn't going to end well.

For anyone.

Normally, this would be Avery's cue to step in and defuse the situation. Her job was to manage the office and clear away the falling debris caused by Dale's erratic temper. Today, she had been expected to bring him a warm lunch since Irene was at her knitting class. What she hadn't expected was to mediate an argument between her boss and a guy who, as of recently, knew what her O-face looked like.

The smart move would be to leave family business between the Donovan family and head back up to the office to finish her day's work. She was already taking off an hour early to go to the hospital. Nothing could cap off her perfect day better than giving Caroline her crown.

Avery had never been good at taking the smart path. She'd spent her whole life trying to follow her heart. Especially when two people she cared for were headed for an argument that would end with a world of hurt. So she positioned herself right outside the doorway and perked up her ears—in case there was an opening for her to help.

"This lodge has been hosting Senior X-Treme on this weekend since my dad was running things," she heard Dale shout.

"I know, and I understand why you're upset," Ty said, and Avery could tell he was working hard to keep his tone gentle. "But this year we are overbooked, down a guide, and we have Cal-SAR coming next week. So unless you want to fail that inspection, we have to reschedule."

"Why?" Dale asked. "I can handle it, been handling this lodge and this trip for over thirty-five years."

Avery didn't want to stick her nose in when it seemed like Ty was handling things pretty well, but she couldn't help but inch closer to press her ear to the wall.

"Fern Falls requires ground transportation, and since you can't drive—"

"I am an excellent driver," Dale argued.

"Not according to the State of California. Plus, I already talked to Mr. Fitz about rescheduling for after SAREX."

"You've only been here for a few weeks and already you're making a mess of things." Dale's tone was clipped and accusatory. "What will people say if I don't show up?"

"I don't know, Dad." Ty's voice took on an edge that was not good. "That you should have hired a new guide three seasons back?"

Avery's hand flew to her mouth, and she silently shook her head, as if the motion could take back Ty's last words.

"Why, son? You applying?" There was a long, tense pause where Avery could hear the hurt and humiliation grow, from both men. "No, I didn't think so."

And that was her cue to step in, bring some much-needed perspective to the situation. But when she stepped around the corner, her chest pinched at the sight.

Dale was red in the face and deflated, as if this had been going on for a while and tension was taking its toll. And Ty, *oh poor Ty*, just looking at him made Avery's heart ache. His body was coiled tight, arms folded across his chest, and his feet were planted in a masculine stance as he stared out at the lake.

At first glance, he looked to be a man in control of his world. But a deeper look showed the emotional wear of a decade of misunderstandings.

"You can be as pissed as you want at me, Dad," Ty said. He sounded so troubled Avery wanted to wrap him up in a big hug. "But you and I both know Mom won't let you drive the company van, nor would she be okay with you heading this trek. And with no one else free who is covered under the lodge's insurance, it had to be rescheduled."

"I can drive," Avery offered gently, stepping all the way into the boathouse.

Ty didn't flinch, which meant he knew she was there all along. Releasing a breath, he turned to face her, and it took everything she had not to go to his side. He looked like that same tired, scared teenager he'd talked about last night, desperate to impress his dad—to make things right.

Ty was a fixer. He didn't just rescue people for a living—it was a core part of who he was. But there was no easy fix for dementia, or for how to navigate through a past that was buried so deep it had planted roots. What he didn't understand was that his dad was too busy trying to remind everyone that he was still useful to acknowledge Ty's offer as anything but unwanted.

"I don't need a babysitter, missy," Dale said, but his smile was hiding right beneath that scowl. Avery could tell.

"You're not helping," she whispered to Dale. "So unless you want me to call Irene, then zip it." Then to Ty she said, "It's a perfect solution."

"Avery," he said, his eyes pleading for her to drop it. But she couldn't. The solution was so simple—everyone just had to get past the hurt to see it.

"I'm covered under the umbrella, I know exactly where Fern Falls is, and the hike out is short," she said. "There are no steep elevations, no cliffs to scale or descend, just a bunch of seniors going out for a day in nature."

"You're not fully trained," he said flatly.

"I know, but Dale is." Avery walked over to her boss and linked arms with him, and the expression on Ty's face made it clear that he felt like she'd chosen sides. "Between my book smarts and Dale's reputation and years in the field, I think we can handle a few old-timers."

"You do realize that those old-timers could solo K2 and build a shelter out of twigs and dust," Ty said.

"Then there's nothing to worry about."

He glared at her for a long moment, and Avery did her best to look like a capable adventure guide. Dale even puffed out his chest a little.

"Except with you two in the driver's seat, trouble is bound to ensue."

"Only the good kind of trouble. Plus, if anything goes wrong, Dale is more than qualified to handle things." She turned to face Dale so that she didn't have to see Ty glaring. It didn't help that she could feel his eyes boring into her back. "You promised to train me, and I've been patient, waiting for the right time. So unless you have a better time in mind—"

"It's settled," Dale said. "I'm taking Senior X-Treme out and training the new girl." He gave Avery's hand a gentle squeeze, then headed for the door. "Be sure you come ready and prepared—the guys and I don't like wasting time. So if you forget something, you go without."

"Yes, sir." Avery saluted, and she could have sworn Dale was chuckling when he walked out.

Ty was not chuckling in the slightest. He looked irritated. The complete opposite of how he'd looked last night when he'd dropped her off at her car and kissed her good night.

He picked up a tackle box and jammed it on the shelf with force. Then he went about wiping down the fishing poles stacked against the wall, making short, jerky wipes with the rag that Avery was surprised didn't snap the pole in two.

"This is such a bad idea," he said when he was done with the first pole.

"We're talking a mild hike to the falls, where they'll fish all day. The same thing they do every year, just in a different location, with a chopper ride back," she pointed out. "How bad could it be?"

He stopped mid-jerk and sent her a long look. "This morning you texted me that we had to cancel scouting the trails. Do you remember why?"

"To take Mr. Keefer fishing," she said innocently, leaving out the reason why Mr. Keefer had called in the first place.

"Right, you told me there was a mix-up in the schedule, that he must have written it down wrong, but since he's staying in the VIP suite I canceled my morning plans," he said, stepping closer. "Which I was really looking forward to."

Avery looked up, and those warm chocolate eyes turned her body to mush. "Me too. But we get to go tomorrow. And for the record, I did think he had the wrong date."

Avery booked every trip, and she hadn't taken a booking from a Mr. Keefer. She would have remembered because he was a guest in their VIP suite. And when she'd opened the schedule and looked at the eight o'clock slot, like she suspected, there was no Mr. Keefer.

So instead of upsetting a guest, and explaining he had the wrong date, she'd sent Ty. It was only after Ty had gone down to cover the trip and Avery had talked to Irene that she'd learned the truth—and from the look on Ty's face he'd figured it out as well. "He'd been waiting at the boathouse for over an hour. In the cold. His poles and tackle box were ready to go, only there was no guide. He said Dale was supposed to meet him at eight."

"He got mixed up," she said. "When I called your mom I figured it out, but you were already gone so there was no point in telling you, but I did apologize to Mr. Keefer."

"By telling him my dad was with another group, then comping him the trip." Ty took her hand. "Angel, you are a horrible liar."

As a rule, Avery didn't lie. Nothing good, she'd learned, ever came from lying. But she didn't know what else to say. Mr. Keefer had paid a ton of money to receive an experience of a lifetime, and Avery wasn't going to let him be left on the dock waiting for a boat that was never going to come.

She found herself in a lot of these compromising situations lately. And she foresaw many more if Irene didn't do something and get Dale to a doctor.

"That's why I offered up the free champagne, hoping to distract him."

"Jesus, Avery." He paced the floor, his hands working the knots she was sure had sprouted in his neck. "Between you and my mom covering for him, it is only making things worse."

"I know," she admitted, but the devastation she knew she'd see in Dale's eyes if she confronted him would break her heart.

"How long has he been forgetting trips and sneaking out and leaving the house in his fucking slippers?" He stopped pacing long enough to look at her. "How long have you been covering for him?"

"I don't know," she said, but he clearly didn't believe her. "I only know that your mom hired me because I needed a job, and she needed someone to keep an eye on Dale. So we made a deal—I would make sure the office was running smoothly and that Dale didn't go out on anything beyond a beginner trek, and she would give me free adventures."

"So you've been keeping him distracted with other stuff?"

"I tell him I need help with booking a trek, or ask if he could go with me to offsite bookings, or show me how to schedule a hike versus a climb."

"Or pretend he's training you so you can make sure he doesn't lose an entire group of guests off a cliff?"

She shrugged. "It keeps him busy and involved without putting him in the way of danger."

"And what happens if he accidently books a trip with a client and forgets? Or worse, what if he actually makes it?" He was angry and frustrated. At her, at his mom, and at the situation. But he was also scared. Scared for his dad and what this meant.

"That hasn't happened until today," Avery admitted.

He was quiet for a long moment, then walked to the end of the boathouse to stare out at the lake. Avery joined him and could see Dale standing on the end of the dock, hands stuffed in his pockets, staring down at his feet.

Avery's attention went back to Ty. She could feel the emotions building and turning inside him. He looked lost and ready to run, and she almost offered him the out. Told him that if he needed to regroup, get some distance, she could handle SAREX. But she knew from experience that running didn't solve anything. If anything, it made it more intense, harder to cope later on down the road.

And there always was a later. Things only lie in rest for so long before they demand attention.

"Covering for him won't do anyone any good," Ty said.

She slid him a look. "Neither will embarrassing him. He's lost so much—I don't think he can handle losing his pride as well." Ty flinched at her comment, and she knew he felt as if he were losing too. Resting her hand on his cheek, she said, "Let me help, Ty."

His eyes softened, reminding her more of the man she'd spent last night with. "Why do you want to help?"

She stretched up on the tips of her toes and brushed his lips with hers. "Because you're not ready to."

◆ ◆ ◆

Ty's last appointment pretty much summed up his entire day. He'd taken a group on a sunset cruise around the lake, which turned out to be the local chapter of the Kappa Gamma Kai sorority from Reno State, who clearly liked to pre-party before departure. Since three of the girls mainlined tequila, and their sorority leader had severe motions sickness, Ty spent the rest of his shift listening to Taylor Swift karaoke and an extra two hours hosing down the boat.

Desperate for a hot shower, a cold beer, and a dinner that didn't come with a side of disappointment, Ty picked up the phone and ordered up some room service. Then he pulled a longneck from the minibar and headed toward the bathroom.

He took a few healthy pulls while the shower heated up. When the steam was thick enough to cut, he stepped under the spray—bottle in hand. The water pounded on his battered muscles while the beer worked on the rest. But no matter how long he stood there he couldn't seem to wash away the argument with his dad—or his conversation with Avery.

What did she mean he wasn't ready to help? What the hell did everyone think he was doing in Sequoia Lake? He hadn't come home for the warm family moments, that was for sure. He'd come back because his family was on the fast track to losing the lodge, a lodge he didn't want or care about. But he was there because his parents cared—and that was enough for him.

Yet at every turn he was being challenged, judged, even blamed for a situation that he hadn't been around to cause. His absence seemed to have done as much harm as his presence. And wasn't that a fucked-up situation.

If he'd been there more he would have seen his dad slipping. But being home meant making peace with the past. It had been fifteen years since that night, and Ty still couldn't get past the guilt. At this point he wasn't sure he ever would.

"Shit," Ty said, shutting off the water.

Wrapping a towel around his waist, he realized exactly what Avery had been talking about. Garrett was the only thing he had in common with his dad, and letting go of the guilt would be like letting go of that connection—like letting go of Garrett. So much time had passed, the guilt was all he had left.

Or that was what he'd thought until last night. It was strange—sitting by the fire with Avery nuzzled against him while he told her about

Garrett felt different. Lighter. How a memory should feel. And for a moment, when he'd held her on the blanket and looked into those soft baby blues, he wondered if this was what life should feel like.

Dragging on clean jeans and a shirt, he padded to the front room and grabbed another beer. He was reaching for the bottle opener when a knock came at the door. Hoping it was room service with a big juicy burger and a double side of fries and not one of his parents asking why he wasn't coming to their place for dinner, he answered.

It was neither.

Oh, there was dinner on the other side of the door, but there was also an extra helping of sexy woman to go with it. One glance at that contagious smile and Ty's shitty day circled right back to how he'd felt that morning when he woke up with her smell on his skin. Then she released those dimples of hers that he loved and—*bam*—it was like the clouds disappeared and a bright light warmed him from the inside out.

"What are you doing here?" Ty asked, unable to stop himself from grinning because gone was the windbreaker, knitted cap, and two braids peeking out each side from earlier.

Tonight, her blonde hair hung loose, tumbling down her back with wisps framing that stunning face. She wore a glittery light blue dress that hugged every place a man would want hugged, and then it flared out at the waist and puddled against the floor. Ty didn't need to see the crown he'd made her on her head to tell him she was dressed as a princess.

He'd never really had a princess fantasy before. But *sweet baby Jesus*, there was something about the way her dress went all the way to the floor that had him itching to see what she was hiding beneath.

She handed him a covered plate. "Bringing you dinner. Your mom said all you have to do is reheat the lasagna for thirty seconds in the microwave, but don't put the garlic bread in there because it will get tough." She handed him the plate.

In the mood for something a little sweeter than lasagna, he set the tray on the table by the front door and leaned a shoulder against the doorframe. "And why did my mom give it to you?"

She shrugged. "I mentioned I was headed this way, and before I knew it there was a care package with special instructions to ensure I didn't just leave it at your door." A little grin bit at her lips. "She thinks she was being smooth, but I'm pretty sure she's setting us up."

Well, that explained her sudden appearance. His mom wouldn't be happy until Ty was married and settled down—preferably here in Sequoia Lake. Which made Avery her ideal match for him. But it didn't explain why Avery was dressed the way she was.

"Why were you headed this way?"

"Because I have a surprise."

"Does it include a pumpkin carriage and magical mice?" he asked, wondering if she had glass slippers on beneath the ball gown.

"No pumpkin, but there is a party, and it will be magical." She held out a paper bag. "In case you say yes, know that you'll have to eat your burger on the way."

"Angel, you come here dressed like that and promising me magic, dinner is the last thing on my mind," he said, grabbing his jacket off the coat rack and his keys off the table.

"Good." With a smile so bright it could light an entire planet, she took his hand. "Then put this on and follow me."

Ty didn't question the plastic sword she stuck through his belt loop, nor did he complain when he was forced to fold himself into her tiny car. But when she stuck a CERTIFIED NOBLE KING button on his shirt, he said, "Noble is something one says about a horse."

"I almost got you the 'It isn't a coronation until someone shows their sword' T-shirt, but since you're crowning a princess, I thought it might be a little inappropriate."

A few minutes later they pulled into the visitors' parking lot of Mercy General. "What are we doing here?"

"Making magic," she said, and a small giggle was all she offered him before she led them through the big double doors and down the hallway toward intensive care.

She bypassed the information desk, paused at the nurses' station long enough to give a wave—and every nurse waved back—then continued through the maze of corridors and rooms.

He was surprised that she didn't seem to notice the smell of ammonia and saltine crackers. Almost as surprised to discover that every person on that floor seemed to know Avery by name. So by the time they reached the second floor, the thousand and one questions that had haunted him since seeing that scar last night intensified. The night had ended so perfectly, he hadn't wanted to ruin the moment by asking about how she'd gotten it, but that didn't mean he hadn't thought about it.

But being here with her appearing so at home in such a sterile space confirmed Ty's fears—Avery had recently spent a lot of time in a hospital. Most likely this hospital.

As a patient.

She stopped in front of room 219 and said, "Oh, I almost forgot." Digging through her purse, she pulled out two surgical masks and slipped one on her face. "We have to wear these."

Ty watched her as she carefully secured the mask around his mouth, her hands shaking slightly. And that was when the panic set it. "Oh my God, is it my dad? Is he okay?"

He reached for the door handle, but Avery stopped him. "No, your dad is fine. Everyone is fine."

Ty let out a breath and waited until his heart rate slowed enough so that he didn't feel as if it were going to explode. "Thank God."

"I'm so sorry to scare you." With the mask on, her eyes seemed even bigger than normal. "I didn't even think that you'd go there. I forget that other people associate hospitals with emergencies."

There was something so odd about the way she said it, about how she'd handled the entire walk up here that had him asking, "What do you associate with them?"

"Hope." He couldn't see her mouth through the mask, but he could tell she was smiling. "And that's why I brought you here. I'm bringing hope to a friend who has a special request that I wanted to share with you."

She took his hand in hers and held it. "That crown you made wasn't for me. I won it for a little girl named Caroline who wants more than anything to be a princess at her very own dress-up tea party. I can't make her a princess for real, but I can make her feel like a princess. So we're having a princess party." She gave a little curtsy. "Since you made this beautiful crown, I thought you should be here when she gets it, to see how big she's going to smile."

If it was anything like Avery's, he wasn't sure he could handle it. "You invited me to a dress-up party?"

Right then, the door across the hall burst open, and three nurses pushed a gurney with an unconscious woman past them and into the hall, calling out orders in frantic voices.

"A princess party," she said, watching the nurses disappear down the hall. When it was quiet again she looked up at him. "For a sweet five-year-old girl who misses playing dress up with her friends, who are scared to visit her because Caroline lost all of her hair during her chemotherapy."

He felt something tighten in his chest, and it took him a moment to speak. "She has cancer?"

"Leukemia, and tomorrow she goes in for a bone marrow transplant, and I promised her I'd make her a princess before she went in for surgery," Avery said, the emotion in her eyes overflowing.

Ty didn't know a lot about Avery's past or this journal of hers, other than she was sick last year and desperately wanted to be an adventure guide. But he was starting to understand it went a whole lot deeper than kissing a stranger or winning a crown for a check in some stupid journal.

Of course Avery would win a crown to make a little girl's day special. It seemed she spent her days making the people around her feel special and cared for. He had no idea who cared for her, though. The woman seemed to have a sweet word for everyone she came into contact with, but as far as he could tell she didn't have family nearby, and besides seeing her at the bar with his mom's support group, she didn't seem to have anyone else to count on.

For God's sake, someone she knew was going in for surgery and she'd asked him, a guy she'd met a few weeks ago, to come to her little party.

"Thank you for inviting me," he said, bringing her hand to his mask. He lifted it up enough to press a kiss to her palm. "And thank you for asking me to be a part of something that obviously means a lot to you."

"It might be shocking at first," she said, repeating her words from the other night and ripping his chest open a little further. "She's going to look so small, and without any hair she appears doll-like, so fragile you'll want to pick her up and squeeze her until she's all right, but you can't touch her until you wash your hands, and you can't take the mask off."

"It will be okay," Ty said gently. "The night will go perfect, I promise."

With a nod, Avery reached for the door, then hesitated for the briefest of moments. He could tell her smile didn't fade beneath the mask, and it was still just as genuine, but there was a sadness behind it that broke his heart.

With a reassuring wink, he opened the door and ushered her in. "After you, my lady."

Avery walked in first, washing her hands at the sink and having him do the same before moving into the room. The second she rounded the curtain she took on the demeanor of a duchess from the Victorian era. He watched her go to the side of the bed and curtsy. "Well, good evening, Princess Caroline."

"You came. You came," a small voice said. "When visiting hours ended and you hadn't come Mommy said you might have to come tomorrow. But I told her tomorrow is my surgery and you wouldn't miss seeing me before my surgery."

"I apologize for my delay, Princess Caroline," she said, not breaking character, but he could hear the emotion in her voice. "I knew how important your coronation was tonight, so I brought along a friend who might help in your crowning. Might I introduce to you the noble King Tyson?"

Avery stepped back and gave a regal swish of the hand, and Ty entered the room with one hand on his sword and one on his heart in salute.

All it took was a glance at Princess Caroline to be thankful he'd placed his hand over his heart—it was the only thing keeping it from breaking. Caroline wasn't just tiny, she was the most precious thing Ty had ever seen. Her skin was pale, her head bald, and she was hooked up to a bunch of tubes and machines. Yet she was smiling as if she were at Disneyland and Cinderella had entered the room.

It wasn't a far stretch to imagine Avery in a similar situation, in a different hospital bed, finding a reason to smile among the million or so reasons not to. He was no longer only impressed by her incredible strength, he was moved by it.

"Are you really here to make me a princess?" Caroline asked, her eyes wide with awe and a strength that was humbling.

Ty swallowed hard, then gave his most convincing bow. "My lady, I come bearing the gift of a princess crown and the vow that I will give you whatever your heart desires."

The sun had completely set by the time they pulled into the parking lot, so Ty parked right next to the back entrance of the lodge. He noticed that Avery was shivering from the cold temperature, so he invited her in for a nightcap—which for Avery he knew meant a cup of cocoa.

Ty led her through the door and down the hall into the commercial kitchen, where he started a pot of cocoa. When it was steaming hot, he topped it with whipped cream and handed it to Avery, who had lost her heels and was sitting on the prep counter—those beautiful curls loose and wild, dancing around her face.

"Thank you," she said, her tongue peeking out to lick the whipped cream in a move that had him groaning.

"You were one shiver away from becoming a Popsicle." He ran his hands down her arms in an attempt to warm her—and because he'd been dying to get his hands on her all night—but he forced himself to tread lightly.

Between watching her come apart in his arms last night, then sharing such an intense and raw evening at the hospital, Ty was pretty certain that he was in too deep.

"I meant thank you for being amazing tonight with Caroline. You made her feel so special," she said. "Even the nurses were swooning when you brought her those roses from the gift shop."

"You made her feel special," he said, parting her legs so he could move closer. "You make everyone lucky enough to be in your vortex feel special." He watched her blush at the compliment, then to make sure she swooned, he rested his palms flat against the counter and whispered against her lips, "You amaze me, angel."

"You make me feel amazing." Her hands cupped his face, and she gave him a gentle kiss.

Ty kept it soft, caressing her mouth, then her neck, kissing his way down the silky smooth skin to the base of her throat, where he could feel her pulse racing. She released a gasp of pleasure, and he sucked her skin into his mouth, leaving a little mark. When he lifted his head,

Avery's eyes were dazed and her mouth curved into a smile alluring enough to have his pulse do some racing of its own.

Normally, this would be the point Ty would scoop her up and carry her off to his bed. But the kind of intimacy he sought tonight had more to do with Avery's soul than her body. Not that they wouldn't get there. He was planning on living this princess fantasy out to the fullest, but first he wanted to understand how a woman got to be so giving and sweet as to spend her night with a sick girl who, it turned out, she'd met less than a year ago.

Ty lifted his head as she opened her eyes, which were lit with desire. "Tell me more about this journal."

Avery picked up her mug and took a sip of cocoa. "It is a living memory journal, filled with unanswered wishes and unreached dreams of people I've met. People who, for whatever reason, won't ever be able to make it happen on their own."

"Like kissing a stranger," he asked.

She handed him the mug. "That was for my friend Bella."

"Bella," he repeated with a chuckle, and for the first time knowing that he was a part of some checklist didn't bother him. "You even told me it was for Bella."

"Yeah." She reached out and traced his lip, coming off with a dab of whipped cream on her finger, which she licked clean. "You thought I meant beautiful, but that worked too. Bella was one of the most beautiful women I'd ever met." Ty had a feeling this story didn't have a happy ending, but Avery's grin grew, radiating warmth and fondness. "She moved to Sequoia Lake senior year, lived in the rental across from mine. She was my best friend, and she passed away a few years ago from cancer."

"I'm so sorry."

She shrugged like it was what it was. "She was the jokester of our group. Even at the end she was cracking jokes. But one night we got to talking about life and regrets, and she said that if she could redo one thing in her life, it would be to kiss a stranger."

"And you saw me and decided I was the surrogate stranger?"

She shook her head, her curls spilling everywhere. "No, every time I had tried to be bold someone got in my way, or I got in my way. Then I saw you, and you were so strong and capable and something clicked. Like with you it was finally okay to live loud."

Funny, because Avery made him feel okay to live peacefully. Around her the world seemed quiet and peaceful and healing. "Is Bella how the journal started?"

"No, it started with a picture of Sierra Point."

Ty felt his stomach bottom out at the image of her making that climb. "Please tell me that isn't why you took the job at the lodge."

"I hope motivation isn't one of your job descriptions," she teased, stealing the cocoa back.

"Saving lives is," he said, tucking a strand of her hair behind her ear to soften his words. "Angel, I spend my workdays rescuing hikers like you from mountains they shouldn't be climbing. So as a certified professional, it is my duty to inform you that you climbing Sierra Point is what we like to call a perfect storm."

"I do strive to be perfect." She took a hearty sip of her drink. "Which is why I'm not going up until I'm confident that you've taught me everything you know."

"I could spend the next twelve months training you and you still wouldn't be ready for that kind of climb."

"I like when people underestimate me," she said without a hint of defensiveness. "It makes it all the more exciting when I make it happen."

He could teach her every trick in the book, and Avery climbing Sierra Point was not going to happen. Just the idea made his stomach sour. But he'd learned that everything Avery did, she did with purpose, and until he discovered her purpose behind this climb, he'd hold back judgment. "Okay, so back to the picture."

"Right." Her smile was back. "My parents spent their honeymoon backpacking and camping in the Sierras. They started in Lake Tahoe and worked their way up to Sequoia Lake. And there is this picture of her, standing on top of Sierra Point, her hands out to her side, the wind blowing her hair back like some kind of Valkyrie. She looked so beautiful."

Avery demonstrated, and Ty had to agree—if her mom looked half as beautiful as Avery did right then wearing sparkles and a look of sheer abandon, then it must be a breathtaking picture.

"You could see how alive and in love she was. Happiness radiated from her." She closed her eyes and smiled as if seeing it in her mind. "I think I get my sense of adventure from her. I haven't had many adventures, but it's been a burning desire inside me for as long as I can remember." She hugged her arms around her chest. "Right before she died she gave me a letter, with instructions not to open it until I was standing on top of Sierra Point. That I wouldn't be able to understand it until I understood my strength."

"How old were you when she died?" he asked.

"Twelve. We moved here when it got really bad. I was eight, and she decided she wanted to live in the place that reminded her how wonderful it felt to be alive. She loved living here."

Ty's chest ached for the mother who knew she'd never see her daughter grow into a woman, and the young girl who had lost so much.

"So when I got sick, I held on to that letter and promised myself that when I got well I would make it to the top of that mountain. And somehow that climb would give me the strength I need to hear what she had to say."

"It's been over fifteen years. You've never once considered opening it?" Avery was one of the strongest people he knew. She didn't need to make some climb to prove her worth.

"Oh, I've considered it." She gave a small, self-conscious shrug that tore at him. "By the time I got into high school, I had written and rewritten her letter a million times over in my head, until I was so scared of what was inside I decided I never wanted to open it."

"Then you got sick," he guessed.

"Turns out some kidney diseases are hereditary. It's rare, but it happens. Mom always said I was a rare treasure," she said with a small laugh, but laughing was the last thing Ty felt like doing. Not when he pictured Avery alone in a hospital bed. "She was on the transplant list when I got diagnosed. The transplant list was longer than her body could wait."

"I know sorry doesn't make it better, doesn't take away the pain, but I am so damn sorry," Ty said. He took in her frail frame, the fact that she didn't drink, the way she held her side when she was tired. And it all clicked into place. "Did you get a kidney transplant? Is that why you were sick?"

She gave a small nod. "I was going to dialysis a few times a week, and it was working, then about three years ago my body created more toxins than dialysis could filter out, and my other organs began to shut down. I spent more time in the hospital than at home, but in the end I was one of the lucky ones and was moved to the top of the list."

But her mother hadn't been. She didn't say it, but he could see the guilt in her eyes, and he understood the lifetime of pain that came from being helpless to make a difference. The same surgery that could have saved her mother had been used to save her.

She was a girl with dreams and a sense of wonder who'd spent her entire life being chained to a hospital. He could only imagine how long her journal list was, how many years she had to dream and plan and wonder. His heart ached from the knowledge of a bright light like Avery confined like that. "Is that why you took this job? To be outside and around people?"

"And to find adventure," she said, and he couldn't help but smile at the genuine excitement in her voice. "Also there was the situation with the coworker."

"Right, the idiot," Ty said, knowing where this was going. He didn't like it, but he knew exactly where it was going.

"Maybe, but I was the one who fell in love with him, so I guess that leaves me equally to blame," she said. "I thought we would marry, explore the world, then settle down and buy a little house on the lake. Only I got sick and he got scared."

"So the bastard bailed," he said, feeling the sudden urge to go to Sequoia National Bank and have a little chat with the senior loan officer.

"This life isn't for everyone," she said, looking around. "At first I thought he was in shock. He'd never hesitated in taking me to my dialysis appointments. But when he didn't come with me to meet the surgeon, I realized that me needing a transplant made it all the more real for him. Too real, I guess."

Ty wanted to get real with this guy. It was obvious to anyone who spent two minutes with Avery that she was an all-in kind of person. She gave of herself and her love so freely, never hesitating to open up and let people into her world. All the way into her world. It's what made her so special—and so vulnerable to disappointment. Having someone bail on her when she was fighting for her life?

That kind of loss must have cut her deep, devastated her entire world.

"I change my earlier statement," Ty said, pulling her back against him and nestling her against his chest. "He isn't an idiot. The guy is a fucking coward."

"At first I was so focused on the surgery and what would happen if we didn't find a donor, I didn't have time to think about anything other than he was gone. I was scared to death, and my rock was gone," she said. "But later, after I was released from the hospital, I realized I wasn't looking for a rock. Rocks are rigid, unmovable, stable."

She crinkled her nose as if she'd smelled pond scum, and he chuckled. "And stable is overrated," he said, repeating her words from that first night at the bar.

"And boring."

"I don't know, I think you're giving stable a bad rap. Stable keeps things moving, keeps things safe."

She turned in his arms and looked up at him. "Stable wouldn't burn rubber down the interstate with only the moonlight as a guide." Her gaze dropped to his mouth and lingered. "And stable wouldn't kiss a stranger in a bar."

"Point taken," he said, loving that with her there was never any guessing. Avery knew what she wanted and wasn't afraid to go for it. So when she leaned up and pressed her mouth to his all he could think was *fuck stable.*

"I'm glad I was the one you kissed," he said against her lips.

"Me too," she whispered, her eyes so full of emotion his throat tightened, because his time here was coming to an end. And they both knew it.

It was going to be hell walking away from her, from this feeling. He could pretend that this was nothing more than a fun, light fling. But he knew from experience that pretending could be more dangerous that lying. Because pretending implied that a part of the lie was based in truth.

"So not a single thing on that list is yours?" She shook her head. "If you could write down one wish, what would it be? And yes, I know it doesn't work like that, but if I were making a journal what would your page say?"

"To go horseback riding through the mountains," she said without hesitation. "When I was little my mom took me horseback riding and I loved it. But when my kidneys acted up I wasn't able to do anything that could bruise them, like contact sports, skiing—"

"Or horseback riding."

She shook her head. "So if I could do anything it would be horse-back riding." Her grin turned wicked. "Or BASE jumping."

Ty shook his head. "Your sense of adventure borders on life-threatening."

"People go BASE jumping all the time and live perfectly normal lives."

"I wasn't talking about you, I was talking about me. Every time you have an idea I'm sure it will give me a heart attack."

"You're sweet."

"God, that's almost as bad as noble."

She fisted her hands in his jacket collar. "Even though you think noble sounds like a horse, I think it's one of the sexiest qualities about you."

He let his gaze run the length of her, taking in the cleavage-hugging top, to the pink-tipped toes peeking out from under the billows of fabric. "My thoughts after seeing you in that dress are far from noble, princess."

"Good thing I turn back into an adventure guide at midnight." She looked at the clock, which read eight fifteen. "Well, I'm sure it's midnight somewhere."

"The clock in my bedroom is set to midnight," he offered.

"Well then," she said as she wrapped her arms around his neck, "what are we waiting for?"

Ty didn't know. He felt as if he'd been waiting his whole life for that next big thing. The next climb or adventure that would finally fill the void in his chest. But right then, looking into the eyes of an angel, he wondered if he'd finally found it.

CHAPTER 15

Avery clutched the lapels of her coat tightly as she walked toward the Bear Claw Bakery for a sticky bun and a little gossip. Liv had texted last night asking if they could meet after her shift ended. Since Liv rarely asked for anything, Avery left work early to find herself in the middle of a spring storm.

A bitter wind blasted her the second she got to Lake Street, rattling the branches of the trees that lined the slick sidewalks, but it didn't ruin her mood—which was blissful with a side of best-sex-ever thrown in.

The storm had hit late last night, right around the time Ty was coaxing her into staying a little longer—not that there was much coaxing to be done. It was well past pumpkin time when he'd walked her to her car, and the storm had dumped more than three inches of rain in the mountains and rivers. It was supposed to add another two inches today, but thankfully the rain had slowed to a drizzle and was expected to clear up completely before her hike tomorrow.

Not that a little rain would stop Senior X-Treme, but Avery was thankful that she wouldn't have to lead her first semi-solo trek in a downpour.

Holding her cap in place, she pushed open the door to the shop, and a warm blast of cinnamon and melted chocolate greeted her.

The bakery was already overflowing with locals looking for a welcome-the-weekend sugar fix. A line of customers clustered three deep by the display case waving pink tickets, while others waited for their number to be called. The air was alive with chatter, and there wasn't a spare seat in the joint.

With its clapboard siding, blue-and-white checked tablecloths, and vintage baking utensils hanging from the exposed wood rafters, the Bear Claw Bakery looked like an old mercantile store from the mining days.

A sticky bun sat on the top rack, catching Avery's eye and whispering her name.

"Avery," the whisper said, only Avery looked over to find Liv waving to her from a table in the corner. She was dressed in her work scrubs, white tennies, and—*bless her*—had ordered two sticky buns and a round of coffees.

Promising the lonely bun on the rack that she'd be back to save him too, she worked her way through the crowd.

Avery set her jacket on the back of the chair and took a seat. She put her hands around the still-hot mug and started the defrosting process, then smelled the rich chocolate rising from the steam. "Sticky bun and chocolate mocha? What are we celebrating?"

"Pax made a friend," Liv said with tears in her eyes. "A real friend, a boy who lives on our block who also collects comic books."

"Liv, that is amazing." Avery felt her own eyes prick with emotion.

Paxton had always been on the quieter side, but after his dad passed he stopped talking to anyone other than his mother. Even then, if someone else walked in he'd abruptly go silent. The doctors said it was an anxiety disorder brought on from living through a traumatic experience, and that he would outgrow it with time and healing.

But no one could tell Liv how much time it would take for a boy to heal after being stuck in a car while his dad was dying. It had been a long, hard year for both of them, and Avery was beyond thankful that Paxton was starting to branch out.

"I know," Liv said, the emotion shaking in her voice. "He didn't talk, but the other boy, Tommy, didn't seem to mind. In fact, he talked the entire hour they sat on the porch flipping through Paxton's collection. His mom said Tommy is the youngest of four sisters, so he never gets a word in at home."

Avery reached across the table to put her hand on Liv's. "Sounds like a perfect pair."

"I'm trying not to get my hopes up, and I don't know why I'm crying—it was *one* hour."

Avery handed her a napkin. "Because you and I both know that a lot can happen in one hour. And for Paxton that one hour was a sign we've been waiting for."

"Yeah." Liv wiped her eyes, then gave a little blow. "I don't know how they managed to communicate, but I heard Tommy asking Paxton his name over and over until Paxton just shut down."

"That must have been so hard for him." Paxton's anxiety wasn't just triggered by people asking him questions, it was also affected by being the center of attention. So most people's desire to calm him down only worked to further agitate him until he spiraled into a panic attack.

"I knew he was about to have an attack, so I walked out and gently explained that Paxton hasn't found his voice yet. The boy just shrugged and said, 'That's okay, I haven't found my taste buds for cauliflower yet either, but my mom said I'm not old enough.'" Liv covered her mouth. "Can you believe it? He couldn't have said a more perfect thing."

"I bet it put Paxton at ease."

Liv sat forward. "It was even better than that. Paxton looked him in the eyes when he said cauliflower and made a funny face and the boy laughed. Like really laughed, and the next thing I know they're sitting on the top step, communicating through boy gestures or whatever, and

Tommy is freaking out that Paxton has the Batman comics with Ace the Bathound in them."

"Paxton loves anything with a dog in it," Avery said with a smile. That boy was obsessed with dogs.

"The best part is that Tommy already asked if he could come back this weekend and bring his collection." Liv reached across the table and took Avery's hands into her trembling ones. "I don't know how to thank you."

Avery started. "Thank me?"

Liv nodded. "I don't know how you knew that he would be into comic books, but it was what he needed to open up, and now he has a friend. My little guy has his first real friend since Sam passed."

As touched as she was confused, Avery struggled to put together what Liv was trying to say. With no luck.

"I am so happy for Paxton, and for you, but Liv, I have no idea what you're talking about."

Liv rolled her eyes. "Your Christmas present."

"I gave Paxton a book on dog breeds that he wanted. Remember, I gave it to him at the tree lighting in town."

"Yes, you gave him the 'book.'" Liv threw up air quotes around the last word. "But then you put the mystery Santa gift on the front porch Christmas morning. Even made little reindeer prints in the snow."

Avery opened her mouth to say she didn't know the first thing about making reindeer feet, when Liv silenced her with a finger, then studied Avery as if looking for a tell, like she was some kind of human lie detector. The survey went on for so long Avery was beginning to wonder exactly what her friend was looking for.

Did she have *just been laid* stamped across her forehead? Or was the warm, yummy afterglow she felt so potent it was visible?

Thankful she hadn't taken her scarf off, Avery crossed her arms and casually sat back. After a few moments, Liv leaned close—so close Avery could see the whites of her eyes—then sat back with a frown.

"Look, I don't know if you put Pax and me in your memory journal, or if giving him those comics was you being sweet and wonderful you, but reading about superheroes has really been a comfort to him. The nightmares are going away, and he's smiling more." Liv lowered her voice. "I didn't say anything before because Paxton loved finding the gifts from his mystery friend, and I didn't want to ruin the fun for you, but this time you outdid yourself, and I had to let you know how special you are to us."

"You guys mean the world to me, and I want nothing more than to see Paxton being a happy, chatty kid," Avery said. "But I didn't leave those comic books on your front porch."

Liv sat there shaking her head in confusion. "It has to be you."

"It's not."

Her friend forked off a bite of sticky bun, eating it as if she were at a complete loss. Then she licked her fork, pointed it across the table, and around a mouthful of pastry, said, "It was left on the porch bench in the same exact place you left me the stargazers for my and Sam's anniversary. You're the only one who knows how hard that day is and that stargazers are my favorite flower."

Avery looked Liv in the eye, so she could see the truth. "I didn't do any of those things, although now that you tell me about it, I wish I had. But whoever did must love you and Paxton a bunch." Avery took a big bite of sticky bun, closing her eyes in sheer ecstasy as the gooey sweetness melted in her mouth. "Maybe it's Grace."

Liv bit her lip while she considered that possibility, then shrugged in acceptance. "Maybe. Now," she said as she leaned in, "are you going to tell me about the handsome stranger you're spending your evenings with?"

Avery froze. They'd been so careful last night not to rouse suspicion at the lodge. Even going so far as to sneak out before anyone was awake. Not that she was ashamed—it was quite the opposite.

Ty was such a great guy, and when he left Avery didn't want to field a million and one questions like she had about Carson.

"Who told you I slept with Ty?" Avery whispered.

"Um, you just did," Liv said, obviously not following the girls' guide to discussing affairs in a public place. "You slept with Ty?"

"We didn't do much sleeping, but can you speak up, I don't think his mom heard you from her house across town."

Another reason Avery had been hesitant to go public. Irene was a romantic, but when it came to seeing her son happily married, she was downright mischievous. The last thing Avery wanted to be for Ty was another person he felt he'd let down. Another problem to fix.

"I'm sorry, it's just that you had sex with Tyson Donovan?" This time a couple from three tables away turned to stare.

"Yes," Avery hissed. "And I'd like to sleep with him again, which won't happen if his mom catches wind."

"Inside voices, got it. I just can't believe it, Ty Donovan." She tipped her head down. "Is his butt as tight as it looks?"

Avery smiled. "Could bounce a quarter off it."

"Wow." Liv shook her head in a daze. "A quarter, huh? What about the rest of him?"

"Perfect," Avery sighed. "And I'm not just talking about his body. He is perfect. Smart, funny, and so sweet." Avery remembered the way he'd kissed her scar, cradled her while they made love. "My scar didn't bother him, and when I told him about my surgery he didn't even flinch."

"Oh, honey, of course he didn't," Liv said. "Only rat bastards would flinch, not a real man."

Ty was as real as they came. He was capable, comfortable in his own skin, and had this way of looking at Avery as if he saw her truth and admired her even more because of it. The guy didn't seem to scare easily either. He approached things with a confidence that was as impressive as it was sexy. In fact, the more she got to know him the more she liked him.

Last night, there'd been a moment when she'd watched him sip from a plastic teacup, and she realized that if she weren't careful she might fall in love with him.

"He went with me to see Caroline and give her the crown. He even made this big to-do about the coronation of Caroline as a real princess. The nurses said she wouldn't let go of the crown, even insisted on wearing it into surgery. Said it was her good luck charm."

"I heard from one of the nurses that her surgery went great."

"Her body is taking well to the transplant." Avery took a deep breath and felt her chest expand with emotion. "You should have seen him with her, Liv. Beneath that big, bad survivalist exterior is a guy with a lot to give and a huge heart. After the visit, he took me to get hot cocoa down at the lodge, then gave me a kiss that said the idea of waking up next to me was as exciting as it was terrifying."

"A kiss can say all of that?"

Avery closed her eyes. "Oh, his kisses say everything."

Like how even though he'd tried to keep things light, their connection ran too deep to be anything fleeting. And although he thought leaving was the only solution, she knew he didn't want to go.

"You like him." It wasn't worded as a question, but she knew Liv was hoping for a specific answer. Too bad it wasn't the answer she was going to hear.

"A lot."

"You know he's leaving."

"In a few days, I know. But I don't want to walk away from something amazing because I'm afraid of getting hurt. Loss is a natural part of life, and I want to live, which means experiencing the good with the bad. And I really don't think that anything bad can come out of this since we are both being open about things."

Liv patted her hand. "I want you to experience everything. You deserve that. I just want to make sure you don't get hurt."

Avery had spent her life taking zero risk and being in a world of hurt. She was ready to enjoy some of the perks of living for a change.

"I'd rather take the leap and fall than spend the rest of my life looking out windows."

CHAPTER 16

The next day, Avery's alarm went off before the sun awoke, much to her annoyance. She was right in the middle of a steamy dream starring one hot mountain man and s'mores. She was pretty sure if she closed her eyes she could pick up where she left off, but she was expected to be at the lodge by six, ready to head out.

Tossing the sheets back with a sigh, she padded to the kitchen, her body aching from yesterday's hikes. She and Ty had scouted out nearly every staging area for SAREX, including where they were going to have the cadaver training for the K-9 team. There had been lots of hiking, lots of touching, and the right amount of stolen kisses. And had she not had this big hike today, there would have been a whole lot more than a steamy dream last night.

Pouring herself the first cup of cocoa of the day, she took a sip and was savoring the hot goodness when she heard a honk. Startled by the noise at such an early hour, she walked to the window and peered out at the white Day Adventure van parked in her driveway.

"Oh boy." Stepping into her boots and grabbing a puffy parka, she raced down the driveway right as the side door slid open and exposed the entire Senior X-Treme gang. And the ringleader of this illegal adventure was none other than unlicensed driver Dale Donovan.

"What are you doing here?" she asked in a low reprimand.

"If we want a good catch, then we have to get there when the fish are waking up," the Captain said, lifting his hat. "So hop in so we can get this party bus rolling."

"You can scoot in next to me," Mr. Fitz offered. "My bench has got seat heaters."

"It's called gas," Prudence Tuttman said from the backseat. "Now can someone turn up the radio? Neil Diamond is playing."

Dale, who had remained silent up until this point, reached for the radio knob.

"Don't even think about it," she hissed, then walked around the van to the driver's side window. When Dale kept his vision forward and didn't move to roll down the window, Avery tapped it—loudly. With a temperamental sigh, he finally rolled it down.

"What are you doing, Dale?" she asked.

"Some of the guys showed up early," Dale said loud enough for the whole van to hear. "Didn't see the need to wait, so when they suggested we save time by picking everyone else up, I grabbed the keys."

"You might be the last in the pickup, but you were the first on my list," Mr. Fitz hollered from the back.

Avery lowered her voice so only Dale could hear. "You promised Irene and Ty. And I promised that this wouldn't happen."

"It's only an hour early."

"It's more than that and you know it."

The shame in his expression said he did know it, and he hated dragging her into his lie.

"Time's a-wasting," Prudence said.

"Please, honey." Dale's eyes were pleading. He was stuck between wanting his old life back and accepting his new one. He didn't want to upset Irene, but he also couldn't stand the idea of people finding out he was slipping.

Dale was a proud man, and an independent one, so admitting to his friends about his state would mean admitting to himself that there was something wrong.

"Fine, give me ten minutes to get dressed," she said to the group.

"Five," the Captain argued. "We've got to go through the drive-through. It's Senior Saturday. Fifty-five-cent drip."

"Ten."

Everyone in the car grinned.

Unfortunately, three minutes in, someone thought it would be funny to rev the engine, so Avery skipped a quick shower, threw on some clothes, tossed her hair in a ponytail, and made it back out to the van before the five-minute mark.

"Scoot over, I'm driving," she said.

Dale moved into the passenger seat, while Mr. Fitz mumbled about his heated seats, and Avery buckled herself in. "What are we listening to?"

"Jimmy Buffett," Mr. Fitz said as Dale cranked up the radio and "Let's Get Drunk and Screw" blared all the way down her street and through the drive-through. But by the time they'd made it up the mountain the only sound coming from the car was Prudence snoring.

Avery slid Dale a glance. For all the singing and camaraderie, he didn't seem to be having much fun. Guilt did that to a person. "You know you're going to have to tell Irene."

She heard him sigh. "Maybe."

"Okay, let me clarify. If you don't tell Irene, I will have to."

"Actually, this falls under work business, and since I'm your boss . . ." He gave a big smile, and Avery could see that once upon a time he had been a charmer just like his son.

"And Irene is my friend."

"I thought I was your friend."

"You are." Avery reached out to touch his arm. "Which is why I'm giving you a chance to talk to Irene. You guys have to get serious about what's happening."

He sighed and thunked his head back on the headrest. "I don't know what's happening—that's the problem."

"That's why you need to see someone," Avery said. "A specialist. And I think you need to let Ty in on what's going on."

"Boy's too busy to bother," Dale said.

"That's not a nice thing to say about someone who has done nothing but help you these past few weeks."

Dale turned toward her, his shoulders sunken and his face lined with tension. "You and I both know that there's more help needed than passing some inspection. And Ty's made a life for himself, a good life that's too far away from here."

Avery got the distinct impression that he wasn't saying it as if Ty was too busy to care. It sounded more like he didn't want to disrupt Ty's life.

"Did you ever stop to think that maybe if you stopped pretending you wanted him gone, Ty might find a reason to stay?" Avery asked gently.

"And give up what he's made for himself to come live on a mountain covered in memories and pain?" Dale shook his head wearily. "I don't want that for him."

Avery had a hard time speaking through the sadness. "Have you ever asked him what he wants?"

Dale's expression said that no, he hadn't stopped to ask what Ty wanted. He'd come to an assumption based on the actions of a hurt and angry kid, never taking the time to see Ty for the amazing man he'd become.

Then there was Ty, so gracious he took the time to make a little girl's dream of becoming a princess come true, yet when it came to his dad he purposely held back. As if withholding that same generosity with his love and affection out of anger—and fear.

"Stop!" Dale shouted.

"I didn't mean to upset you. I just wanted to—"

"No. Stop the car." Dale craned his neck out the side window. "I think I saw brake lights flashing at the bottom of the ravine, in the river."

Avery jerked the van over to the shoulder. She barely had it in park before Dale's feet hit the ground and he started heading back down the mountain road.

"Fitz," Dale hollered over his shoulder. "Grab the flares out of the back. Captain, try to find me a flashlight and some rope."

That van went from hibernation mode to hyperalert, and in a matter of seconds, hands were grabbing, feet were pounding the pavement, and the entire team had deployed before Avery even realized what was happening. She grabbed a cell phone plugged into the lighter and hustled behind them.

By the time she arrived, Fitz had the rope anchored to the base of a hundred-foot pine, and Dale was finishing up a harness made from rope.

"Whoa, we are not going down there," Avery said, stepping in front of the team and the steep incline below.

"We aren't going down there," Dale clarified. "I am."

And wasn't this exactly what Ty had warned them all about? An emergency situation where the old Dale would have been helpful and in his element, but the new Dale was such a wild card, he could quickly become a danger to himself and everyone else there.

"Let me call Harris," Avery offered. "He can be here in fifteen minutes."

"If that car is as deep in the water as it looks to be, then we don't have fifteen minutes," Dale said, and she could see the panic in his gaze. "I'm going down."

"You and what army, Dale?" Avery asked.

Dale glanced at his backup, which consisted of a handful of wiry old men with hip replacements and bursitis. Dale might be losing his memory, but he was still a big man. The only one strong enough to help from up top.

"You get down there, then what?" she added. "Who will lift out the passengers? Me? Fitz?"

Helplessness took over, and she watched Dale struggle between doing what was right in this moment and fighting the past. His sense of duty beat out the memories, and he nodded. "You're right. My going down is not smart." He handed her the rope.

"What's this?"

"A harness. Step in, honey, I'm going to lower you down."

"What?" Avery squeaked. "I'm going down?" She smacked her chest so hard it took her a moment to catch her breath. Or maybe that was the panic at work. "I've never been in a harness. Well, okay, I've been in one twice. Once at the Moose Lodge."

"And you wore it well," Mr. Fitz chimed in.

"Then again on Cedar Rim, but my feet never left the ground."

"If we do this right, your feet will be on solid rock the whole time." When Avery looked over the edge and then closed her eyes, Dale stepped close and put his hands on Avery's shoulders. "If you're too scared, no one will think any less of you."

Avery looked at the forty-five-degree incline, the wet clay and jagged rocks. The river rushing at the bottom of the ravine. Then she saw the taillights cut through the trees and knew someone was down there—counting on them.

Someone had to go, and somehow Avery was the most qualified one there. She wasn't going to let fear get in the way of making a difference.

"Captain, call Harris, tell him where we are and to bring help," Avery said, handing over the phone, and then she stepped into the makeshift seat.

"This harness isn't what you're used to," Dale explained, working to securing it to the seat.

"I'm not used to any harness," she admitted.

Dale paused and met her gaze, his full of the confidence she was lacking. "Good thing I am. I got you, kiddo. All you have to do is step back off the edge and trust us to do the rest."

"Okay," she said, then paused, the reality of the situation settling like a bag of cement. "What do I do when I reach the bottom?"

Dale smiled, confident and warm. "After you unhook from the rope, I'll need you to tell me how many subjects are down there, assess the extent of their injuries, and report that back to me." He handed her a radio that Mr. Fitz had grabbed from the back of the van. "Then you do what you do best, honey. You settle and make them as comfortable as possible until help arrives."

Avery looked down once again to the bottom of the ravine and the rushing waters below, and she felt her hands tremble. Was this the best option they had? There was a lot riding on a woman who couldn't last eight seconds on a mechanical bull without pulling something.

"Dale," she said, meeting his steady gaze. "What do I do if making them comfortable is beyond my ability?"

He was quiet for a long moment. "Let's hope it doesn't get to that."

Avery gave a shaky nod and made her way to the cliff's edge. Sending up a silent prayer that she didn't take one look at the bottom and pass out, she got into position, back facing the ravine, her heels at the ravine's ledge.

"You're ready," Dale said. It wasn't worded as a question, but he still wanted an answer.

"Ready."

"Now when you lean back and sit into it, the harness won't feel as secure because there's less pressing against you," Dale explained. "But what is pressing against you is going to squeeze so tight you'll feel the pressure."

Avery was already feeling the pressure. Rappelling with a normal harness would be hard on her body—hanging off the side of a cliff in a seat made of rope was going to leave a mark for sure. Being bold always left marks, she reminded herself. Some more visible than others, but it was what made up the texture of life.

"Live loud," she whispered to herself, then placed her feet at the edge of the drop-off and took one step backward, then another.

Suddenly the mud shifted under her weight and started to give.

Nearly paralyzed with terror, she grasped the rope as gravel and debris fell, bouncing off the hillside before crashing on the rocks below. Way, way, way below.

Whatever happened to rocks being stable, she thought. Then she remembered she liked the unexpected because it had brought her here, to Sequoia Lake. And it had brought her Ty.

Pulling on her big-girl panties, she fought for balance and won. Mentally flipping through the pages of the handbook, she recalled the right term for this kind of descent and called out, "Down on main."

"Down on main," Dale repeated, and there was a small give followed by the terrifying realization that it was all up to her. All she had to do was step off the cliff.

There was no net, no contingency plan. Four retired fishermen and a ten-millimeter rope were the only things standing between Avery and the jagged rocks below.

"Help," a panicked voice called from below. "Please help me."

Avery knew better than to look down, just like she knew all she had to do was say no and she'd be back on solid ground. The easy decision was to wait for the professionals to arrive. But then Avery thought of Ty, how he'd chosen to stay with Garrett, and she realized that sometimes there wasn't an easy or hard choice. In situations like this, one could act or react.

Avery had an entire journal made from moments like this where someone chose to react to the situation instead of owning the situation. She didn't want to add another page to the book.

"I'm coming," Avery hollered, and, ignoring the burn in her arms brought on from holding her own weight, she sat back and let herself lean into the seat until it felt as if she were sitting on air.

Exhilaration met pain as she dropped over the side. The rope tightened, cutting into her skin and tightening around her organs like a vise, and Avery stopped to absorb the pain. Only the longer she remained still, the worse it got until it became paralyzing.

Rain made the rocks slick, her descent difficult, but her healing body made the journey slow. Her lungs constricted with each inch gained, and her blood raced through her body at an accelerated rate until her hands shook and her body cried out. Partly for release from the agonizing pressure, but mostly because she was actually descending the side of the ravine. Pushing her body past its limits and not crumbling.

Avery wasn't asking permission, wasn't letting fear hold her back. She was in the most life-threatening position since her surgery, and instead of waiting for someone else to save her, she was taking a step into the unknown. Looking past the obstacles and toward the future.

But the lower she went, the more alone she became, and the more isolated she felt, until all she could hear was the roar of the river rushing below and the erratic pounding in her chest. She thought about Ty and how he must have felt that day, alone and scared, wanting to run for help but knowing he needed to stay with his brother.

Then she thought about how this would be different, and how when it was all over she was going to make a page in her journal for herself.

And it was going to include kissing Ty again.

Ty was contemplating hitting the snooze button again when his room phone rang. Hoping it was Avery calling to see if he wanted to meet for a little breakfast in bed before work, he answered.

"Please tell me you're bringing something that requires whipped cream," he said, his voice thick with sleep.

"A car went over the ravine on Highway 79 at the Fern Falls cutoff. Car's in the river, search and rescue is en route, but we could use your help."

"Fern Falls?" Ty bolted up. "Is it my dad? Is he okay?"

"I don't know. I jumped in the chopper the second I heard," Harris shouted into his headset. "I'm headed there now."

Ty was on his feet and looking out the window for the van.

"Shit." It was gone. Ty couldn't breathe past the possibilities. "Avery was supposed to be taking my dad and a group up to Fern Falls. They would have had a full van of seniors. And she was driving."

"Good to know. I'm four minutes out. I can call you when I'm on the ground." Ty heard the blades of the chopper cutting through the high wind in the background. Almost as clearly as he heard the underlying message in Harris's voice when he said, "You know how these things work."

Ty did know how these things worked. And Harris wouldn't be calling in an out-of-area guy unless he knew it was bad. He shouldn't have let them go.

Ty grabbed some jeans and a thermal shirt from the closet, yanked on his boots, and was out the door when he said, "I'm on my way."

Ty made the twenty-minute drive in ten, which was more than enough time to go over every possible scenario in his head—twice. Being part of some of the gnarliest rescues in the area made for some pretty detailed images. So when he reached the scene and saw a complete force of first-responder trucks and ambulances, his heart took a nosedive.

Slamming his truck into park, he leaped out and immediately surveyed the situation with assessing eyes. He saw the Day Adventure van, a few of the old-timers, and his dad, but no matter how many times he scanned the scene he couldn't find Avery.

He walked up to Harris, who was in deep conversation with what appeared to be the incident commander on the scene. "Where is she?"

Harris apologized to the IC, but Ty didn't give a fuck if he was interrupting—he needed to know. Every ounce of cool that he relied on to do his job was gone. All he could think about was Avery.

He had become a pro at separating himself from the emotion, but right then he felt as helpless as he had on the riverbank with Garrett. Like all of the training and skills were useless, and there was nothing he could do to ever make this right.

"She's over there." Harris pointed to a tiny woman in rappelling gear, sitting on the back of one of the rigs.

Avery.

Ty's pulse came to a complete stop. She was soaked to the bone, covered in mud, and hugging what appeared to be a crying teen girl.

Jesus, she was okay. Looked like she'd slid down the side of a mountain, but she was okay—and comforting someone else. She'd probably just had the scare of her life and still had the frame of mind to comfort another person.

Ty released a breath he'd been holding since Harris called, and then he started over. He needed to hold her, make sure for himself that she was okay. Then he'd strangle her.

And don't even get him started on Dale. Avery wasn't alone in her actions. This had his dad written all over it.

"You have sixty seconds with your girl. Then I need you focused," Harris said. "There were three passengers, all teens, all drinking. One was airlifted out, the other is over with Avery, but one we think got dragged downriver."

Which meant this would most likely be a recovery, not a rescue. And in order to bring closure to the kid's family, they would need someone equipped to handle those kinds of currents—and that kind of heartache.

"How far could the kid have gone?" Ty asked.

Harris went quiet—too quiet for Ty's chest to do anything but seize up. And that was when he realized just where he was.

About half a mile upriver from where he'd found Garrett. The sun was fighting to cut through the early-morning fog, the ground was saturated, the river raged below with runoff, and Ty felt like he was that seventeen-year-old kid again. About to walk into a situation that was hopeless—no matter how hard he'd trained or how prepared he was.

"I thought the same thing," Harris admitted. "So we'd all understand if—"

Ty held up a silencing hand.

"I'm good," he said because that was what Harris needed to hear. And what Ty needed to get in his head. Guys who did what they did for a living didn't ask for help or a way out. They ran against the flow. Headed into the river when everyone was running out.

"Sixty seconds. Have somebody bring me my gear," he said to Harris.

Harris gripped Ty's shoulder, halting him. "Before you go nuclear, know that if it hadn't been for your dad's fast thinking, two teens would most likely be dead."

If it hadn't been for his dad, Avery wouldn't be shivering like she'd taken the polar bear plunge from fifty feet up.

He turned and met Avery's gaze. *Bam,* everything else disappeared. The panic, the guilt, the paralyzing fear, the need to vent—none of it overrode his need to see Avery.

"You're here," she cried, getting to her feet and meeting him midway. "You're here."

He wanted to say, "You're alive," but Avery wrapped her arms around his neck and crushed her mouth to his.

He could taste her fear, her adrenaline, and the morning chill on her lips. Could feel her body shake as she burrowed closer into him as if she needed him as much as she needed her next breath. Which worked for him since all he needed right then was her. Like this. In his arms.

Forever.

"Are you okay?" he asked, pulling back just enough to run his hands down her sides, probing for sprains or injury. She winced as his hand passed over her scar. "Angel," he whispered, lifting up her shirt enough to see the angry mark the harness had gouged into her side.

"I'm okay." When he kept inspecting her scar, lightly tracing over the bruising, she cupped his face and brought it back to hers. "I'm okay. A little bruised, a lot cold, but not hurt."

"Donovan, right?" the IC said, coming up behind them. "Charlie Decker. Glad you're here. Harris says you're the guy we need."

It took everything he had to pry his gaze off Avery and to the man in charge. Decker was carrying a dry suit and a harness.

"Yes, sir." Ty took the dry suit with one hand, unwilling to let go of Avery just yet. "I'll get suited up and meet you at the chopper in thirty."

Decker gave him a quick rundown of the missing boy, background, description, necessary information, then left him to get dressed.

"You sure you're okay? You should go to the hospital," Ty decided while making short order of stripping down to his boxers. "Medic," he called out.

"All I can think about is that you're practically naked in the middle of the highway, so I think I'm good," she teased, and he leaned up and kissed her while he stepped into his dry suit.

She ran a hand down his arms, as if needing the contact as much as he did. "Are you going down there alone?"

"Harris will fly me in."

Her face paled. "But then you'll be alone down there."

"I have ten more seconds of not being alone." He cupped her face. "I don't want to spend it talking about work."

"But this is more than work, Ty," she whispered against his lips. "You're going after a missing boy who's the same age as Garrett."

"But it's not Garrett." Not that he hadn't thought it the second he got the rundown on the victim.

"I know, but the girl we pulled out said he's been in that water for hours. Won't he be—" He watched her throat work hard to stay calm, to swallow the word everyone was thinking.

Dead.

"Most likely."

Her gaze went glassy, and he gently pulled her against him, wrapping his body around her tightly. Probably too tightly, but he couldn't seem to let go. She'd experienced enough loss in her life. It broke his heart that she was witnessing this.

"But you're going to go get him?" she whispered.

"It's what I do."

She tilted her head until she met his gaze. "Be safe and know that when you come back, I'll be here if you want to talk or just watch the water lap."

Ty stared at her for a long moment. "Wait, are you worried about me?"

She placed her hand on his chest and gave a shaky smile. "You jump out of helicopters and save lives. I ride bulls for crowns and worry about my friends. It's what we do."

"You think of me as a friend?" he asked, not sure if he liked the sound of that.

"I think of you as a lot of things." She rolled on her toes to give him one last kiss. "In fact, I think of you all the time."

As fate would have it, twelve hours, a busted shin, and a safe rescue later, Ty was still thinking about that kiss.

And the amazing woman who gave it to him.

CHAPTER 17

Avery wasn't worried when the workday came to an end and there was still no word on Ty or the missing boy.

She'd spent most of the afternoon accomplishing as much prep work for the inspection Monday as she could. Partly, she wanted Ty to have one less thing on his plate. Between his dad and the lodge, he was already dealing with so much. Then this boy went missing, and Avery couldn't help but see the similarities to Garrett, which meant Ty had too.

Mostly she busied herself to stop worrying. About the boy, Ty, his relationship with his dad, what was going to happen come Monday when the inspection was over and he was free to leave. She hadn't meant to get so emotionally involved, but Ty was generous and sweet—and noble. It was foolish to think she could have kept her distance.

Kept things light.

Well, Avery sure didn't feel light right then. Not when dinner came and went, and the evening news passed without even a mention of a recovery. But the crushing pain in her chest didn't start until it was time for bed and Ty hadn't called. His absence meant one of two things. They hadn't found the boy, or they had found him and Ty needed time to process. Either way led to heartache, she was sure.

She let out a weary sigh and sat down in the window seat overlooking the mountains. The rain was back with force, tapping her windows and tin roof with a hollow thud. Even though she'd lit a fire that had warmed her cabin, she felt a chill roll over her. Was he still out there, or had he simply gone home and passed out?

Maybe he'd left.

Her heart tried to reject that option, but her brain reminded her that he'd cut out once before and kept his distance from Sequoia Lake for a reason.

After the past few weeks, then the talk she'd had with his dad this morning, it wouldn't surprise her if today was the end of Ty's rope. It would crush her, but it wouldn't surprise her.

She'd said a lot of goodbyes in her life thus far and was able to find peace in each and every one. Saying goodbye to Ty—that was going to leave a mark.

The phone rang, and hope flared as she reached to answer it.

"Hello?" she said.

"Hello, dear." Irene's voice came through the phone. "I know it's late, and I hate to think I woke you if you were having one of your good nights, but have you heard from Tyson?"

Avery sat back down. "No, I wasn't sleeping, I was waiting up to see how things went. In fact, I was hoping that you were him calling."

If anything just to tell her that he was okay, that he'd found the boy and everything had worked out.

"Have you heard anything at all?" Avery asked.

"Prudence stopped by a little bit ago and said they found the boy," Irene said, and Avery's eyes pricked with relief. "He was alive but in bad shape, so they airlifted him to Reno. I stopped by the lodge to see how Ty was doing, but he wasn't home yet."

Avery looked out the window again at the sheets of water sluicing down the street, and a gnawing ache started in her gut. "How's Dale holding up?"

"He walked in the door, said he needed to see a specialist, then went right to bed. Hasn't come out since." Irene's voice wobbled slightly.

"I think this is a good thing, Irene."

"I know," Irene said, sounding anything but good.

A knock came at the door, and Avery jumped to her feet. Walking across the front room, she looked through the front window and saw Ty standing on her porch. Her heart leapt. "He's here, Irene. Ty's here."

"Well, thank the Lord," Irene said, and Avery could hear her playing with her beaded necklace in the background. "You give him a hug from me and be sure to tell him I love him, and if he doesn't come see me by tomorrow morning I'm busting his door down."

"I'll let him know."

Avery hung up the phone and raced to the door. She yanked it open, coming to a full stop when she took in the sight before her.

He was still in the same clothes he'd been wearing that morning. Only now they were soaked through, his face was covered in dirt, and his eyes were lined with exhaustion. He was breathing heavily, as if he'd just climbed up from the ravine and came straight here.

"Ty," she said, glancing behind him to see that there was no car in sight. "How did you get here?"

"I walked."

"From the accident site?"

"From the lodge. I got there and I just couldn't go in."

"So you walked here?"

His gaze met hers but he said nothing.

"The lodge is a few miles away." A gust of wind strong enough to rattle the window frames and splatter rain into her house blew past, yet Ty's hair was so wet it didn't budge. Neither did he.

She opened the door to let him inside, but he just stood there, water pelting his body, a haunted look in his eyes that didn't ring of victory.

"We found him."

"Your mom told me," she said quietly, reaching out to take his hand, which was frozen solid. She gently led him into the house.

"Alive. After ten hours. Can you believe it?" Ty laughed, which turned into a raspy cough.

"That you found him? I never had a doubt," she said, shutting the door behind him, but not letting go.

"The kid had enough whisky in his veins to take the tumble down the hill and a half-mile swim down the river. Lucky son of a bitch managed to grab onto a rock in the middle of the rapids and hoist himself up."

"We need to get you out of these clothes."

He looked down, as if just realizing that he was dripping all over her wood floors. But when he looked up, she realized he wasn't just frozen, he was hurting—and lost.

She unzipped his jacket and hung it on the hook by the door, leaving a slippery path. Next came his shoes. "Here, lift up and let me help you with your boots." He raised his foot enough for her to slide it off, and then she removed the other.

"He was pretty far downriver when I found him," he said as she took off his socks as well. His feet were swollen and waterlogged, and she wondered just how long he'd been standing in the rain. "Banged up, body temp low enough to mess with his heart rate, and too damn injured to move back across the current. So we sat there, waiting for Harris to airlift him out. But there was too much tree coverage, so after the third try I knew I'd have to carry him to shore."

"Ty, I need to get you warm." She wanted to hear his story, listen to him unload everything that he was feeling, but he was shivering, and the way he spoke, almost shell-shocked, made her afraid for him.

"It took more than two hours to get him stable enough to move," he said, as if unable to process what she'd said. "He'd been on that rock for most of the night, bleeding pretty bad, then had to lay there waiting for us to get our heads out of our asses and figure things out." Ty shook his head. "You know what? The kid never complained. Not once."

She reached for his other hand, and he winced. It was scraped and swollen, one of the knuckles bleeding. "What happened?"

"Must have banged it on a rock."

"Come with me," she said, tenderly twining her arm through his and leading him down the hallway. She considered sitting him in front of the fireplace, but he was too wet for it to make a difference. Ty needed a hot shower, some food, and a safe place to process.

He also needed tenderness, something he'd denied himself. Ty was convinced that suffering in silence was a badge of honor—a mistake she'd seen time and again with people in chronic pain. It only served to create distance from loved ones—not from his emotions.

Ty needed connection. The kind that was real and open and allowed one to be vulnerable without the chance of drowning.

He would never admit it, but a part of him acknowledged that need. It was why he'd ended up at her front door instead of his own.

"He had some cracked ribs, a punctured lung, hypothermia was setting in, and he just kept clutching that rock as if he wasn't ever going to let go," he said as Avery led him into the bathroom and cranked the shower to hot. He caught his reflection in the mirror and locked on, straining his eyes as if looking for the answer to all of his questions. "I thought I'd have to pry his hands off, but then I said, 'I've got you, man,' and that was it. He let go. Just like that."

"Because he knew he wasn't alone, and that you did have him," she said. In seconds the bathroom filled with steam and the mirror fogged up, but Ty's gaze never wavered. "Shower's ready. If you set your clothes outside the door, I'll put them in the dryer."

"You don't get it—he just surrendered to blind faith in me that everything was going to be okay."

Avery placed herself between Ty and the mirror and took his face in her hands. "It did turn out okay. You stabilized him, calmed him down, and got him the help he needed. He's going to be just fine."

And so was Ty, she'd make sure of it. He was putting his trust in her, desperate for it to be okay. For him to walk away from this, from the past, and somehow manage to find peace with it all.

Realizing he wasn't going to get in the shower unless she steered him, Avery tugged his shirt up, struggling with the wet fabric, his skin ice-cold against her fingers. He lifted his arms, and she dropped it to the floor.

Her breath caught at the faint purpling on his side, and another coming in below his right shoulder. He'd taken a beating today too.

"It was fine this time." He met her eyes, and that haunted look became laced with confusion—and enough anger to have his hands shaking. "Why this time, though? I've done this same kind of rescue a hundred times, followed the same protocol, and still can't tell you why one makes it and another doesn't."

"Oh, Ty," she said, her heart breaking for him. She didn't have to ask who hadn't made it. The pain etched on his face said it all.

"There's no way that kid should have made it. No fucking way he should have been able to survive," he said. "If it hadn't been for mainlining a quarter bottle of Jack and a random rock, he wouldn't have."

"But he did," she whispered.

Ty was right there in front of her, yet it felt as if he was in the middle of his own ocean. Unwilling to let him drift farther away, Avery stepped into him and held on for the long haul. There was nothing sexual about the embrace, just Avery's way of saying she had him. And she did.

She felt his body cave from the inside, then his arms came around her and he pulled her to him, tethering himself as if she were his lifeline.

"You did too, Ty. You made it through, and now it's time to let go."

He pulled back, his expression breathtakingly sad. "It's not that easy, angel."

"It can be if you let it." Stepping back, she quickly shed her night-clothes and stepped under the hot spray, then reached out for him. "Let me help you."

He stared at her hand for so long she thought she'd lost him. "I've got you, Ty."

She watched his resolve crumble, watched the pain surface, and without hesitation he moved forward, stepping in the shower and into her care. She turned him so he was under the spray, which plastered his pants to his legs and chased the chills off his skin.

Lathering up some soap, she started with his shoulders and then his chest, rubbing and massaging, washing away the river, the storm, and everything that was trying to cling to him. When she got to his stom-ach, she felt it knot and ripple beneath her fingers, watched his pulse pick up when she struggled with the wet fabric of his pants.

"You're playing with fire, angel," he said gruffly, his hands stilling hers, which were inches away from his erection.

"I'm not playing." Any game that had been started had ended that morning when she saw him rappel down that cliff. "I'm moving for-ward, and I'd like to do it with you."

He gave her a weary smile. "Most people would get out of the way of a falling boulder."

She looked up at him through the drops on her lashes. "Good thing I've got wings."

"Driving up to that scene, wondering if you were in that car, going through every worst-case scenario of what could have happened to you—" He shook his head. "It killed me," he said, running his fingers through her wet hair, letting the strands slip from his fingers. "I nearly jumped over that cliff looking for you, terrified that I was too late, that I wouldn't get to you in time."

He broke off again with a hollow groan. "Feeling like that? Like there's nothing I can do to help. It makes me crazy." He cupped her face. "You make me crazy, Avery."

Her eyes stung at the conviction in his voice. The man who put it all on the line every day to rescue complete strangers needed some rescuing of his own. "Crazy is a good start, but I'd like to get to happy."

"I'm not looking to be saved." He needed her to hear the words. To understand. But she understood exactly what he needed. And it wasn't a night of distraction—it was a night of connection.

A night where he could let go and be confident that someone would pick up the pieces.

"No one ever is," she whispered, then let his pants slide to the ground. When he went to pull her to him, she scooted to the side to grab more soap.

She watched him watch her as she bathed every inch of him, taking gentle care around the gashes on his knee and the bruise on his side. She worked her way around to his back, stroking and massaging the battered muscles and tense lines, going deeper when she hit a sore spot, but the tension didn't fade.

He had so much adrenaline pumping through his body he was like a live wire. Taut and needing release.

Slipping her arms around from behind, she ran her palms down his chest to that sensitive spot right below his belly button. He sucked in a breath and his abs jerked.

"Avery," he groaned, slapping his palms against the tile wall and hanging his head into the spray.

"I got you," she promised again, going lower until she did have him. In her hand. Gently stroking and caressing.

When his eyes fluttered shut, she picked up the pace, tightening her hold at the right moments, then reeling back to a feather touch. A combination that had him breathing hard. Had his body coiling until she was sure he was about to go over the edge, and he let himself get there, walk right on the line, back and forth, back and forth.

Ty's hand came to join hers, their fingers interlaced. He didn't take over or try to control the pace. It was as if he needed to know she was there. It was such an erotic sight, watching as they both moved in sync.

"Look up, angel."

She did and found Ty staring at her. His head was tilted and cocked to the side, those whisky pools latched on—intense and hungry. Avery felt her own body respond, felt her core heat and tighten.

"Jesus, I'm going to come."

"I want you to."

And to show him exactly how much, she gave a gentle squeeze, then a not so gentle one that had his groan echoing off the shower walls.

Without warning, Ty spun around. One minute she was behind him, the next she was pressed against the wall, her legs around his waist, the cool tile pressing into her back. And Ty, that hard body of his was pressed to her front.

"I do too, but I want to be inside of you when I do."

His lips crashed down on hers. The kiss had a gentle desperation to it, a desperate longing that was impossible to resist. And his mouth.

Good Lord, his mouth was devouring her with every touch. Taking and taking until she was sure that she would pass out from the sensation. He kissed her until she was shaking from the rush.

Ty turned off the shower and, without letting her down, grabbed a towel and carried her through the bedroom, bypassing the bed to enter the hallway.

"The bed's back there," she said, tightening her arms around his neck, water sliding down their bodies.

"We need to dry off first."

He walked her to the front room and set her on her feet in front of the fireplace. With a gentleness that rocked her world, he slowly dried her hair, then her arms, carefully draping the towel over her shoulders.

"What about you?"

Ty smiled and tugged the edges of the terrycloth until she was pressed against him—all the way against him—and they were sharing the towel.

"I'm supposed to be taking care of you."

"You already did. Now it's my turn," he whispered against her lips. They didn't do much drying off after that, but the heat created between them helped out. The long, languid kisses didn't hurt either.

Ty led Avery backward, snagged the blanket off the couch, and dropped it to the floor. Never breaking contact, he guided Avery down until she was spread out on her back, her arms above her head. "You are so damn beautiful."

Avery's throat closed because he was looking at her—scars and all—with desire. Not a drop of pity or concern, but a desire so raw her body felt the impact.

"Don't move," he said, then in case she was thinking about it, he gave a gentle squeeze to her wrists before running the towel down her arms again, over her breasts, as though memorizing the shape of her waist and thighs, then back up and between her legs—teasing and tempting her.

Drying her off and making her wet at the same time.

He consumed her. His hands were everywhere, rough and possessive, mapping her body and leaving a mark—except for her scar. When he reached there he took his time, careful of its size, his touch almost reverent.

Tears clogged her throat. "I won't break."

"I might," he said. His eyes met hers, and what she saw there had her knees wobbling. It was Ty without a filter, everything on display for her to see. His fears, his hopes, and most importantly, his love. He might not know it, but it was right there staring back at her.

Avery wrapped her arms around his neck and pulled him down until all of those hard muscles were pressed against her and she could feel his heartbeat. "Not on my watch."

"You are an angel," he whispered, then took her lips once again, making his way along her jawline and to her ear, leaving a trail of fire that went all the way down to her heart when he said, "You're my angel."

If that wasn't the most romantic thing ever said in the history of love stories, then the way he held her as she kissed him was enough to know that she was in love. Head over heels, never coming back, until the end of eternity love.

Avery locked her legs behind his, pressing her hips up to slide against him. She felt his body jerk at the contact, only to come back down with twice the friction. She did it again, a long, drugging slide that had her brain going fuzzy and her heart doing crazy things.

When she arched her back, Ty gave a soft chuckle, then slid a hand between them. When he found her wet and more than ready, he said, "And here I thought I had taken care of your every need. Guess I missed a spot."

Ty reached for the condom, and Avery did her best to assist with the process—which led to more kissing and teasing than anything. But soon she was laughing, Ty was groaning, and then she let out a groan of her own as he filled her completely.

Ty slid his hands beneath her, pressing the two of them closer together with every stroke. All the way together, taking his time about it too, and making sure to hit her special spot.

"There," she sighed as he narrowed down the trajectory from a drive-by to a one-way journey to heaven when his fingers got involved. With those deliberate and talented fingers rubbing her sensitive skin, he took her higher and higher and so unbearably high that she was quivering from head to toe.

He sank in even deeper, so exquisitely deep it was as if they were one being sharing the same space. Sharing the same breath as their bodies moved together toward the same goal, connecting in a way that she had never experienced before.

It felt as if he were loving her over and over again, every thrust taking them to the next level, until all she felt was him. His pain, his suffering, his strength, and his love—all knotted up in a complicated ball that began to merge—blurring the lines until all that was left was the two of them. Open and vulnerable, no longer afraid of the possibilities.

Ty felt the shift too because he pulled back to watch as their bodies moved in perfect sync, spoke to each other without words. It was intense and so intimate she knew the second it happened. Felt the moment Ty went all in.

His eyes softened, his body relaxed, and the fight drained right out of him. The need to run vanished because just like he had her, he now believed that she had him too.

Her hands tightened around his neck, and he buried his nose in her neck, holding her close, breathing her in as they made that final climb. Together. Which was why it was so important for them to fall together.

"Let go, Ty."

"Only if you let go with me, angel."

At his request, she tightened around him and her body trembled from anticipation. He gave one last push, that spot of hers lighting up like the Fourth of July, and she was launching into the sky—so fast all she could do was hold on to Ty, who was right there with her. Taking her hand and leaping without looking for the net.

They floated for what seemed like an eternity before coming back down. But even the landing was in unison, Ty holding her close, a tangle of arms and limbs as the fire flickered to hot embers, and their bodies melted into each other.

And when Avery went to reach for the corner of the blanket to cover them, he held her still and whispered, "I'm not ready to let go this time."

CHAPTER 18

Ty woke up to a calm sky and a warm woman snuggled up next to him. Even better, a warm, naked woman who, based on the way her nipple beaded against his hand, was awake and wanted a replay of last night.

"Time to wake up," he said, caressing her in a way that guaranteed to put some good in her morning.

With a big yawn, Avery stretched out, pressing her breast into his hand and that ass all over his business.

She looked over her shoulder, those big baby blues already twinkling, and gave a purposeful wiggle. In the mood for a little laughter after the intensity of the past twenty-four hours, Ty hooked a hand behind her knee and rolled her over—and on top of him.

She let lose a little squeal but didn't fight him any. In fact, she sprawled out over him, making herself right at home. He cupped a cheek in each palm and helped her settle in.

Man, she was beautiful. Her face was pink with sleep, her hair spilling down in bed-mussed waves, and she wore a smile that lit him up.

"Someone's already awake," she said, the sleep in her voice sexy as hell.

"Been awake for a while."

She wrapped her arms around his neck and leaned in for a light kiss. "You should have woken me."

He brushed the hair from her face. "I liked watching you sleep too much."

True story. He was supposed to meet Harris at the station an hour ago for a debriefing. Not to mention Decker, the IC from yesterday, wanted to speak with him about an opening in Sequoia Elite Mountain Rescue. A position Ty was seriously considering. He'd be promoted to lead of the swift water team right here in Sequoia County. A proposition that just a week ago would have been a solid *hell no*. But after last night—after Avery—he wasn't so sure what to do.

Yet every time he tried to convince himself to get out of bed, to get down to the station, Avery would make some little sound or nuzzle deeper into him. So he'd been content to watch her sleep.

He liked Monterey, liked his team and his life that he'd created. But he was starting to like the thought of coming home to Avery a hell of a lot more. One of her smiles was enough to fill the emptiness, lighten his day.

But his days were running out. What had begun as a series of weeks had dwindled down to forty-eight hours, and come Tuesday he was scheduled to start work again.

"Are you hungry?" she asked.

He squeezed her cheeks. "Starving."

"I meant for breakfast."

He nipped her shoulder. "So did I."

"I can whip us up some cocoa, and I have a bag of doughnuts in the kitchen," she said. "How about I grab them and we can have breakfast in bed?"

"Is it a clothing-optional kind of breakfast?" he asked, giving her a smack to the lips, then one to the ass as she scooted out of bed and pulled on a big T-shirt. A damn shame for the view.

Ty put his hands behind his head and watched her walk out the room, enjoying the sexy sway of her hips and how her cheeks peeked out of the bottom with every swish.

"What happened to the naked part?"

She stopped at the threshold. "I'll lose the shirt if you call your mom."

He groaned. The last thing he wanted to do was call his mom. She was going to worry him to death, then get Dale on the phone so they could argue about his decision to send Avery over the ravine. And Ty was still riding the high from last night.

With a smile that spelled trouble, she teased the hem of her shirt until he could see just enough peeking through. "If you call her, when I come back it comes off. If not, it stays on. Your call."

"My phone's dead, remember?" He was pretty sure it was broken from dropping it in the gutter on his way over last night.

"Use mine," she said, then ripped his shirt up and off, leaving her mouthwateringly bare. "In case you forgot your options."

The woman was sexy. And so damn sweet he was hooked.

Ty looked around her room, bright and cheerful with framed mantras on the walls, and imagined what it would be like to wake up there every morning. Watch her flit around in oversized shirts and bare feet, drinking her cocoa and humming to herself.

To know that even after the worst of days he could come home to a warm hug and an even hotter kiss. Hell, just to know that no matter what happened, no matter who he let down, he could always come home. Because that's how big Avery's heart was. She didn't judge, didn't back off when things got hard. Nope, she dug in and held tight.

Knowing he had to call his mom, and knowing she was going to ask him a million and one questions about his calling from Avery's phone, he reached out and grabbed the phone. With one last calming breath, he swiped the screen and it opened to an email from Mercy General titled URGENT.

Thinking it might be about Caroline's surgery, Ty stood up to walk the phone to Avery, knowing she'd want to get the news ASAP. Only his finger opened the email, and it wasn't about Caroline at all. The urgent message from the top transplant center in the area was about Avery.

Ty's eyes surveyed the text quickly, locking in on the last line:

> Your latest blood work had some abnormalities. Dr. Johnson would like to see you at 10:00 a.m. Monday morning. Please call the Transplant Center to confirm.

Ty's knees gave and his body went numb. Slowly, he sank back to the bed, rereading the email until he comprehended what it was saying. The tests were run just a few days ago, and they wanted to see her first thing. He might not be a doctor, but he'd had enough experience with medicine to know when to worry.

And this felt like one of those times.

He pictured her scar, the look on her face when she told him about her mom passing, and his gut raged. He'd been trained to prepare for the worst and hope nature doesn't kick your ass in the process. But he was too fucking scared to acknowledge the worst.

Her mom's outcome had been the worst. Holding Garrett while he slowly faded away was the worst. Knowing that this was so far out of Ty's expertise brought back all of the helplessness and panic, like a noose around his neck cinching tighter and tighter.

Avery had been through so much already, the pain, the loss, and she'd endured it all with such courage. She didn't deserve the worst.

She didn't deserve any of this.

"Cocoa is almost done. So why don't you tell me how hard of a time Irene gave you for being here before we crack into the doughnuts."

Ty looked up to find Avery standing by the door in nothing but bed head, a pair of fuzzy house boots that came to her calves, and her scar. He was going to be sick.

Picking up her shirt, he tugged it over her head, waiting until she poked here arms through the holes before he led her to the bed.

She looked at him and rolled her eyes. "Seriously? She only wants to hear that you're okay. Just think of her worry as overbearing love."

"I went to call her, but an email came in from Mercy General. I thought it was about Caroline and accidently opened it."

Avery must have picked up on the tension in Ty's voice, because her smile faded. "Is she okay?"

"She's fine," he said, his mind racing to find the thread. "At least the email isn't about her. It was about your lab results."

"My lab results?" Confusion hit swift and hard, followed by recognition and a small "Oh" that didn't help his panic.

If anything, it made his chest seize up all together.

Avery opened the email, reading over every line and all of the in-betweens to see if she could gauge what abnormality it could be referring to. This soon after a transplant it could mean anything from too many toxins in her blood to a kidney rejection. While she didn't think it was the latter, she couldn't be sure until she saw her doctor.

"Why didn't you tell me you were having problems?" he asked quietly, taking her hand.

"I'm not having problems," she said, putting the phone down. "I went in for my one-year checkup, and I guess there are questions on the lab results." The date for tomorrow flashed in her head. "Oh no. Tomorrow is the inspection. I promised to help you and Dale. I can reschedule for later."

"I don't care about the inspection," Ty said, and she started at the harshness there. Ty never raised his voice. In fact, the only time she'd ever seen him close to mad was when he'd felt helpless with his dad. "Don't reschedule for that."

"Hey, it's not a big deal," she soothed.

Even though a part of her, who knew just how bad abnormalities could be, felt the familiar fear start to creep in, tricking her into making it a big deal, Avery decided dwelling on it was not how she wanted to spend one of her last mornings with Ty.

Getting caught up in things she couldn't change was a total waste of energy. And putting her life on hold for something that could be as simple as *Drink more water and less cocoa* wasn't how she wanted to live her life.

"It could be nothing more than a clerical mistake in the coding," she offered.

"Which is why you should go," Ty said, taking both of her hands. "That way you can know. I'll call Lance, see if I can push the inspection until the afternoon so I can go with you. That is, if you want."

Normally, Avery would welcome the company, the casual chatter to take her mind off things. But there was nothing casual about his offer. In fact, he looked and sounded uncomfortable, as if the idea of her unknown health unsettled him.

Spun him the wrong way.

"That depends. Why do you want to go with me?" she ventured, holding her breath waiting for him to answer. Hoping it was because he loved her and not because he felt bad for her.

"For answers. You may be able to wait, but I need to know," he said.

"I get that, but it doesn't have to consume our fun morning."

"This isn't fun, angel," he said, and she could hear the worry strangling him. "None of this is fun. Seeing that email, thinking you'd gone over that cliff, wondering if I was ever going to see you again."

"I know, it can be frustrating and scary, but wasting one of our last days together, worrying over something that is out of our control, isn't worth it. Not to me."

"But this is in your control," he said, and her heart started pounding. She was going to lose him. He was listening, but he wasn't hearing what she was saying. "After everything that you've already gone through, what your mom went through, don't you think knowing all of the facts is the best decision?"

His question cut right through her. His concern wrapped around her like a vise, tethering her back to her time in the hospital.

"Control doesn't always make life better, Ty. Sometimes it just keeps the colors from shining through."

"Yeah, well, I want to keep you alive until you're a hundred and seven," he said, and her stomach sank. Avery had accepted that life came with no guarantee, and that happiness had to be about quality, not quantity. Ty wasn't there yet, and she didn't know if he ever would be.

No matter how this ended, Avery was going to lose. And lose big.

"You never answered my question. Why do you want to come with me, Ty?" she asked quietly.

He stared at her for a beat, as if trying to find the right answer. "Because I want to know that everything is okay."

And it was the right answer—for him. For her, it brought a world of hurt crashing down.

"You want a guarantee that you won't get hurt," she said through the tears that were building. "You want to know something is a sure thing before you commit. After what happened with Garrett, and what you see every day, no one would expect you to walk into another risky situation where there is a chance that you could lose someone again. But I can't give you that guarantee. I'll never be able to."

"Avery, I didn't mean—"

"I know." She cupped his face and looked up into those eyes that melted her heart. Only this time they were breaking it. "But I can't tell you if my kidney will fail tomorrow or in twenty years. The only thing I do know for a fact is that one day it will just stop working, and I'll go back on that list. Maybe I'll get lucky and make it to the top, or maybe I'll spend my last week climbing a stupid mountain. But I *will* make it to the top, and that means I can't live my life from test to test or waiting for guarantees that might never come."

"I'm not asking that."

"But you will," she whispered. "I want to have fun even when I should be crying, I want to live even when my body tells me I can't, and I want to go horseback riding through the mountains even though it might hurt. And your nature is to protect, to fix the unfixable. I love that about you and would never want to change that."

"I love everything about you," he said, and the weight of his words pressed down in a bittersweet hit that knocked the wind out of her. "Jesus, I love you, Avery. I didn't want to, but I do."

"Oh, Ty." She walked into his arms, holding on and waiting for the pain to ebb, but it only became more acute, until she felt the tears fall. "I love you too."

"Then why does it feel like you're saying goodbye?" he choked out, and she could feel his throat working to keep the emotion from pouring out.

"My dad was a fixer, a social worker." And so much like Ty she was surprised that she hadn't seen it before. "I watched him worry about my mom day in and day out, the helplessness taking over until she finally said goodbye, and he didn't have anything left to give." She pulled back and gave a watery smile. "You're an amazing man, Ty, and you deserve everything life has to offer."

"Jesus, I just said I love you, and you're acting as if that isn't enough."

"Sometimes it isn't," she said sadly, and he pulled back as if slapped.

"The hell it isn't!" Avery reached out, but he took another step back—and that killed her. "You. Avery. You are all I want in my life."

"Even if mine ended tomorrow. Is that still what you'd pick?" she asked, and even though she knew his answer, it still sliced through her.

"Who would pick that? Tell me. Who the fuck would choose that?" he asked, tossing his hands in the air, and Avery knew it was frustration and pain driving him, not anger. She also knew this incredible, amazing adventure of theirs had reached an impasse that not even a type-one adventure expert could cross.

She looked up into his eyes, at the clear bewilderment at her question, and felt a hollow ache swallow her whole. He was a man who valued life over living. It was why he threw himself into work, put himself in danger for others. It was his nature, and she couldn't fight that.

Life was too hard as it was. She didn't want love to be as well.

"Someone whose desire to love goes deeper than his fear of loss," she said, going up on her toes to kiss him one final time. "And that's what I deserve."

CHAPTER 19

The next morning, Ty was standing on the dock in the butt-ass cold waiting for Brian to bring in the last boat when Dale came walking down the dock, adding another layer to his already craptastic day.

Ty cursed under his breath. He was not in the mood to deal with his dad. To hear about how the boats weren't stocked with preservers yet, or about how the go-bags were still missing their first aid kits, or his opinion on every fucking thing else that was going wrong.

Like how Avery hadn't called him back since she'd shown him the door yesterday. And how he'd hiked eighteen miles yesterday so he'd be too tired to think. But even then he couldn't help but remember how he'd made her cry.

All she was trying to do was live her life by her own rules, find some kind of joy in a world that had given her nothing but pain. Including him.

Jesus, he was a bastard. She'd worked her ass off to help him with the inspection, his family, even caring for him after a bad rescue. And what did he do? Took one look at that email and lost it. Thought about how it would affect him when she needed someone thinking about her needs.

Someone supporting her.

Then again, maybe his support wasn't enough. His love obviously wasn't.

"I've been looking for you," Dale said, as if on cue.

"Been here. All morning. Lining up the new life vests for the inspection," he said, picking up an armful and walking them to the edge of the dock to set them with the others.

"I heard that the boy is awake and doing well," Dale said, grabbing a load and helping. "I also heard that you took a beating against the rocks. How are you feeling?"

Like my heart was ripped right out of my chest. "Jammed my finger pretty bad, but nothing that won't heal."

"I was talking about being down in the ravine." Dale cleared his throat. "So close to, uh, well, you know."

Ty froze, then slowly turned to face his dad. "You want to talk about Garrett right now?"

"It's been fifteen years," Dale said, looking as if he'd aged as much in the last twenty-four hours alone. His face was drawn, his mouth tight with stress, his eyes tired.

Ty let out a humorless laugh. "Might as well round it up to an even twenty."

"We need to talk about it." His dad sounded so desperate Ty almost said yes. He almost said yes because he just wanted to hear his dad get it out, say that he blamed Ty, and then it would be in the open.

"Maybe another time."

"Time is something I'm afraid I don't have. Seeing you go over that cliff, thinking back to that day—we need to talk about it now," Dale said, his voice shaking, and Ty watched in horror as his old man's legs started to buckle.

"Dad?" Ty reached out in time to grab his arm and steer him to a bench, surprised at how light he was when he helped him sit.

Grabbing a bottle of water, he opened it and made his dad drink. After a few swallows, Dale gave the thumbs-up that he was all right.

"The theatrics were nice, but all you had to do was say you wanted to talk," Ty joked, relieved when they both laughed.

"You got your mother's humor," Dale said with a final chuckle. "Got your pigheadedness from me. But I also like to think you got my willingness to forgive a man when he's messed up."

Ty swallowed hard. The need to talk and the knowledge that once they did things could never go back to the way they were had his throat tightening. "Dad, I—"

"Let me get this out before I forget what I mean to say," Dale said with a chuckle, but this time Ty didn't laugh with him.

Couldn't. Not when a new wave of guilt sliced through him so sharp he felt it clear to his soul. His dad's life was changing for the worse, and Ty had been too busy outrunning his past to notice that his dad's future was already set in motion—in a direction nobody would choose.

And that had to be scary as shit.

Dale patted the seat and waited for him to sit. "I knew about Garrett."

Ty's hand went to his pocket, to Garrett's rock that he still held close, and his mind raced back to that night, back to Garrett's plea for him to stay. "I should have gone for help, but I was afraid I wouldn't have gotten back to him in time."

And the only thing worse than losing Garrett would have been knowing he'd died alone.

"Son," Dale said so softly Ty had a hard time swallowing. "We all knew you did everything you could. You made the hard call and stayed when others would have made the easy one and left him by himself. Did you think I blamed you?"

"I don't know, Dad, who else was there? I snuck out, Garrett followed me, I made it and he didn't."

Dale looked out at the lake, and Ty could hear him struggling to breathe. "I never blamed you, ever."

It was like a Mack truck full of *what the fuck* hit him in the chest. "You stopped talking to me, ignored me, pretty much acted like I didn't exist."

"I stopped talking to everyone. You, your mother, my friends, anyone who lost Garrett that day too."

"Why?" Ty needed to know, because he'd needed his dad. Needed the one man he admired to tell him he would be okay. That he'd made the right call and it wasn't his fault.

"Because I knew you'd snuck out," he whispered. "I heard you two plotting and I knew, so I thought I'd see how far you got. Then it turned dark and you still weren't back. Your mom started her worrying, but I told her it would be a good lesson for you two to rough it out in the cold." Dale looked at Ty, and his eyes were misted over with guilt and a loss that shook Ty's world. "I wanted to teach you boys a lesson and . . . Garrett's gone."

Ty didn't know what to say, couldn't form the words to speak. There were too many emotions all raging and knotting in his stomach, red-hot with a burn that would last a lifetime. All this time, he had taken full responsibility for what happened, carried the weight of Garrett's death as if he'd pushed him off the cliff himself. Believed he was the reason his family fell apart.

So he'd run.

Yet the only person who could have understood his pain over losing Garrett was the one man he'd turned his back on. It wasn't hate that had silenced his father, it was a soul-deep guilt that had turned to fear and taken hold.

"Then I chased my other son away, not because I didn't love you, but because I loved you so much I couldn't live knowing you had to look up at those mountains and think about Garrett. I let you boys down, and I couldn't forgive that. So how could you?"

All his life, Dale had been a pillar. For the family, the community, the lodge. Always straight and rigid, towering above the others—a position that made it easy to look down, Ty always thought. There was never any softness, any flexibility in his personality or opinions.

But as he looked at his dad now, all Ty saw was a heartbroken man who had tried so hard to control his world, and when it crumbled around him, he crumbled with it.

Something Ty understood, because just like his dad, Ty had been chasing the wrong kind of guarantees. And in the process they'd both shut out the possibility of a happy, peaceful future.

"I don't blame you, Dad. I never did, and neither would Garrett." Ty put a hand on his dad's shoulder so that he felt the truth. "Garrett and I took the back way so you wouldn't be able to find us and bring us home. We didn't want to be found."

With a jerky nod, Dale turned to look back out at the lake, but Ty could hear the silent tears fall. Felt the sad relief roll off him. Neither spoke for a long moment, just silently sat there, staring out over the lake and a lifetime of memories and regrets.

His father had spent as much time running from love as Ty had. He had to be tired, because Ty felt the heaviness every second of every day. And he was too damn tired to run anymore. His soul ached from it: from the fear, the what-ifs, living in the loss instead of the light.

He'd rather have those last few hours with Garrett than to live with wondering if he'd only been faster. And he'd rather live every second he could with Avery than spend a lifetime looking for answers.

She hadn't said his love wasn't enough—she'd said sometimes love wasn't enough. And it was up to Ty to figure out how to be the kind of man who deserved her. More importantly, the kind of man she deserved.

Ty pulled the rock from his pocket and ran his fingers over the smooth edges one last time, then showed it to his dad. "That night, Garrett bet me his favorite rock it could skip fourteen times and break my record. I was too scared at the time to even guess."

Dale took the rock from Ty and tossed it from hand to hand, weighing it and watching how it reacted to being in midair. "Imagine that." Dale chuckled. "Garrett betting you his favorite rock, only to have to throw the prize in the lake."

"Yeah." Ty smiled. "Garrett never did like to lose."

"Garrett never kept score. He was like your mother that way," Dale said, looking up with an expression Ty hadn't seen in a while with regards to him—good-hearted camaraderie. "What would you guess now? How many skips?"

"Maybe eleven."

Dale considered that while he held the rock, and then he looked out at the lake. "Not too many ripples today, but the wind is minimal. You skipping?"

"Yup," Ty said.

"Then I'm with Garrett. Fourteen."

"Fourteen?" Ty laughed. "It's a good rock, but you guys are way off."

Dale handed him the stone, and when Ty went to stand his dad clasped his hands around Ty's. "It's not the rock we're betting on, son."

Ty swallowed hard, emotions churning in his chest as the unexpected moment washed over them. With that one statement, it was as if the past had faded to make room for the present, and it gave them both hope for the future.

"Thanks, Dad."

With a gruff nod, Dale stood. Both men walked to the end of the dock, and they listened to the waves gently lap the sides. Ty followed the rhythm, his hands working the rock until it was warm under his touch.

"It better go eleven, because if I win this bet you have to call up Aunt Peggy and see if she'll lend me the horse team and wagon."

"If I win, I want to drive." Dale shrugged. "Might be my last time behind the wheel for a while."

Ty slid him a sidelong glance. "What about the inspection?"

Dale waved a dismissive hand. "That Charlie Decker was so impressed with how you handled the situation, he came out to the lodge looking for you. Took one look at the updates and called the head of SAREX to say he was looking forward to another great year out at Sequoia Lake Lodge. So if we aren't back in time, I imagine Brian will handle things. Kid's gotta start taking the lead if he expects to be manager someday."

Ty laughed and it felt damn good. Which was nice since he was planning on a lot more laughter in his future. After he was done giving his brother his last wish, he had another wish he wanted to make a reality.

So when the second wave hit the dock, Ty pulled back his throwing arm and said, "Ten I get the horses, eleven you chaperone."

Then he finally let go.

◆ ◆ ◆

The minutes seemed to drag by as Avery waited for the clock in the office to strike nine thirty so she could head to her appointment. Even though the morning had been busy with clients wanting to book trips and volunteers wanting to be a part of SAREX, Avery couldn't stop thinking about Ty. Or how bad her heart ached.

She'd barely slept from the chill he'd left behind, and even now it was a struggle to keep her head up. And even though she felt as if she were slowly dying, she knew she'd made the right decision. Ty was still afraid to put himself out there, and Avery needed someone who was willing to go all in. But knowing it was the right move didn't stop her eyes from watering every time someone called to ask how he was doing or send their thanks for rescuing that boy. Ty was the town's newest hero, and people wanted him to know it.

And why wouldn't they? He was an amazing man, and she didn't regret a single second. Allowing herself to love him like she did, opening herself up to the possibility of something timeless, was the final stage in her healing. Sure, her body had a little ways to go, and her heart would never be the same, but her spirit was finally healed.

And she still believed that the same was overrated. The unexpected brought color to life, made each moment a gift to be experienced. And even when it brought pain, it was still a reminder that she was alive.

"Your ride's here," Brody said, jabbing a finger toward the front of the lodge. He didn't look at her, hadn't glanced her way all morning since he caught her bawling her eyes out in the break room while sucking whipped cream straight from the can.

Avery looked at her watch. Nine on the dot. "Liv is early. I still have a few things to get in order for the inspection. Can you let her know I'll be a few minutes?"

"No need. I've got you covered." Brody held out a clipboard with a collection of spreadsheets. "I have your checklist here, the info on all of the landing sites ready to go, everyone knows what they're in charge of, and in case I miss something or there is a problem I have your cell number."

He'd also been very accommodating. If she'd known tears were Brody's kryptonite, she would have shed a few months ago.

"Wow, thanks." She stood and slipped on Mavis's red leather jacket. She needed a little bold in her day, and she sure wasn't feeling it on the inside. "I should be back by eleven."

At least she hoped. The more she thought about the lab results, the more nervous she became. Which was why, even after Liv told her it was nothing to worry about, she'd still asked Liv to go with her.

Grabbing her purse, Avery headed out through the front of the lodge, surprised by how many people were standing about. It was as if the entire guest list had left their rooms to gather in the lobby at the same time. And they were standing against the massive floor-to-ceiling windows, staring out.

Racking her brain to make sure they didn't have a celebrity or some senator coming in today, she made her way to the front of the crush and stepped onto the porch and froze.

Sitting in the circular drive was an old-fashioned stagecoach draped with a garland made from pine and orange poppies, and it was pulled by a team of eleven Clydesdale horses. But what had her heart settling in her throat was the man stepping down from the stagecoach.

He had a sword in one hand, a poppy crown in the other, and a charming smile that caused a little bead of hope—the one she'd clung to all night—to grow in her chest.

Ty hopped off the running board, and when his feet hit the ground the crowd parted. He walked up each step, so regal and charming, and her heart, even though it was afraid to hope, leapt.

"My lady," he said and gave a bow. A collective sigh rose up from the female section of the crowd.

"What are you doing here?" she asked.

"What I should have done the first time I kissed you." He took one more step and closed the distance.

"The first time she kissed you or the first time you kissed her?" Mavis called out, and Avery turned to see her sitting in a sidecar attached to Harris's motorcycle. "These things are important."

"The first time I kissed her," he answered, and the crowd nodded.

"You fired me," she said.

"Because I was too afraid to fall," he said, resting his hands on her waist and drawing her to him. "But I'm not afraid anymore."

She couldn't tell what he was trying to say, but she guessed that the horse-drawn carriage was a positive thing. But she had to be sure. She had been wrong before, and her heart would crumble if she allowed herself to hope only to end up disappointed. "Because you'll protect me?"

"Nah." His fingers tightened and he leaned in. "Because we'll be falling together."

She went all melty inside at the romantic nature of his words, felt her resistance dissolve and hope grow until her body wanted nothing more than to fall into his. But the realistic part of her, the part that knew just how difficult and draining it was to love someone with a degenerative disease, questioned if he was aware of what he was agreeing to. If he understood that she needed to be with someone who was all in.

"And what if I fall and you can't catch me?"

"I'm never going to stop worrying about you, Avery. It's what I do. It's the Donovan way, so worrying is how I show my love," he said, repeating her words from last night. "But if that time comes, then I'll just have to trust that you have wings, and you'll have to trust that our love is enough," he said, not looking away, even when the crowd sighed. "But until then, I was hoping you'd go for a ride with me. It's not horseback through the mountains, but it is a horse-drawn trip through town, with one stop-off at the clinic."

Avery felt the tears prick seconds before they spilled over. "You're taking me to my appointment?"

"Yes." He silenced her with a kiss. "And before you ask, I'm going because there's nowhere else I would rather be than with the woman I love."

He said it with so much certainty, and a confidence that refused to be challenged, that Avery felt the hope she'd been denying break free. It spread through her body, warming her heart and blooming into something much deeper.

Eternal love.

"Your love has always been enough," she said through the tears. "I just didn't want to be your regret, the reason for any more pain."

"When love is real and true, it could never lead to regret," he said right before he captured her lips in a kiss that tasted like the start of the best adventure of her life.

EPILOGUE
FIVE MONTHS LATER . . .

A warm summer breeze settled around Avery as she stood on the edge of the highest peak and looked out and over the Sierra Nevada mountain range, her hands shaking as she held her mother's letter. The sun was high, the poppies were in full bloom, and the air smelled of adventure. It had taken most of the summer to prepare for the hike, and a report of great health from her doctor, but Avery had finally made it to the top of Sierra Point.

Only now that she was there, she needed one last moment with the letter, one more time to imagine what it could say. An unsettling fear washed over her at the realization that once she opened the letter, it would all be over. The anger, the hurt, the sadness, the wonder . . . and then what?

"It only gets better," Ty said, coming up to stand beside her and pulling her into his strong, loving arms.

"How do you know?" she whispered, resting her head on his chest while her finger traced the familiar script on the back side of the envelope.

"I know."

She gave a nod, her finger tucking under the tattered lip—then paused, her heart hammering in her chest. "What if I'm not ready?"

"You were born ready, Avery," he whispered.

She looked up and into those warm brown eyes, so full of understanding, and her throat tightened and her nerves quelled.

"You got this," he said with a gentle kiss to her lips, then walked to the other side of the rim, giving her the privacy she needed.

Taking in a deep breath, she closed her eyes and pulled back the fold. When she had the letter in hand, she pictured her mom standing right in this very spot with a smile that could change the world, and unfolded it.

The letter was worn around the creases, and Avery smiled, wondering if her mom had folded and unfolded it many times before sealing it tight. Holding back a small sob, she pressed the paper to her nose and breathed in. Beneath the vanilla scent of the aged paper, Avery could smell faint hints of honeysuckle and lavender—her mother's favorite perfume.

Straining through the moisture already forming, Avery looked at her mother's final words, and every emotion inside of her fought to be free.

"Dearest Avery mine," she whispered.

From the first moment I saw you, you were so very easy to love, which tells me you will be my hardest goodbye. Maybe that's why I am writing you this letter, so that selfishly we have more time, because I know the loss will feel as profound as the love we shared. Just like I know that, with time, the pain left behind will bloom into a place of strength going forward.

Even then, there will be moments when the weight becomes too pressing, and fear will try to creep in. I want you to remember what it feels like to stand right here, in the place where I first discovered I was pregnant and we first met, high above the world. Spread your arms wide and welcome the wind rushing beneath you, whispering past you and giving you the extra push you need to let go and fly.

And know that the weightlessness you feel, the one that is as terrifying as it is exhilarating, that is living life with love instead of fear. You can never be lost when you have love.

With you always,

Mom

Avery closed her eyes and, with her arms out to the side, let the tears fall as the wind circled and wrapped around her, testing her strength and teasing her inner adventurer.

Love was everything her mother had promised and more. Ty had been offered a job with the local search and rescue team, which he'd accepted. It gave him the chance to help out with the lodge and to help out with Dale—who, after starting on a regimen of medication, was holding steady. And Avery . . .

She couldn't be happier that Ty was home to stay. Especially since he'd moved his things in last night, making her home his.

"Well?" Ty asked from behind, his arms coming around her to pull her to him.

She covered his hands with hers and leaned back into him. "I'm ready."

Ty chuckled. "I think Mr. Fitz needs it worded a little differently before he can make it official."

Avery turned to look at the small crowd that was gathered, all waiting to hear her answer. Ty's family, her friends, the ladies from Living for Love, even her father had been choppered in—and there was not a dry eye among them. Including Dale, whose tears had started the moment Mr. Fitz had begun the ceremony. "Thank you all for giving me that moment with my mom, but I'm ready now."

"Wonderful," Mr. Fitz said with a toothy smile, and then he continued the ceremony. "Avery, do you take Tyson Lenard Donovan to be your lawfully wedded husband?"

She turned to the man whom she would spend the rest of her life loving, and being loved by, and the rush of emotion filled her heart. "I do."

Avery slid the band over Ty's finger, and Mr. Fitz, who had been certified over the Internet to perform the services, asked, "And do you, Tyson Lenard Donovan, take Avery Joy Adams to be your lawfully wedded wife?"

Ty brought Avery's hands to his mouth and kissed each and every finger before sliding the ring on. And when he opened his eyes, they were shining with unshed tears and love—for her. "For the rest of eternity, and then some more."

Avery's heart bubbled over with love at the raw conviction in his expression.

"I now pronounce you two married," Mr. Fitz said with a few tears of his own. "You may now kiss that bride of yours."

A collection of hoots and hollers went up, followed by chanting of *kiss kiss kiss,* but Avery was too busy tasting her future to pay them any attention. And Ty seemed happy to kiss her right back, his hands at her hips, pulling her closer, until—

Click.

Avery looked up with an amused smile. "Does that mean you're ready, Mr. Donovan?"

His eyes twinkled. "With you, I'm always ready."

Badass grin in place, he spun Avery around and clicked the last few carabiners in place. Then tethered her to him. Together, they walked to the edge of Sierra Point. "Ready to fly, angel?"

"Page twenty-three of *our* life journal specifically said birthday-suit BASE jumping," she teased. "I'm pretty sure that requires us to be naked."

"Oh, the naked part will come as soon as we land," he whispered, his mouth nuzzling her ear. "I promise you that. In fact, once I get you out of that outfit, you'll be naked the rest of the honeymoon."

"That might make for some interesting day hikes."

"It's called living loud," he said. "Now close your eyes."

Avery did, then put her hands out to the side. With the wind whipping past them and the warmth of Ty's arms holding her, she whispered, "Let's fly."

READ ON FOR A SNEAK PEEK
OF MARINA ADAIR'S NEXT
HEARTWARMING ROMANCE
FROM HER NEW SERIES,
SEQUOIA LAKE

Available Fall 2017

CHAPTER 1

After ten years of working graveyards in the ER, there wasn't much Olivia Preston couldn't handle. She was skilled, calm under pressure, and knew how to take charge in the most life-threatening situations. Yet as Liv walked around to the back of her car and saw Superdog Stan crumpled near the bumper, lying in a puddle of his own stuffing, a button eye hanging on by a thread, panic bubbled up until she could barely breathe.

With her heart thundering in her chest, she scooped up the patient and raced across the parking lot, bursting through the doors of the closest shop. The sun had just risen, the day had barely begun, and already she had a code red on her hands.

"I need a needle, the thickest thread you have, sanitary wipes, and something to pack wounds," she called out to Mavis, who stood by the checkout counter flipping through a stack of gossip magazines.

Mavis Bates was the owner of the fastest senior scooter in town and Pins and Needles, Sequoia Lake's one-stop shop for all things quilting and crafty. When riled, she had all the softness of a knitting needle.

"The needles are on aisle five, thread aisle six," Mavis said without looking up from the magazine—clearly not catching the urgency in Liv's voice. "I've got an applique class starting in ten minutes, so just leave your total by the—*Oh my*." Mavis practically purred, her eyes wide in appreciation. "I can see how Beckham was nominated the sexiest man alive, but I still think it should have gone to Channing Tatum."

"Mavis," Liv snapped, burying the panic and taking charge. Story of her ever-loving life. But for Paxton, she'd buck up and do it. Her six-year-old wasn't going to suffer. "I need you to focus."

Mavis looked up and when she saw the patient, gasped. "Good heavens. Is that Stan?" She dropped the magazine and rushed around the counter. The older woman's face showing all of the worry and desperation, Liv knew better than to give in to it. "What happened to him?"

"I don't know," Liv admitted, hating those simple words that had somehow managed to define the past two years of her life.

The same words she'd recently vowed never to fall victim to again.

"I was next door at the Bear Claw Bakery having breakfast with Paxton," she said, her voice cracking on her son's name. "We'd just gotten served when he realized Stan was missing. I went out to look for him and found him in the parking lot. Lying there, crumpled next to my back bumper."

"Poor thing looks like he was run over." Mavis ran a hand over Superdog's torn ear with a seriousness that Liv felt to her core. "Does Paxton know?"

Liv's palms went sweaty at the thought of Paxton's crooked smile disappearing, the one they'd worked so hard to find again—the one so much like his father's. Her heart tripped when she imagined that light in his eyes they'd worked so hard to recover going dull.

"No," she said, breathless. "He's still in the café eating his big-boy breakfast. Shelia is keeping an eye on him for a minute. Smiley face pancakes with the works to get him through his first day of summer camp. You know, a fun morning to ease him into a new routine."

Paxton had a hard time with change, just like he'd had enough heartache in his little life that he deserved some fun. They both did. It was the main reason she'd signed him up for Superhero Camp. Her brave guy wasn't a social butterfly by any means, but he loved comic books—and pretending to be invincible for a few weeks wouldn't hurt.

Only thinking about leaving him at that camp was nauseating. And part of her considered taking this as a sign from the universe, a good enough reason to march next door and admit to Paxton that his sidekick, Superdog, was down for the count and camp was canceled.

That it would be so easy to give up bothered her.

She hated how controlled by fear they both were. Hated the setbacks that would surely arise if Paxton found out his favorite stuffed toy had been reduced to deflated and tattered roadkill.

"Poor thing, his morning needed to go smoothly," Mavis said quietly.

"It still can," Liv said as if it were suddenly that simple. After a trying two years, followed by a disastrous year of kindergarten for Paxton, her family was desperate for a perfect start to what she'd hoped was going to be a perfect summer.

"There isn't a seam I can't stitch or a fabric you can't clean," Liv said, channeling her inner nurse. She'd made a career out of fixing life-threatening problems. "A little extra padding and some TLC and all will be good as new."

Maybe it was that simple, Liv thought as clumps of stuffing floated to the floor.

She knew firsthand that, once broken, things could never be the same. But for Paxton, she let herself believe that everything could be fixed with a simple stitch, because Stan wasn't just a stuffed animal—sadly, he was her son's best friend. And the last present he'd received from his dad.

"I need a needle, stat," Liv ordered, sticking out her hand as if she were in the OR, prepping a patient. Or donning her Supermom cape to save her son's world.

Mavis pulled out a sewing kit from beneath the counter. "I've got a variety of needles and thread here. Cotton balls are on aisle three, and I'll go and find my special cleaner so we can get the dirt off him."

Liv selected her tool and threaded the needle, when she felt Mavis pause at the end of the counter. "You okay?"

She met the older woman's concerned gaze head on. "I'm going to be."

"Thank God," Mavis mumbled. "All this warmth and support was weighing on me. My heart can't take it."

Good thing Liv's heart was strong enough to take on the world if need be. Because thirty-seven balls of cotton, nineteen of the best vertical mattress sutures Liv had administered since nursing school, and a few silent prayers later, Superdog Stan was one knot away from resembling a toy dog instead of a dog's toy.

And Liv was one step closer to being the Supermom she knew she could be. So when Mavis approached the counter from behind, she said, "I'll need your finger on this spot. Push and push hard."

When no finger appeared, Liv said, "Finger, spot, push. We're talking life or death here!"

She was about to cut Mavis a look when a hand reached around and a finger landed on the thread. Only it wasn't a pudgy, arthritic pointer. It was a strong, masculine index finger attached to a hand that looked capable enough to balance the world in its palm.

Liv turned her head to see who this hand belonged to, and froze.

Her hero looked more Paul Bunyan than Superman, in a gray tee that clung to his biceps, a ball cap pulled low, and enough stubble to take that ruggedly handsome vibe he had going on to the next level.

But it was his eyes that got to her. Gunmetal gray with a hint of amusement and a spark of excitement she'd been missing as of late.

"I didn't mean to keep you waiting," he said, his voice a low thunder that shook her to the core. "I was just trying to figure out which one you meant."

"Which finger?" she asked a little too breathy for her liking.

"No, which spot." He grinned and—*bam*—it was powerful enough to jumpstart spots she'd long thought shriveled up and dead. Spots she'd promised to Sam for eternity.

"But now that you bring it up," Mr. Bunyan said, "both are equally important. So why don't you show me exactly what you need, so I can be sure to get it right."

Liv's belly pitched low. Just because she hadn't dated since college didn't mean she couldn't recognize flirting when she saw it. The fact that the flirtation was directed her way was both thrilling and terrifying. Reason enough to create some much-needed distance.

"That's okay. I've got it," Liv said, moving away from him—and his more than capable arms. Arms that had ink peeking out from beneath the sleeve and bulged when he crossed them over his chest.

But Mr. Bunyan didn't leave. He stared at her for a long moment, studying her as if he had something important to say. Just when Liv thought he'd turn and leave, he smiled instead. But this smile felt different. Still flirty, still wickedly tempting, but now it was softened with an emotion that sucker punched Liv every time.

Kindness.

"Of course you got it." He reached out and placed his finger on the knot again, with a look that meant business. "But doing it with someone else is a hell of a lot more fun."

ACKNOWLEDGMENTS

Thank you to my editors, Maria Gomez and Charlotte Herscher, for believing in my work and giving me the push I need to make this series the best it can be. And thanks to the rest of the staff at Montlake, for everything you do that goes into making a book a success and for letting me be a part of the best team in publishing. Team Montlake forever!

A special thanks to my amazing agent, Jill Marsal. Some authors have agents, and I am one of the lucky few to have an agent who is also my friend, my confidant, and my business partner. I couldn't imagine taking this journey with anyone else.

Finally, and most importantly, to my husband, Rocco, and my daughter, Thuy. You are my biggest supporters and my biggest motivators. If love were people, I'd be China.

ABOUT THE AUTHOR

Photo © 2012 Tosh Tanaka

Marina Adair is a #1 national bestselling author and holds a master of fine arts in creative writing. Along with the St. Helena series, she is also the author of the Eastons, the Destiny Bay series, and the Sequoia Lake series. She currently lives with her husband, daughter, and two neurotic cats in Northern California.

As a writer, Marina is devoted to giving her readers contemporary romance where the towns are small, the personalities large, and the romance explosive. She also loves to interact with readers, and you can catch her on Twitter at @MarinaEAdair or visit her at www.MarinaAdair.com. Keep up with Marina by signing up for her newsletter at www.MarinaAdair.com/newsletter.